# THE MAN WHO SOLD
# THE WORLD

**by**

**IAN ADRIAN**

Myrna & Ulrich,
    May you enjoy reading
this book as much as we
enjoy having you as friends
and neighbors.

Ian J. Adrian

WingWays Productions LLC

# CONTENTS

*To my mom, Samara Adrian, who taught me how to write
and gave me the freedom to dream.*

# THE MAN WHO SOLD THE WORLD

# CHAPTER I
## The Intruder

The cat, gunmetal gray, crouched in the bushes that ran along the quiet suburban street – the boundary line of its territory. An intruder had been trespassing regularly, in one of the four-wheeled chariots so ubiquitous on this planet, coming and going into the home building as if he belonged there. Tonight the cat would put an end to that.

As the vehicle's headlights came into view, the feline prepared to attack. It was ready, ready for anything except the broom that swatted it on the backside.

Spinning around to face its attacker, the cat's eyes lit up a bright fluorescent green like a cold-hearted demon. They powered-up to incinerate the attacker with a quick energy blast. But, alas, the attacker's infernal broom came down again, knocking it on its side.

Confusion followed. The broom kept coming down. The cat scurried to escape, but not before getting a good look at the short-legged, gray-haired man holding the broom over it menacingly. Recognition filled the small feline's eyes. It was the same elderly man who had been harassing it for the last several days.

The man seemed even more erratic than usual.

"Get out, you stupid cat!"

Knowing its limitations, the cat chose a tactical retreat. It fired a quick blast from the laser gun under its tongue setting the broom head on fire.

The elderly man's jaw dropped. "What the-?!"

He let out a startled scream and threw the smoking broom to the ground.

Distraction created, the cat scurried around to the side of its home building. With a twitch of its whiskers, it vaulted onto the vines running up the walls and climbed to the third story window conveniently left open by its owner.

Sticking its head into an elegantly appointed apartment, it found its mistress, Diana, in her usual place, working at a Parcae Model 6 computer console situated in the center of the urban chic living room. Her slender hands waved left and right, conducting the multi-colored streams of light that emanated from a shiny metal rod protruding from console. The flickering effect of these lights gave the room a crazed, discotheque feel.

The cat studied its mistress's face trying to ascertain her mood. Being a robot, it could not appreciate the beauty in its mistress's high cheek bones or how nicely they framed her perfectly straight nose. But it found her eyes, the color of burnt almonds, usually more readable.

Deciding all was safe, the feline leaped down to the floor and made its way towards its mistress who was now preoccupied by holographic projections of various colored orbs that appeared and disappeared like pictures in a slide show. As each successive orb appeared Diana commented on it.

"Take the price down to 3.2... Arrange a showing... Get a second opinion on the valuation..."

Each orb was marked with a unique string of symbols that named it. The final one to appear was marked 5jie6c. She bit her lip.

"Lot 5jie6c. Unique selling points: high quantities of magnesium, chromium, and silicon."

With that, she pushed a discreet button on the console. The last orb hologram disappeared as the entire console transformed from the multi-transverse computer it was, into the tastefully understated sofa and side table that was its disguise.

Without turning her head, she said to her feline companion, "IO, I know you weren't out there causing trouble like you've been told not to." She moved to rise, but IO was too fast for her, leaping onto her lap and looking up at her with wide, plaintive kitten eyes.

Diana's face stayed stern.

"You, my little friend, have been overzealous at doing your job. I don't know exactly what you've been up to out there. But, I'm pretty sure it's been causing trouble." She crooked an eyebrow. "Don't make me turn you off."

The cat lowered its head and let out a plaintive toot of apology.

Diana's stern demeanor disappeared entirely. She petted the short hairs along its back a few times before moving to push it off. The cat resisted.

"What are you doing? You know I need to get dressed. Tonight's the big night. I am going on a date, of sorts."

She pushed a little harder, but IO stood firm, its eyes flickering green.

"Oh, no, you don't!" With that she lifted the cat by the back of the neck and bopped its nose with her finger, "don't even think of it!"

Chided, the feline's eyes reverted back to yellow. It leapt off its mistress's lap and took its position on the side table. Back hairs still standing, it watched its mistress pull the lid off a black, lacquered wood box and run her finger along the tiny, cloth-covered scrolls within.

"Hmm…just might be the most important night of my career." She muttered to herself as much to IO. "What to wear? What to wear? Ah, yes." She selected one of the scrolls, pulled it out enough to reveal a shimmering, black fabric, its surface dusted with silver.

"This one always stops them dead in their tracks."


Leaning his head back onto the car seat, Orion rubbed his fingers along his temple trying to relieve the throbbing pressure. Stan, his follically challenged, work obsessed best friend and co-worker at the Polymer Mutual Company, had been nice enough to give him a ride home. But, for much of the ride, the car pointed at the setting sun forcing Orion to squint. The blinding glare abated when they took the last turn and pulled up to the three-story apartment building Orion called home. The trip ended, unfortunately, Stan's ranting had not.

"…And then Bernie, from payroll, you know, that idiot who put the popcorn in the microwave for thirty-minutes. Boy, if I hadn't caught that he might've burned the whole place down. Well, at the very least, he'd have smoked up the office and we'd've had to evacuate the building again. Oh, his excuse was, catch this: he thought he had typed in three minutes not thirty. Yeah, that's what he said. Do you believe it?! I mean, if he can't even get the numbers on the microwave right, how are we trusting him to get the numbers on our paychecks right? You see, that's why the company's having all these problems. We got people who…"

Orion tried to nod, but his eyelids were drooping, the throbbing in his head made his co-worker's usual rhetoric unbearable. So, when Stan loosened his tie and shifted in the seat to get more comfortable, Orion made his escape. Grabbing his suit coat, he pulled the door latch and stepped out of the mud-colored sedan. Stan kept talking, but Orion ceased listening, his attention suddenly and wholly captured by someone else.

A woman, divinely elegant, had emerged from the front entrance of his building. In the glow of Stan's headlights, her ensemble shimmered, affecting the impression of an old time movie star. In a slow, dream-like motion, she descended the front walk, her floor-length satin gown sparkling with her every movement like a night sky awash with silver stars, her hair styled with a crown braid wrapped into a tight chignon, held together by a sparkling net that framed her moon-white face. A generous black and white striped dress scarf draped her long, elegant neck. The effect, as a whole, should have produced an over-the-top-effect; but to Orion, she was the most beautiful thing he'd ever seen.

It was his closing the car door that caused the woman to turn. When their eyes met, he froze, energized, exhilarated, yet hesitant and a little frightened. His mouth closed but he was unable to do much else but stare. The power of this stunning, regal creature seemed infinite. Though she was like no one he had ever seen before, she seemed as connected to him as a twin. His world was somehow right because she was in it.

Her visage stayed cold and restrained. But her eyes widened at the sight of him and stared just a little too long. She turned back to the silver Bentley limo waiting for her and disappeared into it, the door closing behind her.

Until the Bentley pulled away, Orion was frozen in place.

Stan was forgotten; the question, "So, what time do you need me to pick you up on Monday?" went completely unheard.

Orion sauntered up the front walk that led to his building, a modest, three-story walk-up, just pretentious enough to have a name - "The Atlas Building" - displayed on the carved plaque affixed to the roof just below a one foot statue of the god Atlas holding the Earth.

On the front porch of the building, sweeping aggressively was its gray-haired owner and superintendent, Uri. Though the definition of a kindly old man, Uri was someone Orion usually avoided. Even exchanging a friendly greeting with the dowdy octogenarian would inevitably lead to being forced to listen to a lengthy speech on whatever mundane astronomy-related subject had recently caught the old man's interest. There would also be the invitation to come to Uri's apartment to have tea. Orion still remembered painfully the three hours spent listening to Uri describe different types of nebulae. His landlord had a slideshow with prints of every kind of nebula that existed and happily talked at length about each one. For the big finale, Uri displayed a picture of the great Orion nebulae, which he left up for an extra five minutes to let Orion take in all the glory of his namesake. Orion would have made an excuse and left but knew his rent check was going to be late.

Orion wasn't thinking about that now.

"Hey, Uri."

Uri spun around holding a broom with the bristles burnt off.

"Orion! Hi. Say did you see the meteor shower last night?!"

Orion quickly pointed down the street to the Bentley which had, stopped, waiting for the light to turn. "What was that?"

Uri looked at the direction he was pointing to. "Oh, that was a limousine. You know; a big luxury car."

"No. I mean who was that gorgeous woman who got inside?"

"Oh, you noticed her? That was Diana. Out of this world, huh?"

"Yeah, to say the least. So, you know her?"

"She just moved in. Staying in the unit above yours."

"Wow, no offense, but she looks like she could stay in a lot nicer building than ours."

Uri's blank face did not seem to understand the remark. He unconsciously ran his hand over what was left of his thin gray hair. Shifting his weight from one short, stubby leg to the other, as if not sure what else to do, he stayed silent for a few seconds, then returned back to his original interest. "Yeah, that meteor shower was amazing."

Orion inwardly sighed. There was going to be no getting any more information from the old man.

Uri pointed to his watch. "It peaked about one in the morning."

"Did you catch it?"

"No, no. Somehow I must have missed that."

"That's okay. I took lots of pictures."

Stan's honking inadvertently saved Orion.

Still in his car, Stan made a "What's up?" gesture with his hands.

Orion smiled widely and gave Stan a broad wave good-bye before slipping inside the Atlas building.

Opening the door to his apartment, Orion regretted that in his rush
to flight, he had obtained no real information on the new tenant. All
he knew was her name, Diana, and that she lived on the third floor in
the unit above his.

Thinking of her exhilarated him like nothing ever had; his chest
tightened, his mouth grew dry. Oh, how she had glowed! The image
of her goddess-like face seared itself into his mind, creating a stirring,
restless feeling. Filled with this energy, he circled his living room
several times; mouth slightly agape in a silly smile. This ended with
him taking a seat on the arm of his couch. There, the enthusiasm that
had swelled up inside him, gave way to another, darker emotion.

Whether it was the way she dressed, the mystery of her identity,
the beautiful car, or simply the vitality she seemed to possess, Orion
felt strangely hollow in comparison. His broad shoulders lowered as
he looked around at the sad reality of his oppressively bare-bones
apartment furnished with items that were more castoffs from other
people's lives than any reflection of him.

After throwing his jacket down on the well-worn, tweed couch,
he generously watered a poinsettia so shriveled up as to be past the
point of recognition. Out of the corner of his eye he spotted a bulge
that had formed in his ceiling with a crosshatch crack in the center of
it as if something of great weight were pushing it down. A wry smile
passed his lips. Even the ceiling was threatening to come down on
him. He pondered this only for the length of time it took to soak the
rock hard soil that had shrunken inside the pot; then forgot about it.

Dead plant watered, he turned on the TV to break the loneliness that filled the space. To his annoyance, the television's color settings had reverted back to default. He pulled up the television's menu screen and set the colors to normal. He never understood why the TV manufacturers didn't set the default settings correctly. Why not have the television settings set to reflect colors as they are, not the weird colors they always started out with when the set first turned on?

He returned to the couch. The sound of a glum reporter discussing subjects like miners trapped in a copper mine collapse and the widening of the holes in the ozone layer were mere background noise to the one thought racing through his mind – Diana.

Sinking into the couch and lost in contemplation, he failed to notice the pair of slanted, golden eyes rising into view just outside his open window.

Precariously balanced on an extra thick vine growing along the Atlas Building, IO's hind legs wobbled a bit as it stretched its slender body up enough to peek over the windowsill of its intended target.

It looked to either side and, seeing no one was watching, set its attentions to the room. A quick scan revealed that it was indeed empty except for the fair haired intruder slumped on a couch, apparently hypnotized by the signals emanating from the flat energy screen across from it. The intruder raised an arm. Alarmed, IO ducked out of sight. Waiting a few seconds IO peeked over the windowsill and found the intruder rubbing his head while still entranced by the energy screen.

Raising its head fully above the windowsill, IO opened its mouth wide enough to allow the small brass gun barrel to protrude from under its tongue. Holding its head still, it took aim at the intruder. Just then, the vines underneath its hind feet shifted a little. The feline regained its footing. Then the vine under its hind legs pulled away completely!

IO's front claws caught the window ledge. It pulled itself up onto the windowsill and took the shot. A loud clap sounded from below, jostling its aim. The shot misfired! The target missed. Another loud clap sounded. Flustered, IO gave an aggravated, guttural moan as it retreated up the vines back to the safety of Diana's apartment.

The loud clap outside the back window caught Orion's attention. He looked over to the half-open window, but, seeing nothing, returned to daydreaming about the most divine girl in the world.

Only later would he notice the hardened puddle where his foyer lamp had been.

# CHAPTER II
## Apollo

Cruising in and out of the illuminations of the overhead streetlights, the Bentley's engine hummed with minimal noise. Inside its sleek charcoal grey interior, the passengers it carried heard nothing beyond their own conversation, and through tinted windows, saw more shadows and ambiguities than the actual world outside.

Diana had so far spent the trip listening to her host pontificate on his myriad business philosophies which all seemed to revolve around two things: how great he was and how to get your opponents before they get you. She was appreciative of his instruction, though, for he was the acknowledged expert, the master of their shared field. If she were ever going to be at his level she would have to absorb as much of this free advice as possible.

Unfortunately, her companion's liberal dispensation of advice was just slightly more pronounced than his remarks on how nice

Diana looked this evening. To most women, these little flirtations would be more than welcomed because, as well as being massively wealthy and influential, he was blessed with a perfectly chiseled face and steely grey eyes that seemed to look into you and through you simultaneously. These were all signature traits, of course, of the man whose name was legend throughout the universe: Apollo.

Diana knew that to succumb to the wiles of Apollo would be to no longer have him as a business associate, but as a lover, and that would not get her what she wanted. Any appeal she had to him came from being just out of reach. His reputation with women was well established. He always wanted what he couldn't get. That's how she would maintain control.

Apollo sipped his drink. "More?"

"No, I'm good." Diana was subtly nursing the liquid gas concoction for as long as she could. "But, I was curious about the Laurent Quadrant. I've heard you've a deal going there."

"The Laurent Quadrant. Oh, have you been there? The southern hills of Quantar are absolutely stunning at the right time of the planet's revolution. The light convenes upon them just so, to produce brilliant magenta hues across its blue grass fields. The feeling they'll bring out," he whispered leaning in closer to her, "is like a kiss from your first love."

Diana instinctively blocked the attempted kiss that followed by raising her glass. "So, the Laurent Quadrant deal? How are you seeing that play out?"

Apollo pulled back, his voice sobering up a bit. "The deal…" he began. Diana felt his eyes fix on her with a growing frustration at being unable to bring her closer to him, his flattery pushing her away rather than bringing her closer.

Suddenly, his gaze broke, the muscles in his face relaxed, his usual confident air returned. "The deal," he repeated, "the execution of the deal. Yes, that's where hides the heart of Diana, isn't it?"

She let through a hint of a smile as she looked him straight in the eyes. "Yes, Apollo, I want to learn all the tricks; all the angles. That's what I'm after. You've known that since before we met."

"Of course I know. Once I heard of your latest deal, I made certain to learn everything about you including your past. You were a young lady from a planet no one had ever heard of, the up and coming star that had just peaked above the horizon. You created a buzz just a few revolutions ago when you brokered the deal for the Super Asteroid Belt in the Hugos System. Everyone was so impressed by that one. Yes, the Hugos deal changed everything. Suddenly, all eyes turned to you and, for an all too brief second in time, you were the talk of the moment. But then came Galleos."

Diana lowered her gaze.

He continued, "Galleos, the nebula that legend says endows any who pass through it extraordinary powers. For eons, many a fool and dupe have devoted their lives to finding that mythic place. And then you, some upstart from nowhere, had not only found it, but its owner too, a recluse who you had convinced to put it up for sale. What a laugh."

Diana lifted her head to protest, but Apollo held up his finger.

"Yes, we know how that turned out. That debacle wiped out your career just as it was beginning. Who could trust you after that blunder? Even your success with Hugos could not make up for that fiasco. Afterwards, I couldn't find any trace of you. No doubt, you couldn't find work. I mean, what potential client would risk their property being associated with your brand?"

Apollo paused. Diana's mouth was clenched, her face reddened with anger. Indignant, her eyes met his.

He grabbed her wrist, a little possessively.

"And, yes, my dear, I looked into it. That's why I'm here. Any fool could see it wasn't your fault. You were only really guilty of believing what you wanted to believe and overlooking the facts. You were played like all the others before you in a con older than time. You did what we've all done at one time or the other. You just made the mistake of doing it on a galactic scale with an audience of billions. But now, like a comet, you've returned. And with a tail that's definitely much nicer to look at. You've jumped back on stage with the most outlandish all or nothing deal I've ever seen. If you pull this off, you'll shoot higher than before. If not, then there's no coming back. They won't allow it."

He pulled her wrist to him. His face moved closer to hers, compelling her to face him. He spoke with slow and deliberate intonation.

"What I want to know, what I need to know is can this little girl from a planet no one's ever heard of pull this off?"

A hint of apprehension washed across Diana's face. It disappeared as quickly as it came. She knew Apollo could not help but see it. He was so very close to her.

"Can she…," he asked, "Do it again?"

Diana nodded involuntarily. "Yes, she can. I mean, you're here aren't you? The great Apollo has journeyed all the way to this little spot on the map just to put in a bid, along with an offer to personally mentor me. Or is there something you want more than that?"

This time it was Apollo who refrained from comment. With a perplexed look he studied her face as if trying to determine who was playing whom. He was given the answer when Diana adroitly extracted her arm from his hand and leaned back in her seat. She was ready for the next round.

He pulled himself together, faced forward and raised a finger in the air. Three different miniature, translucent orbs appeared before him. Each depicted a section of the galaxy. With a slight twitch of his finger, two of the levitating orbs disappeared. The remaining sphere expanded slightly and rotated slowly until he saw the spot he wanted and touched it with his index finger. The orb promptly disappeared.

Diana observed his actions from out of the corner of her eye. Her expression indicated disinterest but her voice did not.

"What are you up to, Apollo?"

He just smiled and leaned back into his seat, settling himself in for the journey ahead.

Though one could feel nothing, the light shadows from the misty, flickering street lamps faded; the windows were now black.

"Where are you taking us?"

"Somewhere you'll find interesting."

Seconds later, a hint of a bluish light shined through the windows.

"Here we are." A tiny smirk gave away his joy at what he was about to show her.

The door on Diana's side opened to reveal a landscape of jewel-toned beauty; a large expansive plain of blue sands fringed with pink-edged mountains.

Exiting the Bentley, she felt the temperature shift. It was hot, but not uncomfortably so. A steady breeze caressed the folds of her gown as she took one look at the sky, covered with streaks of black and grey clouds. "Impressive. Where are we? This isn't the Laurent

Quadrant…?"

Apollo emerged from his side of the car pulling out and affixing a maroon knee-length cape with fur collar.

"Try coordinates 35098746353-hu8j"

Her mind raced through an internal map of the galaxy, eyes widening once she placed the name.

"Lathius?"

He nodded and pointed her over to the lone artificial structure in sight – a metallic silo sticking out of the ground, a little over a meter high. Diana instantly recognized it as one of the tools of the trade – an Index Drill. An instrument that, once plugged into a celestial body, can report a variety of facts about it. Instinctively she walked to it and placed her eyes over the small screen at its top to read the measurements. Her jaw dropped at what she saw.

"Ilithium. Pure ilithium. The entire planet's crust. There's enough here to-."

"Power half the civilized galaxy?" Apollo spoke with even more pride than usual.

She knelt down and ran her fingers through the blue sand. "It's soft like silk."

"And a million times more valuable. The mineral ilithium content of the seven moons and planets in this system could power the populations of three galaxies."

"I've never felt ilithium this pure, before… But Lathius Nine isn't for sale. It has never been for sale."

"Lesson one from your mentor – everything is for sale. And our job is to join the right seller with the right buyer. That is what I have done here."

"But who could ever afford this? The owner, Lana of Litheon

would never sell."

"Lana of Litheon would, if she were in debt enough. But, if that were true, she couldn't let anyone know because it's only her appearance of unlimited wealth that keeps her credit good. So, now that she's in urgent need of cash, her priceless property all of a sudden has a price. When I was tipped off that her debts had reached dangerous levels, my group contacted her with a secret offer for lot 6yx13a. The transaction will be made, the new owner will quietly extract the ilithium, selling it through back channels, and no one will be the wiser."

"A sale like this – the commission for you would be..."

"Yes, it will be the deal of the millennia. Yet, no one will ever hear about it."

An errant wind swept past them. Diana, still kneeling, struggled not to be knocked over. Apollo, his cape flowing behind him, offered his hand. Her eyes squinting from the blue haze of ilithium dust being kicked up in the air, accepted the help.

The wind died down and Diana wiped some of the blue dust from her face. In the far edge of the plain, she saw a large blue funnel take shape but then fall apart as quickly as it had been born. Looking around at the beauty and untapped wealth that surrounded her, Diana was more than astounded at Apollo's maneuvering and manipulations. So much so, she didn't realize he hadn't let go of her hand.

"It's really just a game," he drew her closer to him. "The winner is the one who controls the pieces and the board itself. There are not many like us, Diana. Few can see the big picture, act upon it, mold it and make it their own. Fewer still can pull off the deals that can't be done."

He leaned perilously close to her. Lost in his speech, she had not realized the subtlety of his approach. She noted once again his chiseled features and steely grey eyes framed by arching, thick eyebrows that were a slightly darker shade of his pale red, shoulder length hair. This was a man who exuded all-consuming, unobtainable power. With each breath of his, she felt the power he exuded. Knew she could drown in him and be subsumed whole.

His lips pressed against hers, strong and forceful. But, the feel of his lips became a release from the unknowing anticipation of what his kiss, his touch would be like. It brought her back to reality. She pulled away from him, but he lurched forward, his lips locking on to hers with smothering intensity.

Diana forcefully pulled back with a weak, "No." Quickly, she turned away towards the Bentley. "I think we've seen enough here." His hand reluctantly let go of hers as she pulled away to return to the vehicle.

The Bentley's doors opened simultaneously and Diana climbed in. "Are you coming?"

A slight grin crossed his face. "Is there a reward if I do?"

She gave no answer as she tried to compose herself.

He made his way to his side of the limo and stepped in. The doors closed behind them both and the Bentley ever so softly lurched forward, beginning its journey.

He leaned over only to meet Diana's cold shoulder.

"There's only room enough for one on this side."

He retreated, visibly frustrated. "You can't control everything, Diana. You must give a little."

She crooked an eyebrow. "This is your definition of mentoring?"

He felt a twinge of shame from the rebuke and was rendered

speechless by it, for shame was not an emotion he was familiar with.

Diana watched as the blue specks and flashes of light faded as the windows became black. Apollo's chariot had taken flight.

It did not take long for Apollo to compose himself. He waved his hand and three translucent orbs materialized before them. "Okay, then. Here is your situation. You have three interlocked deals - lot 2vfdj5i, lot 4o83q, and lot 5jie6c. The selling of each lot is contingent upon sale of the previous one. That was stipulated in the deal you made with the owner. So, if you meet the reserve on all three, then you pocket the commission for all three. If not, then no commission for you on any of them. Interesting deal, but I guess it's how you were able to get it."

He enlarged the first orb. "So far, you've successfully closed out lot 2vfdj5i." The first orb disappeared. "That leaves two."

"Lot 4o83q and 5jie6c," Diana interjected. "These are things I already know."

He repressed a smile. She was pushing his buttons, again, but he wasn't going to let it show. "But, per your agreement, the next lot to be sold is 4o83q." The left orb was magnified. "This is the landmine in the deal. A badly located asteroid field comprised largely of inert gasses which you have to sell at an inordinately high reserve."

She nodded, "Relatively worthless, I know."

"So, how do you pull it off?"

"You have an idea?"

"Yes. You forgo the bidding and sell me both lots at the reserve price."

The offer caught her off guard.

"Just sell you both at the reserve price?"

"Yes, then your problem's solved. You'll have closed the huge deal and I'll have secured lot #5jie6c at a price I can live with. Win, win."

The audacity of the offer is what took Diana's breath away. The third lot, 5jie6c, was bound to end up getting extraordinarily more than the reserve amount. Though, having lot #4o8q3 taken off her hands would definitely make everything so much simpler. His offer was intriguing at the very least, as was he.

"Well?" he asked before noticing the white specks from passing streetlights slowly emerge in the windows. "Oh, we're here."

The Bentley came to a stop. The doors opened. Apollo stepped out. Diana followed suit and found herself in front of a black skyscraper, back-dropped by the night sky, and towering above all the other buildings on the block - Apollo's lair.

Diana had heard of this place, but seeing it in person filled her with awe shaded by a twinge of foreboding. Every aspect of the structure was designed to connote bold, unmitigated power and wealth. Wide lines of silver, in bas-relief, began from the ground and ran straight to the top of the building, leading into the tower's glorious crown which was decorated by brilliant gold suns modeled on each of the four sides. Inside the extending rays of these suns were small planets of various sizes. But, what caught her eye were the large round windows in the center of each of the suns, for these were the only points of light emanating from the entire structure.

Apollo didn't have to follow her eye line to know what she was looking at. "Yes, they are up there."

Her eyes widened. Could it be true? Was he toying with her? As she stood there, she could faintly hear their voices, even from so far below. She swore she could!

He continued, "Just like in the old poem our mothers used to tell us, *'for in twilight they met, just before the beginning and after the end. The Lords of the Cosmos doth plan and scheme, while we mere mortals lie in pleasant dreams.'* They like to think of themselves as the 'Lords of the Cosmos' those fools up there. But, then again, maybe they are. The mighty powerbrokers who arrange the buying and selling of star systems and whole galaxies as lackadaisically as children pushing game pieces around a board."

Diana's eyes stayed transfixed on the windows. "The Titans, they really are up there?" she whispered, almost reverentially.

"Yes, quite. They're happy to freeload in my building. But, I make them pay the price." He noticed her eyes were still transfixed upon the tower's crown. "Yes, Diana, you can hear them. That is because you were meant to be up there, not down here. But, you can't understand what the voices say. That will only come when you are invited into their inner circle."

Diana looked away for the first time and eyed Apollo quizzically. "You are in the inner circle, right?"

He did not answer.

She continued, "That's what everyone says."

He looked her up and down as his coy demeanor surrendered a sly smile then, almost casually, he walked over and positioned himself by the large revolving door entrance to the building.

She began to join him but wavered. Apollo could see this lovely, magnificent creature was not easily swayed. But, his closing ability was legendary for a reason. "Come on, Diana. There's only one way to get up there." He motioned to the slowly spinning revolving door. "We have to see you through these last two deals. Then you'll be invited. You'll be one of them, just as it should be."

She shook her head. "It is well known what happens inside your place, Apollo. How many other women have passed through those doors, lured in by your promises? I know that I would be neither the first nor the last."

"You would be neither, Diana, because there is none like you. There never has and there never will be. Why else would I have come all this way to meet you?"

Diana took a few steps closer to the door. Apollo reached his hand out to her. She took it, but as he led her through the revolving doors, she asserted, "But, it's only to discuss business."

"Oh, of course," Apollo said, his voice assuring. "Of course..."

# CHAPTER III
## The Shed and the Cat


The first light of day found Orion in his so called kitchen expertly pouring milk into his cereal to achieve the proper milk/cereal ratio. It was Saturday, so there was no need to be awake at the crack of dawn, but he felt too keyed up to sleep. Only his blonde hair, which looked like someone had assaulted it with a vacuum cleaner, revealed the restless night he had endured.

Though he could not quite recall them, he knew that his slumbers had been filled with wild and vivid dreams. These ended when, in the wee hours of morning, he had opened his eyes and sprung upright with the inexorable feeling that he'd been asleep his whole life, until this moment.

The new sense of being truly aware gave him the impression that his every action held special import. When he made his bed, it was absolutely the most perfectly made bed ever. The housekeeping staff at the Waldorf-Astoria could do no better. When he brushed his

teeth, it was as if a dental hygienist had come in and performed the
most extensive cleaning possible. Even when he adorned his robe
he tied the belt like an Eagle Scout in his prime. A sublime clarity
washed over everything. And now he was finishing the creation of
the perfect bowl of cereal: a mixture of Muesli and Rice Krispies
with a smattering of Cheerios sprinkled on top. He leaned back on
the counter to partake the first spoonful, but stopped. Through the
window, he spied a Bentley limousine, *the* Bentley limousine, pulling
up in front of the building.

Reflexively, he shrank down beneath the window; head just
high enough to keep the car in sight. His newly discovered neighbor,
Diana, emerged from the rear door. Orion's eyes widened. She was
magnificent. He couldn't explain it, but even in the dim, morning
light he felt he understood her like no one else he'd ever encountered.
Still in her shimmering evening dress, she ascended angel-like up
the front walk as if her feet never touched the pavement, her chin
confidently thrust forward with those perceptive almond eyes that, he
guessed, could alternately cut a person down to size or raise them on
a pedestal. He couldn't help but break into a silly, smitten grin.

The scene turned less dreamy when the man who had picked her
up last night emerged from the back of the limo. Orion straightened
up from his semi-crouching position for a better view of the
attractive and ridiculously well-dressed man accoutered in an elegant
chocolate patterned, caped, three-piece suit. An enormous arrowhead
shaped diamond was pinned to his tie. Worst of all, he was blessed
with a full head of hair an Irish king would envy, bested by thick
eyebrows that were just short of being untamed. Orion instantly
envisioned him being a famous conductor returning from an after-
opera party.

As his grin faded, a series of questions flooded Orion's mind. Was this man her lover? Had she spent the night at his place? Of course, she did. Why else would they have been out all night? The logic of a creature like her dating someone like this impossibly handsome man seemed annoyingly matter of fact.

The man ran after Diana catching up to her just before she climbed the steps. Orion's window was ajar enough to let him hear their words.

"Diana, wait!"

She reluctantly slowed and came to a stop.

The man hurried up to her, "I should apologize." He offered his hand.

"Sweetness and butterflies, I don't care what you do." She waved him off and continued walking.

"I know I come on a little too strong. It's just…"

She halted and crooked an eyebrow.

The man softened his voice a little. "Maybe, I've gotten too used to getting whatever I want."

"Then this will do you good. When I work, I work."

"I know. That's what makes you so snip, snip, cut the devil." He gave her a wink.

She ignored him and continued walking to the door.

He followed. "Wait. Can I come up, and maybe…?"

She turned and extended her hand to shake his. "Good day, Apollo. I will see you in two rotations, when it's time to work."

Hearing the gentlemen's name, Orion cocked an eyebrow in bemusement. He heard the front door close with harsh finality. The man named Apollo looked at it for a second, then smiled smugly and returned to his limousine. Seeing all this made Orion's heart beat faster. He stood up and took a long, deep breath.

"Nothing happened last night." His silly grin returned.

The Bentley's rear passenger door opened and Apollo stepped in. As the limousine pulled away, Orion realized for the first time that there was no driver in the front. It was hard to believe, but the front seat was completely empty. Also, Apollo hadn't opened the door; it had opened for him, almost like there was an invisible chauffeur.

Questions kept building in Orion's mind. Then, it dawned on him that Diana lived in the unit above his and she would have to take the stairs up because there was no elevator. Abandoning his masterpiece-in-a-bowl on the counter, he ran to his front door, stuffing feet into slippers. Realizing he needed a reason, he ran back to the kitchen, pulled out the trash bag and rushed it back to the door, losing a slipper in the process. He opened the door just in time to hear...nothing.

Had he missed her? Maybe she had run up the stairs. Maybe, she stopped to get the mail? On his one slipper, he carried the half-open bag of trash to the stairwell looking down - no one in sight and nary a sound. He then walked to the other side of the stairs, looked up and let out a gasp.

At the top of the stairwell was a gray, tight-coated cat with brilliant yellow eyes looking down at him. He rolled his eyes, feeling silly being startled by a cat.

"Hi, kitty."

Curiously, the cat didn't flinch, didn't even blink. Like a chameleon changing its skin, the feline's eyes shifted from yellow to deep green. Orion took a double take. Yes, the cat's eyes were now green. With a sudden jerk, the little creature's head pushed forward, its eyes glowing. Orion instinctively backed up, retreating until he felt the wall behind him. There was nowhere to run.

The cat crouched into attack position then stopped. Its eyes dimmed, distracted by something outside the window. Orion snuck a glance out the window and saw Diana stepping into a gardening shed. He shook his head. So that's where she went!

Looking back he noticed the little gray creature was vacillating, its gaze alternating between him and the window. When the cat looked back to the window, Orion darted full tilt across the hallway and into his apartment, locking the door behind him.

Once inside, he flashed back to Diana going into that gardening shed, which was odd because there had never been a shed in the backyard before. Orion quickly changed into shoes and moved for the door. He opened it no more than a crack when he saw, to his horror, that freaky cat, standing in front of his door, its eyes luminescent green. He slammed the door shut.

Immediately, he heard little scratching noises on the other side of the door. He stepped back. The sounds were like a pet dog asking to be let back inside. Knowing this was one pet that he definitely wasn't opening the door for, Orion looked to the window. He was only one flight up, but it was a long flight. The scratching grew louder.

Opening the window, Orion, dressed in slacks and a t-shirt, carefully tested the vines growing alongside the building with a few tugs then stepped out to climb down them. Portions of the vines broke and tore turning his descent into a slow, clumsy fall.

On the ground and covered with leaves and a ripped shirt, he remembered Diana and scurried around to the backyard only to find his landlord attacking a clump of bushes with a spray can of pesticide. The shed door was closed.

Uri turned from the bushes. "Orion? You're up early. What

brings you out here?"

Orion stared blank-faced. "I…uh…just wanted to say, hi."

The old man looked a little disconcerted at being distracted from his spraying.

"What happened to you? You look like you fell out the window or something."

Orion pointed to the shed. "So, is that new? I don't remember seeing this before."

Uri half looked over, "Oh, you noticed that, huh?" He then walked a few steps away to spray another set of bushes.

Orion was at a standstill. He didn't want to just open the shed with the owner there. Heck, he didn't even know what was in it. Maybe, he could try another course of attack. Moving over to Uri, he asked, "So, that new tenant. Um, what was her name? Diana? I saw her coming out of that fancy limo."

Uri spoke while spraying. "Yeah, she's quite a lady."

"So, what does she do for a living?"

Uri let off a few more sprays before answering. "She's in real estate. You know, where people buy and sell property."

With that, he wandered off around to the side of the house, Orion presumed, to molest the bushes in the front yard.

"Real estate," Orion pondered to himself. Alone, in the backyard, he suddenly felt a little silly. What was he doing? There must be a million things more productive to do than tramp around chasing after one of his fellow tenants just because she's hot and a little mysterious. And, when he stopped to think about it, real estate would explain everything. Though, not rich herself, she might have to hobnob with moneyed people. Real estate agents usually drive something nice to impress their clients. She could be dressing up for

the same reason. That annoyingly well-dressed man she was with
is a client. He's got a limo, so he picks her up so she can show the
properties. But, in the end, he wanted her to do a little more than
she was willing to do to earn her sales commission and she shut him
down.

Orion had to laugh at himself. Maybe, he actually hadn't gotten
enough sleep last night. Why else had he constructed this elaborate
mystery out of next to nothing? Pulling a couple of the vine leaves
out of his pants, he moved to go but then a weird, recurring pulse
sounded. Spinning slowly around, he realized the noise was
emanating from the shed.

As he took a step forward, he noticed the light in Diana's window
turn on, then that weird cat jumping on to the sill and looking down
at him. So, it was her cat?

Orion eyed the shed, again. It was, by all appearances, a simple,
double door, green, wood-framed gardening shed like the ones
you find in backyards across America. The pulsating rhythm was
definitely coming from inside. In fact it had become louder. He
gathered up his courage. If he was going to look inside he better do it
now. Tentatively, he stepped up to the shed and grabbed the latch.

The last feeling he knew was that of an energy shock knocking
him down while sending deadly electrical currents through every
nerve of his body.

# CHAPTER IV

## The Daily Grind

Diana had two more properties to sell and little time to do it. The deal she had gotten herself into stipulated that the three lots be sold before one full rotation of Ribula's Moon – a universally understood unit of measurement often shortened to the word Rib. The moon was now seven eighths of the way into a full rotation cycle. What was worse was that lot #5jie6c had not been drawing the amount of attention she had calculated it would. Lot #4o83q had drawn none, but that was expected, given its content value and location. No, it was the lack of interest in lot #5jie6c that increasingly weighed on her mind. Something of a more radical nature would have to be done.

Combing through the extensive lists of possible bidders, she paused on one name that stood out – Lord Boibemad IV. First, because of his vast wealth, but second and more intriguingly, because he was Apollo's longtime nemesis. The sparring between the two in much publicized property deals was the stuff of legend. One of their clashes had become so hostile, with the two sides leveraging their backers' assets to the hilt that it ended up not only being one of the costliest acquisitions in history, but bankrupted the famous Ulysses Tri-system Conglomerate in the process. Furthermore, when Apollo ended up the winner and proud owner of the Virgilius star cluster, he lorded it over Boibemad by not allowing any businesses associated with his highness entry into the cluster, thus bankrupting several more of them. Boibemad had never before suffered such losses.

With this in mind, Diana could not suppress a grin as she drafted an invitation to Boibemad to pay a visit to the property, which highlighted possible uses and listed all the mineral deposits #5jie6c had to offer the lucky bid winner. The pitch was pretty standard except for the endnote where she added that she felt obligated "to inform his highness that the financier Apollo has shown interest in the property, and has visited it several times. I mention this only in light of the less than friendly history between you. Of course, if his highness chooses to stay away for that reason, I wholly understand."

Opening his eyes, Orion found himself lying in his own bed, a slight numbness throughout his body. His toes tingling almost painfully, he wiggled them a little to wake them up. Turning his head, achiness ran throughout his body. The room seemed empty.

"Hello?"

He heard nothing. Residual fatigue forced his eyes closed again.

Memories softly crept back into his mind, Diana walking past him on the way to the Bentley, her movement akin to a lovely apparition floating past, arousing more than just physical elation, but coming as the answer to a question he did not know. Other memories pushed their way in; the cat at the top of the stairs with the glowing eyes, Uri showing him snapshots.

"Did you see the meteor shower last night?"

These were part of other memory snippets, none of which explained to him how he ended up here in his bed.

The cell phone rang. He reached over and around until he found it on his nightstand next to the clock which read eight-ten in the morning. Fumbling with it he located the talk button.

"He-. Hello."

It was Stan. "Hey, where are you?! I'm out front. You're not gonna make us late, again, are you?"

"Stan...? What day is it?"

"What're you talking about?"

"Tell me, what day is it?"

"Monday."

"Monday?!" Orion bolted upright, immediately realizing he was naked as the day he was born.

"You coming down?"

Orion instinctively pulled the covers back up.

"I'll be down. I'm just having...issues."

Scrambling to get dressed, Orion didn't know why, but he knew it shouldn't be Monday. What was the last day he could remember?

Was it Friday? That's when he saw Diana. Saturday? That seemed kind of fuzzy, but he remembered seeing Diana and that Apollo guy arguing out front. He remembered Uri talking to him about Diana being in real estate. But, that's it, nothing else.

Fingers anxiously tapping the steering wheel, Stan looked to the car clock then back to the front door of the Atlas building. His face tightened into an angry knot.

He caught sight of himself in the rearview mirror, scrunched up face and glaring eyes and immediately took a deep breath, exhaled and forcibly relaxed his face. Pointing his chin down, he examined his hairline. Though receding, his dark brown hair had at least had the decency not to turn gray. But his face. Quickly tilting his right eye up to the mirror, he slowly ran a finger over the "character lines" that surrounded it, even wistfully pulling the skin to see if the little creases might straighten out. They didn't.

Looking back to the building then to the clock, he hit the steering wheel.

"Why is he always late?"

Suddenly, there was a limo parked in front of him. He hadn't noticed it when he arrived. It must have pulled up while he was lost in thought.

The door to the apartment building opened. Stan perked up until he realized it was only some lady. He had never seen her before.

Whoever it was, she was dressed like a model in a get-up worthy of an Alexander McQueen fashion show. With brisk steps, she descended the walk and disappeared into the back of the luxury car.

Totally frustrated at this point, Stan was about to call Orion again, but saw the building door open and his ever-tardy workmate emerge. Finally! But, when his fair-haired friend stepped out onto the front porch, he froze staring straight ahead.

What the hell is he doing? Stan thought to himself. Past the boiling point, he beat the car horn.

With the honking and the Bentley pulling off, Orion snapped out of his trance, ran over and got in.

"Where the hell were you?!" Stan barked. "And what're you doin' making like a statue in front of the building?"

As if his friend had said nothing, Orion quickly asked, "Did you see who got into the car?!"

"Well, yeah, some lady, I think."

"Was she absolutely gorgeous?"

"I don't know. She was okay, I guess."

"And the car, did you notice there wasn't a driver? The doors opened by themselves and then it just drove itself off."

"Huh…?"

Stan didn't even know how to begin to answer that one. He looked his co-worker up and down for signs of inebriation or something worse.

"Are you high? I knew there'd be trouble once they legalized marijuana."

Stan bristled when he felt his friend grab his arm.

"Did you see that?"

Stan shrugged Orion's hand off.

"Not so hard. Look, I don't know what you saw. It was just a car that some lady got into."

"An amazing lady!" Orion's gaze drifted towards the sky as he went on. "The way she dresses, like from another time. Her clothes always glowing, even in the daytime. Her eyes, brilliant, precious gems that look right through you and her hair, it's always covered, but I bet it's perfectly wonderful to look at, to touch."

"LSD," Stan determined. "That's what you're on."

He pulled the car out but stopped abruptly when a massive white and black spotted dog ran across the street in front of them.

"What the hell was that?!"

"A Great Dane-Saint Bernard mix."

"It was friggin' huge!"

A middle-aged woman in a light blue bathrobe and bunny slippers scurried past.

"POOPSIE! POOPSIE! COME TO MOMMY!"

The dog ran between two houses and out of sight, the robed woman following.

Stan shook his head and looked at the car clock.

"Jesus, we're fifteen minutes late!"

The light turned red. Stan slammed on the brakes.

"It just doesn't stop!"

He noticed a couple of wrinkles on Orion's suit sleeve.

"It wouldn't hurt to use an iron once in a while. They're looking for any reason to lay people off, right now."

Orion's eyes were fixed straight ahead.

"I've got to find out more about her."

"About who?"

"Diana, the woman who got into the limo."

Stan shook his head as he hung a right.

"Don't want to get personal. But, maybe this could all be part of that eyesight problem you have. You know, where the colors and stuff are off."

Orion grimaced. "That's not really a problem. I know what I'm looking at."

"Well, if she's all that you're saying. I don't think you should be worried about this lady. Limos, chauffeurs: doesn't sound like you two travel in the same circles."

"No, it's not like that. She lives in my building; in the place above mine. She's a real estate agent."

"Good," Stan ran a yellow light. "Then she'll be able to support you when you're out of a job for frequent tardiness. Polymer's busy cutting down its staff like a Thanksgiving turkey and here we are offering ourselves up on a platter.

A symbol of the capitalist dream realized, the Polymer Mutual Insurance Company's white, twenty-story tower had stood in the center of downtown for over a hundred years.

In the beginning, the maverick upstart insurer specialized in indemnifying the paddlewheel steamboats that majestically sailed along the nation's rivers. This proved profitable enough to let the owners hire new staff. As the gambling and showboats disappeared, the company switched to indemnifying landlocked structures. Auto insurance followed once horseless carriages proved more than just a fad. By the early 1960s, Polymer Mutual had branched out to eight locations across three counties. But providence truly fell in 1972 when the state legislature passed a law mandating all drivers must have car insurance.

As a result, Polymer Mutual roared to its apex becoming the 23rd largest insurer in the nation. Times were so good a forest fire couldn't burn through all the money it was bringing in. Government regulations loosened; diversification became the new buzzword in the board of director's room. Within the span of a decade, the company's holdings expanded to shipping, an agricultural conglomerate, and even a chain of "home-style" restaurant- gift stores that ran along the highways of the Midwest. It couldn't last. When the market crashed, reality hit like a daredevil motorcyclist crashing into a mountain side. The company, like so many in the industry, found itself swamped with unrecoverable loans and faulty investments. Bankruptcy was imminent.

Stan cracked the door to the vast, open-design office space that comprised the third floor of Polymer Mutual's headquarters. He peeked to either side of the main row dividing the analysts' cubicles and the call center cubicles. A tinge of sorrow overcame him as his eyes scanned the large number of empty cubicles, the results of the last spate of layoffs. The occupants scattered throughout the remaining desks seemed too busy peering at their screens or speaking into their headpieces to notice any latecomers.

Feeling safe, he slipped in and made a beeline to the far end of the analysts' section. Orion crept close behind passing under the large digital clock that read nine-fourteen a.m. Unnoticed, the pair slipped into their respective chairs.

Orion's cubicle was next to Stan's, which was more in the line of sight of their manager, Mr. Ogleby. Stan sat straight up so Mr. Ogleby would see the top of his head if he happened to look his way.

After ten minutes, he felt safe enough to roll his chair back to find Orion blankly looking at his monitor.

"Hey, O, we've got a ten o'clock meeting, remember?"

His friend snapped out of the trance he'd been in.

"Oh…yeah."

Stan's voice grew dark. "What's wrong with you, today? We were over fifteen minutes late this morning because of you and now you're half awake at your desk."

Orion nodded absent-mindedly.

The soft thumping of ladies' heels on the light beige carpet caught both their attentions. A knock on the wall dividing their cubicles followed as Lorraine, from two rows over, peeked in. She flashed her signature smile that, with her big wide eyes and frizzy strawberry blonde hair, always made Orion flash on that cereal box character – the beaming sun with two scoops of raisins in its hands.

"Morning, guys.  So glad you could make it in, today."

Stan furiously motioned for to her to lower her volume.

"Morning, Lorraine."

He returned to his screen.

Not one to be ignored, Lorraine moved to the cubicle opening where they could see all of her, though neither took the opportunity to enjoy the view.

"And good morning, Orion."

Getting no response she continued the conversation throwing in plenty of theatricality.

"What? I'm good, thank you. Why, yes, this is a new top. How sweet of you to notice."

Orion's eyes stayed glued to his monitor.

She leaned forward, eyes squinting trying to figure out why Orion's screen settings were so weird. A stack of papers next to him caught her eye. On the top sheet she could make out the word "REJECTED" stamped in dark purplish ink. She shook her head pityingly knowing from experience that the others in the stack were marked the same.

She stepped over to Stan's wall.

"So, Mr. Terrance, you do anything exciting last night?" Her voice was tinged with a bit of naughtiness. His lack of response made her scowl. "Hey Stan, I'm talking to you. I expect to have one-sided conversations with blondie over there, but I thought we were pals."

Stan's response was dry. "Just going over my pension benefits plan. It keeps telling me that I'm going to end up with four dollars and twenty cents a year less than I'm supposed to. It's killing me. How's a guy supposed to get ahead?!"

"Oh, Stan, you crack me up." She let out a little snort. "You ready for the meeting?"

"Yeah, we're ready. Just hope it doesn't last all day."

"Let's hope it does." she entered his cubicle and strategically leaned her rear against the desk just inches from his keyboard.

"I was talking to Kwesi up in Accounting and he said that the company has only thirty days, maybe sixty before all the money's gone. He says they gotta do something. It's gotta be big and fast."

This grabbed Stan's attention. He swiveled his chair around, taking only a quick glance at the cleavage displayed through her strained blouse buttons.

"A month, huh? Damnit, I knew things were messed up, I just didn't know it was this bad."

"Yeah, it's bad up there. I was talking to Bernie-."

"Bernie?! He's half their problem. I've had to contest two paychecks this year because the amounts were wrong."

"Geez, Stan. Don't you hear anything? They moved him to our section, yesterday."

"What?!" Stan's jaw dropped.

She nodded. "Word is that Accounting wanted to get rid of him. I mean, we all saw it coming. He was such a mess. Oh, my God. You know, he couldn't even work the buttons on the coffeemaker."

"You're tellin' me?!"

"Well, Ogelby has some sort of bromance crush on him and let him transfer into our section."

Stan clenched his fists.

"I hate it when incompetent people keep getting the breaks while the good people get the heave ho."

"There's talk that with Bernie coming they have to let at least one of us go?"

"Really?! Who do you think they'd cut?"

She grew pensive as she tilted her head in Orion's direction.

Stan put his hand to his stomach.

"No...they wouldn't..."

Her voice became hushed.

"Why not? Everyone thinks he's a bit weird. He doesn't talk to nobody and half his stuff comes back rejected."

"It's just taking him a while to get the hang of things."

"It's been a year."

Stan's head pulled back in surprise.

"That long?"

She nodded. "You're the only one who'll work with him. But, how long can you keep covering him? Hanging with him is holding you back." She jabbed a finger into his chest. "And you and I both know who'll end up correcting those forms."

Stan tensed up.

"Stop beating up on him, you and everyone else. You just don't get to see how smart he is. I could never have done the DuPont analysis without him. He figured out workarounds to problems I didn't even know were there. It's just the little things he has trouble with."

"Like processing any kind of paperwork?"

Stan's jaw clenched. His eyes looked down at his keyboard.

Lorraine's voice softened.

"I know he's your buddy from college, but-."

He shot her a look of warning.

She raised her hands in surrender and picked herself off the desk to leave. Before stepping out of the cubicle she looked back.

"Honestly, when we go in there we might all be getting the sack."

Stan's shoulders fell as everything hit him.

"It could be today, huh?"

"Well…" she stuck out her lips.

"Damn…"

He sunk in his chair letting the news soak in.

A phone rang. She looked back to her cubicle. "Oh, that's me."

With a flirtatious wink she wandered off.

Orion hadn't heard a word of the conversation taking place in the adjoining cubicle. He was wholly absorbed in a calendar he had pulled up. At first he didn't believe it, but as he filled in the sequence of events that had comprised his weekend, the clearer and more disturbing it became. Deeper and deeper he dug into his memory. But, it seemed true. He had lost a whole day.

"Orion, Orion, wake up." He came to with a sudden jolt. Stan was peering down at him from over the dividing wall.

"Were you daydreaming again? They're saying that we might be heading into our last meeting."

Orion blinked several times still a little dazed.

Stan rephrased. "In five minutes, you, me, and all the other analysts might be walking into that conference room with jobs and coming out with pink slips."

Stan punched the cubicle wall with the side of his fist startling Orion.

"Damnit. I thought I'd be in management by now. In a few minutes, I'll be lucky to have a job." He looked at a pre-occupied Orion.

"Don't you care?"

His co-worker turned away from the screen.

"I do...care."

"It sure is hard to tell, sometimes. Your mind's always in the clouds. I wish you could be down here on earth with us giving a damn about what happens at Polymer."

Orion tensed up. "That's not fair. I come in here every day just like you. I know this place is sinking into the ground. All those empty desks I pass when I refill my coffee? How can that not affect me?"

Stan moved to Orion's side of the wall, took a seat in the extra chair.

"Well, you never seem to show it. The others talk about it, O'. How you think you're too good for them."

"I don't think that!"

"Well, you don't act like part of the team."

Orion put his head in his hands.

"I do what I'm supposed to do."

"You do the minimum, everyone knows that."

Stan immediately regretted the words the moment they came out. He looked away, ashamed.

"I'm sorry, I didn't mean that. I... "

Orion leaned in.

"I know that I'm not as fast as the rest of the group. And no, this isn't the first choice of what I'd like to be doing but, I'm doing my best. You stuck your neck out and got me this job. I appreciate that. I do. But for the last thirteen months I've been watching people get let go, people with families. People who really want to work here. And I sit and wonder why not me. Why don't they just fire me and let one of them stay? If I thought it'd make any difference, I'd quit."

Stan shook his head.

"No, don't say things like that. You're smart, really smart. I know this because I'm here with you everyday. The others don't get to see that. You don't let them. We've got a section meeting every two weeks and not once have you ever said one word; something, a suggestion, even. That's all you'd have to do. Then everyone else could see. They'd know you care, that you're in it with them."

Orion nodded, though his eyes looked more through his friend than at him.

Taking a long exhale, Stan leaned back in the chair, gazing at the ceiling. A wistful look came into Stan's brown eyes.

"You know what's been going through my mind this whole time watching the company collapsing? I wanted to come up with the solution, something that would save Polymer. At night, I try and try to think of a way, some kinda trick, anything that the big wigs might have missed. And when I came up with it, I'd reveal it to them in a glorious presentation. They, of course, would be so grateful, they'd give me a big office and everything would be as it should. Things'd be going so good that they'd be able to hire all the people back."

Sallowness washed over his cheeks. He bowed his head, his gaze falling to the ground.

"I just couldn't do it." His hand grabbed what was left of his hair. "I've been rackin' my skull for a whole year, but couldn't come up with one goddamn solution to get us out of this mess."

Orion stopped short of putting a hand on his friend's shoulder.

"Stan, we're just analysts here. That's what they pay us to do. We didn't create this situation. The president and the board did. They're the ones who messed everything up and only they have the power to fix it. We just have to have faith that they will."

"But, it's all falling apart."

"Trust them to do their job like they trust us to do ours. Be the best analyst you can be, that's all anyone can expect of you. Control what you can, disregard the rest. Look at me. I'm just a low-level employee putting in a day's work. I can't change the fate of the mighty Polymer Mutual Insurance Corporation any more than I can change the weather. And honestly, I wouldn't want that kind of pressure."

A bit of the gleam came back to Stan's eyes.

"I would, so much. I keep thinking and thinking there's gotta be some way."

"Please, stop killing yourself. For the last year when I looked at you, you know what I saw?"

"A man trying to make a difference?"

"A man whose blood pressure is rising as fast as his hair line."

Stan met his friend's earnest stare with a swift punch in the arm. His fist met solid muscle.

Orion looked at the spot where he had been hit.

"What was that for?"

"Talking about another guy's hairline is verboten."

Stan took to his feet.

"When you finally start showing some signs of your age, then you can crack on mine."

Orion followed suit but stumbled a little getting out of his chair.
Stan held him steady.

"Whoa, you okay? I didn't hit you that hard did I?"

Orion nodded. "No. I don't know."

"What do you mean?"

"I've been a little out of it. I think I lost a day." Orion blurted out.
"Sunday, I don't remember Sunday."

Stan broke into a wide grin.

"Yeah, Saturday nights can do that, alright." He gave Orion a slap
on the back. "Can't tell you how many Sundays I lost in college."

Stan took a glance at the crowd growing by the conference room
door. "Looks like the sheep have begun to gather. Maybe, we can
pretend we didn't know about the meeting."

Stan jumped as the voice of their manager, Mr. Ogleby, a
smallish black man with a booming nasal voice, sounded throughout
the floor.

"Attention. Attention, Everybody, if we could have all the
analysts to the conference room. Thank you."

Orion put a hand on his friend's shoulder.

"Stan, let's go get fired. Then we can go to the bar early and I can
watch you drink yourself sick."

Stan grimaced.

"You almost make this sound fun."

Minutes later, the pair rolled into the meeting and took their
usual side-by-side seats at the oval conference table. Lorraine
presumptively took the seat next to Stan. A young lady with dark

bangs began to take the empty seat next to Orion, but realized he was there, froze a half-second, then took a seat several chairs away by herself. With all nine analysts present, owl-eyed Bernie included, the group was still ten short of filling the table.

Stan's rigid countenance, not unlike that of a prisoner facing the firing squad, was shared by almost everyone seated. Orion sat head down, looking more like a defendant waiting for the jury to return but dreading what will happen when they do. Being surrounded by others in the same situation made it slightly better, but distressingly more real.

At the other end of the table, Mr. Ogleby entered the room with a sandy-blonde haired woman, just over six feet tall. Orion was brought back from his thoughts when Stan, suddenly ghost white, kicked his leg and nodded to the visitor. Orion's eyes widened with understanding when Mr. Ogleby introduced her - Linda Polymer, the president of the company.

Ms. Polymer, four generations removed from the company's founder, was blessed with patrician good looks and spoke and carried herself in the manner old money demands.

"Good morning, all. It's good to see everyone. I want to start off by saying that I will not pretend that you are unaware of the financial difficulties the company has been experiencing. This also means that I do not have to waste time explaining them or how they came about. The recession has affected the whole economy. Instead, I will get to what brought me here today."

Several of the analysts leaned forward with baited breath.

She continued, "I came here today to introduce Polymer Mutual's newest program. Called 'Express Yourself', it gives employees a chance to tackle a problem that is outside of their usual responsibilities."

The lights dimmed. A picture of a doctor examining a patient came up on the screen behind her.

"This slide illustrates what our company is all about. A patient, usually insured by his employer and fully covered with Polymer Mutual, happily goes to the doctor whenever they need to because we're covering the expenses. The doctor, also Polymer insured, knows he is safe to make mistakes because we will be there to cover him if he gets sued. Thanks to Polymer's coverage, it's a win-win for everyone."

The slide changed to a couple of smiling twenty-somethings in business attire running hand-in-hand up a flight of stairs.

"Now," she leaned forward and put her hands squarely on the faux walnut conference table. "We are seeking new ways to attract younger customers, specifically, people in their late twenties and early thirties. We've grown so much over these last decades, but it's vital that we further draw in this potential market. This would normally be a management function, but we've decided to put a team of two of you in charge of this."

On a notepad, Orion doodled the face of a cat with glowing eyes.

Ms. Polymer waited for the screen to change to a cartoon image of a man and woman working on either side of a desk.

"They would work together to develop ideas. So, here's your chance. Anyone interested in the challenge? We need two people interested in making a real impact on the insurance business?"

Stan's face looked like a kid who had just been picked to come off the bench. His hand shot up so quickly it startled Lorraine, causing her to spill coffee on her lap.

"I can!" he exclaimed with a crackle in his voice.

Ms. Polymer looked pleased, Ogleby less so. He spoke directly to Bernie, who was hunched forward on his elbows.

"Anyone else want to be on the committee? It'll mean long hours, but it's a real chance to shine"

The dark haired girl brushed her bangs off her eyes, her mouth twisted as if thinking about it.

Orion felt Stan's eyes on him. He looked away, but jumped a little when his friend gave his foot a kick. Linda Polymer caught Orion's sudden jerk and became aware of the stunning, blond haired man sitting towards the rear end of the table.

Ogleby's eyes were squarely on Bernie. "Is that it? No one else wants to jump in? Be part of the team?"

Bernie adjusted his glasses. His hand didn't fall back to the table but hovered just above it, not quite high enough to be a committal.

Stan's mouth opened in horror. He put his mouth to Orion's ear.

"Come on! Volunteer. This is my chance to do something. Don't make me be stuck working with him!"

Brow furrowed, Orion put his pen down.

The girl with the bangs lifted her hand an inch off the table.

Both Ogleby and Stan's eyeballs were pushing out of their sockets.



Diana sat on the edge of the bathtub running the lyso wand over her nude form. Slowly passing the yellow metallic rod over her long, alabaster leg, its warm, laser bristles extricated and disintegrated all the grime that had built up since the previous day. She had made it to her toes when the ring of an incoming message sounded.

Slipping into a sheer, rust colored negligee she made her way to the computer bank. The message played, activated by her presence.

"Attention: the great and mighty ruler of Acreon, Septon, and Deonis, and third son of Alteron, Lord Boibemad IV has read and deigned to accept your invitation to view lot #5jie6c."

# CHAPTER V
## Diana Meets Orion

Soulful strains from L'Elisir D'Amore wafted through the apartment coming from nowhere and everywhere. Guided by the light from his bedroom, a pajama clad Orion was dragged by an invisible hand to the old GE refrigerator which hummed sporadically like a drunk clearing his throat. Against his will he was forced to grab the plastic-coated handle and pull the door open.

The music swelled as a tsunami of fruits and vegetables burst out and flew around the room, many coming to rest in mid-air. Getting to his feet, he whirled around, finding himself inside a dazzling galaxy of produce. From the smorgasbord of foodstuffs hovering around him: bananas, peaches, apples, broccoli, pears, and more; he plucked a white onion.

With quick motions, he peeled off the layers. But, the more he peeled, the bigger the onion grew. Eventually, it grew too large to hold and he dropped it to the floor. It fell into single layers which blackened and blew away like dried up flowers petal in a wind gust.

A low, guttural howl sounded as if from a large mammal crying in pain. He pivoted to where the noise emanated from and saw a pair of disembodied cat eyes watching him through the window. The horrible moaning sound turned to one of despair, like that of the death throes of a wildebeest giving its final plaintive cry.

Orion fled from the green feline eyes but no matter where he ran in the apartment he couldn't escape their menacing gaze. He tried the front door, but the knob wouldn't turn. The wailing sound grew louder. He looked back. The suspended fruits and vegetables dropped to the ground as if they just couldn't resist gravity, anymore.

A cat's paw punched through the kitchen window. Glass shards flew across the apartment, a few whizzed past Orion's head. The disembodied leg matched the cat he had encountered on the stairs the other day.

Finally, the knob turned. Orion escaped, slamming the door behind him. But, in the hallway window, the glowing eyes reappeared, staring directly at him. Another set appeared in the window just above the first; then, another next to those.

Orion had to get away. He flew down the stairs to the front door of the building. Through the door's window he saw the Bentley Limousine pull up to the curb, its rear passenger door open. It was waiting for him.

Behind him the cat howls sounded, moving nearer.

Shoving open the front door, he bolted down the walk and jumped into the back of the limo. The door closed behind him with a definite thud, the locks clicked into place. He yanked at the door handle, but it wouldn't open. He was trapped.

A guttural yowl sounded from the front seat. To his horror, the cat from the stairs, a dark steely gray, peered out from over the drivers head rest. Most disconcerting was the chauffeur's hat it was wearing. It stood on its hind legs, its front paws resting on the steering wheel.

Orion kept trying to open the door. It wouldn't budge.

The four legged driver talked in feline mews and yowls. But, Orion, somehow, understood what it was saying. The small animal asked where he wanted to go. He said, "The Atlas Building."

The feline looked at him and grinned demonically as the limo lurched forward.

Orion watched in horror as the Atlas Building went out of view.

"Where are you taking me!?"

Orion woke up shaking and in a cold sweat. He was in his bed. It was that stupid dream again! The same as the last four nights.

The clock on the nightstand read eight fifteen. Even for a Saturday, it was too early to get out of bed, yet, too late to go back to sleep. He wanted to forget the nightmare. He'd meditate on Diana. Thinking about her still made his pulse rise. His mind had just started playing back the conversation between her and that Apollo fellow when he heard a knock at the door.

Robed, he answered the door. It was Uri.

"Good morning, O. Hope I didn't disturb you."

"Well, it is-." A quick look at the clock revealed it was half-past ten o'clock. Where had the morning gone?!

Uri held up a packet of batteries, "Just going around changing the batteries in the carbon dioxide detectors."

Orion stepped out of his way. "Sure, come in."

Along with batteries, the small old man pulled in a short ladder which he clumsily set up under the $CO_2$ detector.

Orion, suddenly hungry, prepared a bowl of cereal.

His landlord eyed a nine volt battery in his hand before beginning his ascent.

"I've really fallen behind on replacing these." Uri made it two steps up the ladder before he started to look a little dizzy. Weakly, he took another step, but it looked like he had used all his strength. He leaned to the side causing the ladder to wobble a little.

Orion tried hard to focus on eating his bowl of cereal, but couldn't take it. With a look of resignation, he set down his still crunchy cereal.

"Here, Uri let me do that."

"No, no. I'm okay."

Uri tried to take the last step, but realized he couldn't.

"I-..."

Orion helped him down.

"Here take a seat on the couch."

Uri plopped down on the couch and immediately looked very comfortable.

"Thanks, O. Guess I'm not as young as I used to be."

Orion squinted suspiciously as he evaluated whether he was being played or not. Soon his attention was wholly engrossed with trying to figure out how to remove the detector; not as easy a task as he had assumed it would be.

Uri spoke, almost more to himself.

"It gets harder and harder keeping this place going. All the maintenance, nothing seems to work."

"Yeah, this place is kind of a wreck."

"Every day, it's something new that needs fixing. And that's on top of all the regular stuff that needs taking care of. I just work and work and I don't know for what."

"Yeah, you are always working. I've been awoken many mornings by the beautiful sounds of your banging around the trash cans and tangling with the raccoons you find inside."

The old man nodded forcefully.

"Miserable pests!"

The angry tone quickly subsided and a touch of melancholy penetrated his words.

"Miserable me.... I don't think I can do it anymore, O."

"Do what?"

"Run this place. I think I've reached the end of the line. It's come to the point where I'm not sure what I'm even doing it for, anymore. Or who…"

"Come on, it's not as bad as all that."

"It's not the same without her, the missus, not since she passed away. Getting this place, that was her dream. Without her, I'm just going through the motions."

"I have to admit, I know what you mean. I feel like that all the time."

The old man let out a long sigh.

"I'm thinking of selling this place."

The new battery in, Orion reaffixed the case.

"Hm, that's an idea…"

"You think?"

"Sure, why not."

"Well, what about the place. Who would take care of it?"

"The new owners of course."

"I'd want someone who'd take care of the tenants, keep the place up the same way I have all these years."

"They might do that or they might tear it down and build

something better. Once you sell the building it's out of your hands; not your responsibility."

"But, O', I wouldn't want you to lose your home."

"It's fine. People move all the time. This," Orion motioned to the apartment around him, "is just where I'm living now. I don't expect to be here, forever. In fact, I think it'd be good for me if you did sell it and I was forced to move on."

Uri squished out his cheeks as he pondered this.

Orion stepped off the ladder and handed the old battery to his landlord.

"You only live once, Uri. There's more to life than just keeping up an old building. You've done a great job, but sooner or later you've got to let go of things."

He picked up a cheap lamp and shook it. "This is just a material possession. It's replaceable. Your time with the living is not. What matters is that you get to do everything you want while you're still around."

Uri took to his feet.

"You make good sense, O."

"It's what I'd do if I were you."

The gray-haired gentleman folded up the ladder.

"Okay, I'll get out of your way. Other's to do."

Orion's eyes darted up and to the right as a thought passed through his mind.

"You're going to do all the apartments?"

Uri had just opened the door, "Yeah."

"And mine's the first one you've done?"

"Yeah… Why?"

After a quick shower, shave and wardrobe change, Orion walked
with Uri from apartment to apartment changing the smoke detector
batteries. Uri was simple, but he was no dummy. To Orion's chagrin,
his gray-haired landlord started them on the bottom floor, so they
had to do every single unit before they got to Diana's floor. To
speed things up, Orion began doing the whole job himself while Uri
happily gossiped with the tenants.

Early afternoon arrived before they finally made it to Diana's
floor. Orion immediately proceeded to her door.

"Not yet," Uri motioned him to stop. "We're starting on that end
of the hall."

"What?! But-."

The small man determinedly made his way to the farthest door.

"We always start at this end."

Dejected, Orion cast a longing eye towards Diana's door then
meekly followed.


Diana had worked for several hours at her console. The machinery
was silent to the naked ear, but the computer was marking trillions of
minute changes in the two lots' properties. Anomalies were reported
and communicated to Diana, who would then transmit them to
potential bidders. The perceived value of the lots shifted accordingly.
Too many anomalies and the price would decrease. No anomalies
and the price would remain firm, or occasionally rise slightly.

A knock came at the door. As Diana crossed to answer it, the computer console swiftly transformed into a sofa, two chairs and a coffee table.

She broke into a wide grin at the sight of the old caretaker. "Uri. What a nice surprise."

"Diana," he gave a slight bow, "Just coming round to change the carbon dioxide detectors."

He stepped in.

Diana's gaze turned vacant when she saw Orion coming in with the ladder.

Before he could say anything, she had turned back to Uri.

"The carbon dioxide detector…?"

Uri pointed to the ceiling.

"Yeah, the battery in them has to be replaced once a year."

Diana examined the detector as if seeing it for the first time.

"Oh, yes. I hadn't even noticed that little thing up there."

She eyed it, fascinated.

"Why would you want to detect carbon dioxide? It's relatively worthless."

Orion crooked a wondering eyebrow as he set up the ladder.

He motioned to Uri, "The battery."

Uri fished a nine volt out of the package and handed it over.

He motioned to Uri, "The battery."

Uri fished a nine volt out of the package and handed it over.

"Oh, I'm sorry. Where are my manners? Diana, this is another roomer in the building. He's a really great guy. His name's Orion. Orion, like the constellation."

A flash of recognition came to her eyes.

"Orion? Oh, hi there. My name is Diana." She extended her hand to him. A bit surprised, he took it but just held it, having the feeling that he was supposed to kiss it, but not brave enough to try.

"Like the constellation." He repeated, suddenly unable think of anything else to say.

"Of course," she replied. He observed her perfectly trimmed eyebrows rise a bit, crowning a fetching smile.

"Orion's been here for two years now." Uri proclaimed then added, "He shares my love of astronomy."

Orion replaced the detector cover and climbed down the ladder. To his horror, he suddenly realized how much dust had collected on his burgundy, V-neck sweater he had sported for the occasion and quickly tried to brush it off.

Uri continued. "Diana's in real estate like I told you the other night when you were asking about her."

Orion shot Uri a, *don't talk about that* look.

She added, "I'm just a broker."

"Never needed a broker, I always rent."

"Renting is like throwing money away." She shot back. "Everyone knows that."

He gave a mischievous grin. "I don't throw it away. I give it to Uri. For his retirement."

She laughed; a bit too long and hard as if it had been awhile since she had last done so. As she laughed, her cloche slipped off her head, revealing the top of her head.

When Orion saw her hair for the first time, he fell breathless. Her slightly wavy locks were an amalgam of soft reds and browns with golden strands scattered through whenever the light shone upon them.

Sensing his gaze, she replaced the bonnet as if taken by modesty.

"Well, that is a good cause."

Orion eyed the apartment.

"You've really decorated the place. How long have you lived here?"

Uri interjected, "A week, like I was tellin' you."

Orion's mouth fell open.

"Really?! It was way over a year before my place looked this lived in. And how you've decorated it…"

He eyed IO, standing on the fireplace mantle in its statue form.

"This piece… You know, it looks just like-."

He reached for the stone feline statue, but immediately had to use two-hands.

"Wow, it's heavier than it looks.

The jade green eyes of the statue lit up. A green targeting dot pinpointed the spot between Orion's eyes.

Diana's hand shot out.

"No, wait!"

Distracted by her, Orion failed to notice the ray gun extending from the statue's mouth.

"What?"

"Don't touch that!"

She grabbed IO and replaced it on the desk, giving it a stern look of admonition.

"Sorry." Orion said.

"That's okay." Diana smiled apologetically, "So, what do you do for a living?"

Uri volunteered an answer. "He handles insurance. Large accounts. Isn't that right, O?"

Orion shook his head, unsure as to what Uri was talking about.

"Uh, yes. Large accounts. That's what I do."

"And, when he's not doing that, he's showing people a good time - especially the ladies."

Diana saw the blonde haired man blush in embarrassment and disbelief. She looked him up and down, liking what she saw.

"Is this true?" she teased.

"Yes, that's what I do. I show people a good time. 'Especially, the ladies.'"

She beamed with delight at the red-faced man's unease. He hurried to fold up the ladder.

Uri added, "You know, if you want, Orion could show you a good time."

"If I want a good time," she nodded suppressing a grin.

Orion pushed the ladder onto Uri.

"Okay, Uri, I'll take it from here."

He gently pushed Uri to the door closing it with the old man on the other side. He then turned around, looked her in the eye.

"Um, so, would you like...?"

"To have a good time?"

They both smiled.

# CHAPTER VI
## When Stars Cross

Pasticci's was one of the last family-run trattorias in the city.
Tucked away at the end of a sleepy, otherwise residential street, the
establishment provided its customers – most of whom were regulars
– homemade Italian cooking in a cozy environment. Best of all, the
prices were still affordable, making it Orion's ideal choice for his
date with Diana. Even if she was a huge eater, he'd be able to afford
it.

Despite being set a half flight below ground level, the quiet
eatery at the end of the street had tall, open windows that allowed
passer-byes an excellent line of sight to the eating area. The
restaurant glowed from the colors of old wood, mottled brick, mortar
and the golden light that filters through grape vines. Clay pots, arm
length striped ewers, and tarnished copper bowls nestled between the
simple tables and chairs that lined both walls worked to recreate an
alley in a small Tuscan village. Above each table, pictures hung, not
always straight, that looked, intentionally of course, as if they'd

been purchased at an Italian yard sale.

Orion motioned his date to the stairs that led to the swinging entrance door and watched her descend the concrete steps in yet another of her radiant costumes: a low cut, shimmering dress seemingly composed of crushed diamonds. Despite that, when she walked, the fabric ebbed and flowed like eddies in a tidal pond. Her tiara was embedded with miniature diamond swirls framing a single, large, deep black ruby, cut perfectly round.

Well aware of how she tended to dressed, Orion had made sure to wear his best and only suit. His dapper appearance had been aided by a video he had found that demonstrated how to tie a Windsor knot. Another video he found showed him how to properly shine his shoes.

Hurrying to greet them, the owner, who spoke with the hint of an old world accent, pointedly seated the rather glamorous looking couple at a table by the front window so that persons on the street could see what a classy restaurant he was running.

Orion moved to pull Diana's chair out for her, but their eager host got to it first.

She was about to thank him, but was distracted by screams emanating from the kitchen. A dark-haired, sweet faced girl, probably seven or eight, though made to look even younger by the pig-tails in her hair and the adult-sized apron she wore, ran out of the kitchen holding up a birdcage with two birds in it. The owner smiled weakly and said with a roll of his eyes: "My daughter." He quickly stepped over to the mischievous child and wagged his finger, scolding her in thick Italian.

As Diana and Orion watched the scene play out, she asked him, "Oh, do you think that's what they're going to serve us?"

Orion grinned. So, she did have a sense of humor. How cool.

He retorted, "I think someone's not big on having birds – live ones at least - in the kitchen."

They watched a little more.

"Fascinating," said Diana. "I wonder what that means."

"What?"

"Well, he's telling her that she won't be allowed to keep the birds. He doesn't want them having eggs, that her mother should learn to say no to her once in a while. Now he's asking her why she couldn't get a normal, quiet pet like a cat."

Orion didn't know any Italian, and was suitably impressed that Diana did. He would have remarked on it, but part of him felt a little ashamed at not knowing any other languages. She was so amazing. Who knew how many other languages she might be fluent in?

He picked up his menu and began perusing it.

Diana followed his example and did likewise, but quickly looked baffled by what she was looking at. There were names of items she assumed she could order, but the menu had explanations that made no sense to her. She looked back to her dining companion, his eyes moved back and forth as he read over the options.

Done, he looked up.

"The mussels here are excellent." He informed her.

She read the description carefully; her brows furled a bit, "I just do not understand. What are mussels?"

"What do you mean?"

"What sort of food are they?"

Orion tilted his head a little, not understanding. How could she not have heard of mussels? So, he went the literal route.

"They're seafood."

"From the ocean?!"

He nodded.

Her face widened in amazement, "Bees and butterflies!"

Before he could formulate a response to this, Diana abruptly straightened up as if someone had poked her in the back.

"Oh, I'm so sorry." She said, "I just have to take this."

He hadn't heard a ring or even a vibration, but was taken aback as she dramatically stuck out her middle finger. To his further surprise, she began speaking into it.

"Yes, I did get the numbers."

Orion watched, dumbfounded, his date flipping him the bird while talking into it.

"No, I really can't hear you, either." She told the finger. "I'm going to have to switch."

She fished into the gold-lined clasp purse at her side and pulled out a bizarre looking cell phone with a tiny spinning satellite dish on it.

"Yes, I can hear you, now.... Okay, once the official survey has been submitted, we can finalize the deal.... No, the pleasure is mine."

Orion's eyes popped as she folded the full sized phone from regular size into a fingernail sized wafer and slipped it into her purse.

"Sorry."

Before he could ask any of the myriad questions currently filling his head, the waiter came to the table to take their order. Diana patiently listened to the specials then remarked that she was parched.

The waiter promptly drew her attention to the wine list on the back of the menu.

"Is champagne good?"

The waiter leaned forward to look at the list.

"Which one?"

"I don't know, any of them. Is champagne something that is good in general?"

Orion's jaw dropped. "You've never had champagne?"

She shook her head.

He directed the waiter to the middle priced of the three selections. "We'll each have a glass, thanks."

To Diana he exclaimed, "Wow, your first champagne. This will be great."

"Hmm," she smiled wickedly, "it's not often that I get to try some of the local fare. It is quite the stone spitting the gull, huh?"

"What…?" Orion said half to himself.

She picked the menu up, again. "So, you think I should try these mussels?"

"Uh, yeah, they're great."

"Then I shall. A night of firsts!"

He could hold back the question no longer. "Where are you from, anyway?"

She paused at the question as a wave of shame crossed over her face.

"Oh, a small place. You've never heard of."

"Try me."

The champagne arrived. Seeing a chance to change the subject, Diana quickly grabbed her glass. "Champagne, I presume?"

He nodded.

"That's it, kind of a bubbling wine." He raised his glass. "To building mates."

She followed suit, raising her glass, but almost dropped it when he inexplicably bumped his glass against hers. She observed him drink deeply from the champagne flute so she did the same.

"Bees and butterflies! That's strong!"

Orion almost snorted his champagne through his nose upon hearing this. She was definitely, like no other woman he'd ever met before.

Almost immediately a saucy look came into her eyes:

"Going to have to go slow with this one."

She set the glass down; a slight cloudy feeling was chilling her brain cells. Suddenly, she saw how attractive the man across the table was; really, really fine! His deep ocean blue eyes, thick blonde hair, and easy smile were making her warm and tingly. He didn't put on superior airs like someone else she could name. She was glad she was getting to know him. She was going to be glad to get to know him even better later that night. Yes, suddenly there was no question about that.

Leaning in she asked, "So, why are you here?"

"Here?"

"I mean this is a really out of the way place. I never thought I'd find one of our kind in a place like this."

"Our kind?" Orion looked around at the restaurant and the staff. "The place isn't so bad. You think it's no good?"

She shook her head, "You have to admit, it's certainly not what one would call a destination spot. But, I was really trying to find out a little about you."

"Oh."

She finished off her glass like it was soda pop.

The waiter returned and asked what they wanted. Diana pointed to Orion, "You order for me."

He did. Before leaving, the waiter remarked upon Diana's empty glass.

"You're right, look at that. I'd love more. Wait." She pulled up the wine list and pointed to the most expensive champagne. "Let me try that one."

Orion craned his neck trying to see if she had ordered the one he thought she had. Seeing the price, his face contorted unpleasantly.

The waiter took no time in bringing a replacement glass which she quickly slurped up.

"This stuff is great! I can't believe I've never had it before."

"I can."

When the waiter arrived with their food, she asked for a third glass. Orion broke into a cold sweat visualizing money flying out of his wallet!

Eyeing the bowl of mussels before her, Diana cringed and slowly poked at them. The sight of these little creatures that appeared to have mouths opened enough to reveal squiggly insides turned her stomach. Finally, she reluctantly picked one up looking afraid it might bite her.

"What's this?"

"Mussels. You eat them."

She looked at it oddly, then took a bite out of it.

CRACK!

Orion's jaw dropped.

All heads in the restaurant turned their way.

"Oww!" Diana held her hand to her mouth.

Orion stood up to help her. "No, no. You eat the inside."

He grabbed one and opened it to reveal the meat inside. She winced at the contents.

"It's good." He assured her. "Really."

"This is from the ocean?"

He nodded.

She put the mussel in her mouth, but was too grossed out to chew.

"I-. It's alive. I think it's moving!"

"Just chew."

She shook her head "no."

"If you don't chew it, then you'll just have it sitting there in your mouth."

Turning green, she took a sip of champagne. Instead of alleviating the situation, now, she had champagne and mussel in her mouth.

"Just swallow. You can do it." He pumped his fist in support.

The ridiculousness of it all become too much for her, champagne pushed up through her nose.

He reached over and wiped her face with a napkin.

"Maybe you should just spit it out."

Totally nauseated, she violently lurched forward, spitting the lump of meat back into her bowl.

He shook his head. "Swoosh! What a waste."

Her face was flushed.

"It'll be okay." He wiped her mouth, again. "I can't believe you've never had mussels before."

"No. And never will again."

She broke into giggles at her "joke."

"They're a lot like oysters."

"Do you eat them alive, too?"

This time he laughed, shook his head at the "joke."

"Wow! You know, Diana, it's like you're from a different world."

"You mean trans-dimensionally?"

"Umm..."

The waiter reappeared. He had witnessed the scene from afar and was desperately strategizing how to save his tip.

Diana pushed the bowl of mussels away.

"Please, take these away. I will incinerate anyone who ever tries to make me eat these again."

The waiter walked off with the bowl of mussels past the girl with the bird cage who was looking sullen at the prospect of having to lose her new pets.

Orion weakly told her, "I'm sorry. Maybe that wasn't the best thing to order."

She didn't respond. Just sat looking like she was about to throw up. Orion took on a disheartened air as the date more and more seemed like the final flight of the Hindenburg. Spotting a chance to distract his date and change the mood, he motioned the little girl with the cage to step over.

"Wow, those are two lovely little birds you have there."

This perked the girl up a little and she raised the cage so the couple could better see them.

"Their names are Polly and Colombo."

The sight of the two little finches did the trick in distracting

Diana from the trauma she had just endured. Curious, she put her finger to the cage and smiled.

"Polly and Colombo? You named them? Why?"

The owner, horrified at the sight of his daughter annoying his customers with her birds, rushed over.

"Lucia, get away from these people. They are trying to eat."

Orion raised his hand.

"That's okay. We wanted to look at these two beautiful little birds."

The little girl smiled proudly and gave her father a *see* look.

"So," Orion asked the girl, "which one is Polly and which one is Colombo?"

The girl thought for a second then decided, pointing them out as she answered.

"Polly. Colombo."

Orion smiled. "You know, you can tell your father that he doesn't have to worry about having eggs with these two."

"Why?" she asked.

"Because Polly's a male."

Both the girl and her father were confused.

"What?" the girl asked.

The owner was curious, too. "Why do you say that?"

Orion pointed to the foreheads of the two small animals.

"Their markings are both male. See the stripe on each of their foreheads? Only a male would have that."

The owner and his daughter peered into the cage. The girl shook her head.

"I don't see a stripe on the birdies' heads!"

Perplexed, the father put his hand to his chin. "No, I don't, either."

"Look closer." Orion pointed directly at the stripes on the tops of their heads. "They're quite prominent."

Both father and daughter looked perplexed, shaking their heads and staring at the birds.

Diana, however, did. She pointed to the tops of the birds' heads, too.

"Yes, look at that; wide bright stripes, almost impossible to miss, really. That's the sign of the male?"

"Yeah. That's part of how they attract the females."

"What about those smaller lines on the wings and the tail?" Diana pointed to the stripes.

"Oh, wow, I hadn't seen those. Yeah, those're male markings, too."

The owner shook his head. He didn't see anything and looked increasingly frustrated that the two customers were either crazy or having fun at his and his daughter's expense.

"Come Lucia."

With a strong jerk, he pulled the little girl away and back towards the bar. The last thing she could be heard saying was, "Why don't I see no stripes!"

The waiter reappeared at their table. Diana displayed a broad, intoxicated grin.

"Oh, yes. I'm glad you're here. Give me that menu, again."

Orion's heart skipped a beat.

"The menu?"

"Yes, I'll just try something else."

"Try mine. We could switch." Orion pushed his plate to hers.

"Nonsense, you enjoy your meal. I'll just try some other things. This 'veal', is it good?"

As Orion looked at the listing, all he could say was, "At that price, it better be."

"Ah," the waiter chimed in, "It is truly excellent!"

She pointed to several other items from the appetizer and entrée sections each of which, of course, were "excellent".

"Okay, I'll take all of them."

"Yes, miss. Of course." In a flash, the waiter had grabbed the menu and was off to put in the order.

Orion felt dizzy, calculating in his mind all the food his date had just ordered - four entrees and three appetizers.

"You want to eat all that?"

She crinkled her nose. "No, just want to try all of them. This is fascinating. All these different foods, I've never done this before! Bees and Butterflies!"

The waiter, with help, brought out a succession of dishes for the glamorous couple by the window. A side table was set up, when room on their table ran out.

Diana was gnawing on a lamb chop when she asked, "Mm, mm. This one beats old bulls! So, you've tried all these foods?"

"Yeah, it's Italian. Everyone has."

But not all at one sitting, he thought to himself. He had given up calculating the cost of this dinner three entrees ago.

She lowered the chop and emptied her fourth glass of champagne. "You… are a very interesting person. What do you do for a living? Oh, yes, Uri said insurance. You must be a very big person in the industry."

This time, the wave of shame passed over Orion's face.

She pointed the lamb chop bone at him. "Maybe, we should work together, you and me. Insurance goes hand in hand with real estate. But, I don't have to tell you that." She let a giggle slip out.

"Uri kind of exaggerated my job. I'm in insurance, but as an analyst. In the section I work in, we basically figure out how to give the minimal amount of coverage for the maximum amount of customer fees – not really much to talk about, but a job's a job. I'd leave but I can't imagine any other job being different. Though, until a week ago, I couldn't have imagined any woman being different. You're certainly one of a kind."

Diana blushed at the compliment, though imperceptibly as her cheeks were already bright red. The glaze over her eyes gave him the feeling that she hadn't understood much of what he had just said. Her body was so completely relaxed it was remarkable that she was staying upright.

"I don't know what this insurance analysis is all about, but," she reached across and put her hand on his, "It sounds like something you don't like and you're not proud of. So, why do you do it?"

He felt her pity and it stung.

"Well, I-. I don't know. I never thought about it."

"You seem too talented to be spending your time doing things you don't like and, much too smart."

Orion pondered this a moment.

"Smart enough to see when I'm being flattered and criticized in the same sentence. I can see why you're successful at what you do. So, what's it like to be a real estate broker? All excitement, high power and adventure?"

She finished chewing a ravioli.

"The bulk of my career, so far, has been selling minor properties that have already been stripped of their most valuable assets. It's so highly competitive - the business - I fight tooth and nail for even the smallest deals."

"Bad as all that?"

Her visage turned intense.

"Not any more. Because I'm working on a deal that could change everything. If I pull this one off, I can break through to the big time. No one will remember Galleos. All those years of running myself into the ground will be redeemed because I'll finally have made the deal that changes everything."

"This big deal, does it have something to do with the guy who picks you up in the big car in the mornings?"

"Oh, you mean, Apollo? Sort of. But, he's in a class all by himself. He's the one we all look up to."

"With a name like that he'd have to either be an amazing realtor or male stripper. But, look at me picking on someone's over-the-top name." Orion motioned for the check.

"He wrote the rules on property acquisition. There's no one like him. The way he can ascertain an asset's real potential and double it is almost magical. But you know what?"

He shook his head.

"He can make a broker's career or crush it. You're either with Apollo or against him and no one lasts long who's against him."

The check came. Orion couldn't help but notice how long it was. He didn't bother looking at the total.

"So, you work with this pleasant sounding guy?"

"I've emulated him professionally. That's why I know to be very careful when I'm around him. My guard always has to be up. He says he wants to be my mentor but I know better."

She pointed a finger into Orion's chest.

He took out his card and laid it on the bill. There was no way it would cover this bill. Maybe, he thought to himself, he could offer to come back to the restaurant tomorrow night and do the dishes or sweep up in the kitchen. Perhaps they'd have him do deliveries. With a bill this large, it might take doing all three, several nights in a row.

The waiter returned quickly with the card.

"I'm sorry, it didn't go through."

"What?"

Orion fumbled through his wallet. It was for show as he knew there was only ten dollars in it.

"I-."

Before he knew it, Diana whipped out her card - a shiny platinum card with no writing or markings.

"Don't worry, I'll cover it."

The waiter eyed the card suspiciously.

"It's good everywhere." Diana said.

The waiter walked off with it.

Orion eyed Diana.

"I'll...I'll pay you back."

"Don't worry about it." She smiled coquettishly, brushing her leg against his.

The waiter returned with her card and receipt.

"No," Orion continued, "I was supposed to take you out."

They got up, Diana just barely. Both men moved to help her. She held up a hand to stop them.

"It's okay."

She tried to take a step, but too woozy, fell onto Orion who caught her and wrapped his arms around her. He gave the jealous waiter a *back off* look.

Diana seemed very comfortable in Orion's strong arms. Her eyes closed, savoring the moment.

He pointed her to the door.

"Come on. Let's get you home. And, okay, you got the bill tonight, but I'm bringing you dinner tomorrow. Deal?"

She nodded carelessly, running her hands along his well-toned arms.

"Sounds marvelous."

The walk back to the Atlas building was achieved only by Orion holding up his date. Not used to being helped with anything, she would fight him occasionally but, in her current state, eventually gave up trying to walk independently. Besides, in his arms, she could feel the muscles through his shirt and warmth of strong arms, comforting, reassuring.

They entered through the doors of the Atlas building laughing, arms around each other. Their talk had devolved into nonsense more than anything else.

"…and that's just the half of it!" Diana laughed through her nose finishing a fantastical story about the planet Emoss.

"Yeah," he helped her up the last step. "You've definitely had enough champagne for one night."

They stopped at Orion's door and hesitated.

"I'll walk you up to your place."

She shook her head.

"I don't want to go to my place."

She clung to him, kissed him on the cheek.

"Oh."

"I want to keep feeling like this, warm and safe."

He pulled her close and they kissed, then kissed some more. His kiss was firm and aggressive. Hers was receptive, willing, taking in and enjoying the sensation of being connected. His arm held her up, the back of her head ended up resting against the door, her eyes closed.

He broke it off. She, very drunk, started to fall again before he caught her. He looked into her eyes.

"I think we better call it a night."

"No!" she protested.

He looked into those lovely almond eyes of hers, cupped her face in his hand. Her fragrance filled his nostrils; exotic, yet extremely feminine. Letting her go was the last thing he wanted, but she was fading fast.

He turned her to the direction of the stairs and started walking her up. She resisted but was too weak to put up a fight.

Half awake, she felt herself being carried up the stairs like a baby, leaning against a muscular chest. She didn't like this, not one bit, but felt herself being lowered back onto her feet at her door almost as quickly as she had become aware of being aloft.

"You have your key?"

She looked confused. "Key?"

He turned the knob, found the door unlocked and opened it.

"You go to lullaby land now. Tomorrow night, I'll come up with some dinner so we can have a really nice second date."

With a kiss on the cheek and one last inhale of her lovely fragrance, he nudged her through the door, and made sure it was shut.

As much as one could ever know anything in this world, he knew she was the one for him.

# CHAPTER VII
## The Job

To Stan's amazement, Orion was already waiting for him at the curb when he arrived in the morning. With pep in his step, his co-worker jumped into the car.

"Good morning, Stan."

"Good...morning?"

Orion hummed while checking himself out in the side passenger mirror.

Stan didn't know what to make of this.

"Are you okay, O'?"

"Yeah, why?"

"You just seem really effervescent today."

"Really?" Orion looked up at sky. "Wow, what a beautiful day!"

"The sky is darkening. It looks like rain."

The Bentley drove up alongside the Honda and parked in the spot in front of them.

As if by clockwork, the front door of the Atlas building opened and Diana emerged.

She paused for a split second, startled at seeing Orion. In a moment of dread, her eyes apprehensively darted back and forth between the two cars at the end of the walk. She quickly regained her composure and fixed her eyes straight ahead.

Stan couldn't help but notice the smile that appeared on his friend's lips as the flashily dressed woman strolled across the front walk and stepped into the limousine in front of them.

In the backseat of his Bentley, Apollo watched, too. Diana's averted glance was something he definitely noticed. Looking behind him, he studied the good-looking man with golden locks staring intently at her. The man's expression was intense; love struck, even.

Orion craned his neck a little as he watched Diana disappear into the grey limo, the door closing itself behind her. The four wheeled chariot pulled smoothly from the curb.

He turned to Stan.

"Did you see her?!"

"You mean, that lady who just got into the car?"

Orion corrected him, "That amazing, lovely, wonderful, divine lady who just got into the car."

Stan cocked his brow. "I guess."

Orion looked as excited as a kid who had just learned what happens on Christmas morning.

"We went out last night."

Stan's face showed genuine surprise. "You and the girl next door?"

"I took her to Pasticci's"

"That dive?"

"It's a nice place and it's all I could afford."

"Exactly. I just saw this lady get into a limousine and you can barely afford a cheap Italian dive."

"She ended up paying."

"She paid?!" Stan shook his head, started pulling the car out. "No wonder she didn't give you the time of day."

"I tried to pay…but couldn't. She'd never tried Italian and wanted to try all of the dishes. It's cool, though. I'm making her dinner tonight."

"Yeah, you're place is really gonna wow her after she's back from drinks at La Rocques in the limo."

"Hm, you have a point."

"Look, I'm not sayin' it won't happen, but it's pretty obvious you two are from different worlds."

The first two hours of Stan's morning had been spent cleaning and organizing his desktop. This included wiping the monitor, dusting the keyboard, replacing the mouse pad, changing the trash bag, and even stocking the min-fridge with those cute little Coke cans you can only get from the store way across town. Like a bird in mating season, Stan had made his nest as inviting as possible for his special visitor. Now, with the invitee seated in his guest chair, Stan was ready to dive into the business at hand.

"And here are some of the ideas I've been able to come up with so far." he pointed to his computer monitor. "Not fully flushed out, but together I'm thinking we can…we can…"

He suddenly realized he had lost the attention of his co-worker.

"Bernie. Bernie, over here."

The uninterested looking man finished his text, read through it, then looked up at Stan through horn-rimmed glasses, nodding to continue.

"Okay," Stan resumed, "so the first of these ideas involves a game show where people can come to our website to play the game. I'm not sure how they-."

The cell phone ringing was bearable, but Bernie's answering it was not.

Stan gave a menacing glare to no avail.

"Hey, I thought we were having a meeting here."

With phone to ear, his co-worker raised a finger to indicate he would need a moment then turned his back to him.

In disbelief, Stan leaned back on his desk, his eyes shooting daggers at his co-worker who obliviously sauntered off down the aisle. Towards the end of the aisle, Bernie passed Lorraine who spotted Stan and made a bee-line towards him.

He quickly ducked back down into his cubicle, but Lorraine's head popped in through the cubicle doorway a second later. This time, though, she was minus her usual ear-to-ear grin.

"Stan. Got a moment?"

"Now's not a good time."

She entered and took a seat.

"By end of the day Friday, Polymer will have ten fewer employees. I heard it in the parking lot from a source who was informed by another reliable source who may or may not be from HR."

Stan waved her off.

"Come on Lorraine, this is what you told us last time about that big meeting."

"That was different. No one really knew what the meeting was about so it was guessing. This time is for real."

His color turned pale, it was too much for him.

"Why are you telling me? What am I supposed to do?"

Lorraine gave a look of sympathy; put her hand on his shoulder.

"Oh, no, I didn't want to make you feel bad, sweetie. Just wanted to give you a heads up."

Too overcome by the news, he didn't notice her hand maternally brush his elevated hairline.

"It's alright. It's not you I'm upset with. It's that dope, Bernie. We've yet to have a meeting on the project."

"Weren't you meeting just now?"

"For five seconds. Then he gets a call and walks off. It's killing me."

"Oh, that's horrible." Lorraine rolled her chair over, rubbed her hand up and down his back. "I wish there was something I could do to help."

"I'm getting seriously worried. What if we don't have anything to show in the meeting?"

She wrapped her arm around his back and gave an affirmative squeeze.

"I know. It's all so crazy. How can they expect you, an analyst, to come up with some revolutionary plan that no one's ever thought of inside of a few weeks?"

"And I'll be personally letting the president down. There goes any chance of a promotion in the next five years. Who am I kidding? With the path this company's heading down, there won't be any Polymer Mutual five years from now."

Despondent, his head fell into his hands.

"All because I couldn't come up with anything."

Lorraine continued to rub his back.

In the distance, just above the office's ambient tone, a melody sifted through. Someone was humming, and the song was cheery; the kind of tune that invoked birds chirping and sunny, blue skies. Stan lifted his head, he recognized the tune. It was from an old musical, with words like, 'put on a happy face'. His features mutated from despair to annoyance the longer the tune continued.

He rose to find out who the culprit was and immediately detected it was his cube mate.

"Is that you humming?!"

Orion, who was lackadaisically leaning back in his chair, gazing off into space, casually swiveled around to face Stan, a hint of sparkle in his eyes.

"Oh, sorry. Was I bothering you?"

"Well, yes. Some of us are trying to save the USS Polymer before it sinks for good."

Lorraine rolled her eyes as she made her exit.

Orion spoke, a seemingly permanent grin plastered on his face.

"So, how'd the meeting with Bernie go? Can't wait to see the plan."

Stan signaled his co-worker to stand and with a nod of his head, directed him over to Ogleby's window where their manager could be seen sharing a laugh with Bernie.

Orion raised his eyebrows. "How long did you two-?"

"Five seconds if you include 'Hello'"

"Hmm."

Stan leaned in. "I-. I don't know what to do about this assignment. I try and try to think of something, some plan that will increase revenue and save the company, but I can't. Polymer Mutual's in a real sinkhole. We've tried everything that the competition's doing but it's just... I don't know."

Orion got up.

"You gotta stop blaming yourself for everything. Management couldn't come up with anything and now they want two analysts to do it?"

"Not two, just me. Bernie won't even talk to me unless I trap him in the file room or something. If I could just have someone to run a few ideas over..."

With a sudden gleam in his eye, he looked up to Orion.

"Say, could I-?"

Orion immediately shook his head and backed up an inch.

"No, Stan. You know I wouldn't be any help to you. I'm no good at this insurance stuff. Besides, I'm swamped with all this work."

"I just found you daydreaming at your desk. You were humming the soundtrack to the "Bye Bye Birdie for Christ's sake."

Orion stepped back.

"Look at this spreadsheet I got up. You know how they kill me. I'll be lucky to have it done by Friday."

Stan observed the monitor. "The weekly cal-report? You could knock that out in a couple of hours."

"You could, but some of us aren't so great at these reports. That's why I should be getting back to work on it."

Orion turned his chair around to take a seat.

"Wait," Stan raised a hand to stop him. "I'm really dying here. I've got myself into this spot and now... I don't know what to do."

For the first time, Orion truly realized the extent of his friend's desperation. He looked beyond to their manager's window and saw

Ogleby shaking Bernie's hand like two beer buddies saying good-night.

"I could give you thirty minutes."

Stan's eyes widened.

"I need two hours."

Orion recoiled.

"No, I just can't spare that much time. Not today."

Stan motioned to Orion's computer screen.

How would you like to have the cal-report done by tomorrow?"

"What?"

"Not only done, but what if it was your first perfect cal-report?"

"You're losing me."

"If you sit and let me run by my ideas with you for a couple of hours, I'll do your cal-report."

His fair-haired friend reflected on the offer for a second. One last look at the spreadsheet seemed to decide him.

"Okay, but you'll do the whole report and it'll be perfect like yours?"

Stan nodded.

"Once it hits the auditor's desk, you'll never see it again. I'll even put a couple mistakes in mine so yours looks even better."

"A perfect cal-report..." The brightness returned to Orion's appearance.

"Okay, I'm going to pull my chair over and we'll look at the problem. But, I can't promise I'll be much help."

For the next three hours the two discussed the problems and tossed ideas back and forth. For Orion, it was a fun game; dreaming up new realities and different ways of doing things. For Stan, it was as if someone had handed him a flashlight and pointed him to the building exit. He had never seen Orion so alert and insightful. His energy infected Stan. For hours, ideas were suggested, built upon, then destroyed, then built back up in new variations.

Five o'clock rolled around, by which time the two had moved to an empty conference room to more easily write up their ideas on the large marker board. The problems were complex with the new government oversight of the industry, health insurance companies would be forced to cover more people. Many of the loopholes the companies had used to get out of covering certain individuals would be gone. So, while the company would end up insuring more people, it would be making less money off each person. Lastly, many of the competitive incentives they could offer their customers would cease to be an advantage because all carriers would quickly start providing the same incentives.

By six-thirty, the key to the problem had pointed to combining beneficiary groups. The two of them knew that the problem was almost solved. At six-forty, Stan noticed Orion grabbing his coat.

"Wait, where are you going?"

"Home."

"But, we're so close."

Orion gave a not entirely apologetic shrug.

"Got a date."

A plethora of frozen food boxes and containers cluttered the counter top that ran along the kitchenette wall. With the intensity of a master chef at a Michelin-starred restaurant, Orion carefully spooned out potatoes au gratin from a plastic food container into a yellow

Tupperware serving bowl.

With not a little pride, he looked over the collection of serving dishes full of food that almost looked as if he had cooked them himself.

Italian, i.e., lasagna was Orion's specialty, but he and Diana had eaten that last night. So, for their second night together, he was expanding his repertoire by preparing a traditional meatloaf with mashed potatoes and asparagus tips. The potatoes came out of a box in powder form, the asparagus tips were pre-frozen, but the moist mass of delight, this meatloaf with its delectable juices dripping down its sides, and three perfect lines of ketchup for zing was completely homemade.

Too preoccupied with carefully placing the food on the serving plate, he failed to notice the grey Bentley limousine pulling up in front of the building.

With a zip in his step, and tray in hand, he almost danced up the stairs to Diana's floor. This was going to be a great night.

He knocked on her door. No answer. He knocked again with the same result. The different reasons she might not be answering gripped his mind. Why wasn't she answering? Some possibilities were simple, others were not. What if she had second thoughts? What if she never answered?

As if in answer to a prayer he heard her lovely voice. But, it didn't come from within the apartment. No, it came from downstairs. There was another voice, too. There was definitely another voice besides hers. Their footsteps! They were now coming up the last flight of stairs. It was too late to do anything. Orion froze.

Diana came into view on the stairs, Apollo just behind her.

Apollo was finishing up his sentence. "Small place; but it does have its quaint charm."

Diana nodded. "I've got the presentation ready. I'll admit I tweaked it, though, when I found you were going to see-."

The two of them stopped in their tracks on seeing Orion holding the tray, frozen like a rabbit hoping to not be seen by a predator.

"Orion?" Diana looked shocked. "What are you doing here?"

Orion's feet were still frozen in their tracks. All he could mumble out was a weak, "Having dinner?"

She moved past him to open her door.

"Excuse me."

He stepped out of their way.

Apollo's eyes looked from the two plates of food to Orion's stunned face.

"Quite a lot of food for one person," he quipped.

Diana opened the door. Apollo shot Orion a knowing smirk as he followed her in.

Left alone, Orion skulked back down the stairs to his apartment. He wanted to get as far from her door as possible.

Later, slumped on his dilapidated couch, Orion nursed his misery.

The empty food packages strewn across the counter fit in perfectly with the rest of the apartment: fading wallpaper, a bulging brown-spotted ceiling, and second hand furniture; the portrait of a of a life going nowhere. Each day was just something to pass through, not to enjoy. Before, it was bearable. Now, his lack of success on any level felt like digging out of a self-dug grave.

If only he hadn't met her.

# CHAPTER VIII

## No Trespassing

Though, she worked feverishly to hide it from Apollo, Diana's thoughts, while working on how to move lot #4o83q, kept straying to the man she had cold-heartedly rebuffed at the door. Had he really made a meal for her with his own hands? How would one even do that? Obviously, it could be done. But, getting all the ingredients, and then actually, with your hands, cutting and heating and whatever else would be required. No, it was too much to imagine. Then he brought it to her! It was such a crazy act that it was somehow very touching.

"What do you think?"

Diana's thoughts slammed back to Apollo who had apparently broken off his interminable talking to ask her something.

"I'm sorry?"

"I said, what do you think?"

She covered for herself. "Well, it's something to think about, isn't it? Hmm."

"It's just one way we could approach it."

"Yes, rather an intriguing way."

"So, we should go for it?"

"Um...What do you think?"

Apollo harrumphed to himself and gave a knowing look. "Oh, I wanted to apologize."

"For what?" she asked.

"For interrupting your plans, tonight."

"Oh?"

"Your visitor. The one waiting for you when we came up."

Diana almost reflexively rebuffed the direction the conversation was going.

"Oh, just a neighbor. Now, about lot number two. I don't understand how we'll get interest in it without flipping some of the numbers."

"Where did you meet him?"

Apollo saw every muscle on her face grow taut.

"I-. I don't know. As I said just a neighbor."

"Well, why is he here?"

"Who knows? There are a million reasons he could be here."

"Doesn't it seem rather odd, someone like him happens to appear at this time and place?"

Apollo pressed on. "Maybe, we should find out why he's here."

Diana collected herself.

"Well, feel free to ask him why he's here. I don't care one way or the other."

"Yes," Apollo smiled. "Diana only cares about one thing – work."

She could sense, in his tone of voice, a mix of deprecation and a statement of fact. She held his gaze as she responded.

"Correct. We're here to discuss how to move lot #4o83q, not engage in discussion of my personal life."

The Atlas building faced north. On certain mornings, when the clouds were few in the sky, the light of the rising sun hit directly on the structure's eastern façade. This light, especially at certain times of the year, turned the windows a brilliant blue. The illuminated panes became opaque and the effect produced the illusion of depth. One might fancy they could plunge their hands into the soft shimmering surface, if they had enough imagination for such things.

Stan, waiting out front, was definitely not the imaginative sort. His thoughts were on the proposal they had devised. He perked up when he saw his workmate emerge from the front of the building and only a few minutes late to boot. Orion walked towards the car, but paused, apparently distracted by something. Stan uneasily followed his line of sight. A diminutive man in a light blue, three-piece suit had just stepped from the sidewalk onto the front yard. Stan's gaze returned to Orion who continued toward Stan, but kept glancing back at the little man walking toward the Atlas building.

When he finally opened the car door, Stan coaxed him, "C'mon, O'. Get in. We can still make it on time, today."

Orion nodded, taking a seat.

Stan held up his phone.

"Want a laugh? I had already pulled this out of my pocket as I was turning the corner, because I'm so used to having to call your sorry ass to see why you're not up."

He dropped the phone into the cupholder and pressed the

ignition.

"We might even have time to work on the presentation, today if I can get through my reports. I looked on my computer this morning. Ogleby's put in another twenty requests already. Twenty. I can't understand why he's loading me down so much. He know's I have this special project to do for the president."

Orion was not paying attention. His sky blue eyes were still on the little man who had diverted from his path and was now walking around the building. Orion pursed his lips and, to Stan's disbelief, climbed out of the car to follow the funny little man.

"Wait, Orion, no. We're gonna be late. Where are you going?" Stan yelled and pounded the dash in frustration.

Stan's voice might as well have been a gentle breeze wafting through the trees for all the effect it had on his friend.

The strange character with eccentric hair drew Orion in. He had to follow, find out where this mystery figure was going, even if he couldn't say why.

Rounding the back corner of the building, Orion froze in his tracks as he spotted the petite man standing in front of a shed. Curiously, he didn't remember there being a shed back here. Peeking around the corner, he realized it wasn't a man at all but a boy, maybe seven or eight. The suit he wore was an old style three-piece suit; perhaps, the kind that a railroad tycoon from the 1800s might have worn. But, where traditional buttons would have been, there were round, fluorescent, white crystals. They were also the inverse of the ascot which was patterned black with white streaks. Another distinguishing feature was a chain running into what Orion could only assume was a pocket watch. The chain was white, thick as a finger and easily distinguishable against the sky blue of the suit.

Lastly, and hardest not to notice was the boy's blonde hair, pulled up almost a foot high like one of those troll doll toys.

The boy hovered around the shed looking at it, occasionally extending a hand towards it, but never quite touching it. Stan's car horn honked.

The boy's head spun round. Orion jumped behind the building. A second later, though, the slender lad stepped around the corner, eyeing Orion with a menacing air. Dramatically, he stretched a hand toward Orion, who knew the end had come.

"Identify yourself!"

The boy's words boomed as if a giant had uttered them. His pale, ethereally light blue eyes, heavily mascaraed, squinted as if the sun was too bright for them.

Orion didn't know what to say.

The boy's hand came down. Too impatient to wait for an answer, he stalked back to the rear of the building. Orion followed and found the boy standing beside the shed. Orion approached, struggling to compose himself, to control his fear of this…child.

"Who are you? What are you doing here?" He asked the youngster whose head barely reached his chest.

With a steady arrogance the boy's head turned toward him.

"You are to show me?"

"Show you what? Who are you?"

"Boibemad."

"Boy be…"

"You are my guide? Take me to yesterday!"

"Sorry? What do you want to see?"

"Lot 5jie6c is my destiny"

"I…don't know what that is."

The little figure gesticulated wildly. Orion tried his best to interpret.

"The shed. Is it in the shed? I don't under-."

"I want to eat the red ants and kill their eyes!"

"What?!"

"The wasp cries in my bloody toenails!"

"Okay, now, that just sounds gross."

"Sing dark for pie is blood bright!"

Beyond the point of exasperation, the little figure stomped off to the front yard. Orion watched long enough to see the boy start down the sidewalk and out of sight.

Looking back, he noticed the shed. Was that always there? He walked up to it. There was a lock on the door, but it was unbolted. A quick back and forth told him that no one was around. He moved to open it, but some inexplicable impulse told him not to. He backed away.

Stan's honking horn brought back the reality of having a day job. He rushed back, but not before looking up to Diana's window. There, looking down at him was that cat, its eyes brilliant yellow.

# CHAPTER IX
## Supernova

The shadows had grown long and dark in Orion's apartment as the sun slowly fell below the horizon. Taking a seat on the couch he stared at one of the larger cracks on his ceiling as he waited for his frozen dinner to heat up.

His thoughts throughout the day kept returning to the odd little visitor that morning - a child who spoke like Moses descending Mount Sinai, dressed like a vintage antique clothing model with hair like a seventies punk rock star. A shooting star might be a more apt metaphor, as the man-child had disappeared as quickly as he had appeared.

Despite its brevity, the incident had been so vivid that Orion was able to play back every second of the odd encounter as if he'd recorded it. When asked his name, the trespasser had responded, "Boy be mad." Was this his name or just another of his weird verbal explosions bordering somewhere between riddles and mad ranting? What did he want in the backyard? Surely, it wasn't to get something out of the gardening shed.

Eventually, Orion's meditations, lacking any new facts to sustain them, played themselves out. They were replaced by others as odd thoughts crept in; things he had not thought about in ages: a childhood memory of falling off the jungle gym and being tended to by his mother; sucking the icing off his birthday candle at Chucky Cheese; telling his overjoyed parents he'd finally agreed to go to college, and meeting Stan in a Physics for Philosophers class. Before Stan he'd never kept a friend for more than a year. He'd meet kids in school or in the neighborhood and they'd hang out for a while. He guessed they wanted to stay friends, but he never felt motivated to make an effort to keep them. He never initiated. He didn't know why. Slowly these scattered thoughts dwindled down to only one: except for Stan, he had closed the door on everyone in his life. He never even talked to his family anymore. He should call them.

His life was sinking into a growing miasma. These feelings were something that had been with him for as long as he could remember. He had always felt alone, separate from those around him; always the observer, never the participant. Love was there, but not the fully consuming kind that it seemed to be for others. All that changed when he first saw Diana. Why, how, he didn't know. But having her in his life was like getting a free pass from the dreariness of life. She was the answer to the question, is this all there is? And what a beautiful answer she was; the North Star guiding the ship back home after a long voyage.

But the stars had all faded. She had thrown him away. For him the sky was black.

The beeping of the microwave triggered the reflex to remove the dish of macaroni and cheese. The scalding hot container hurt his fingers. He barely noticed.

A knock at the door startled him. He wasn't expecting anyone.

He opened the door to find Diana. She smiled, a little tipsy with a half-emptied bottle of champagne in her hand. In her other hand was a half-empty wine glass which she held up seductively.

"May I enter?"

Seeing her at the door erased everything bad.

He stepped out of her way and motioned her in to get a look of the form-fitting white silk number she was wearing.

"Yes, of course."

Without warning, her lips pressed firmly against his. Once he broke out of his shock, he pulled her close to him. His hands slid around her waist and up her back.

She felt his warmth enshroud her, his hands running up and down her back, taking possession of her. Her lips were burning as they alternated between his lips and face. It was too much. Her legs grew weak. The bottle in her hand slowly slipped out of her fingers and dropped to the floor.

Holding her firmly with one arm, he closed the door and steered her to the couch. Her scent was intoxicating. She was soft, yet perfectly firm. He showered her face and neck with kisses as he lowered her onto the couch. With a swift movement, he laid on top of her, covering her face and neck with a flurry of kisses that became one long kiss.

Suddenly, Diana pushed back against him, fighting him off.

"No, stop!"

Orion fell off the couch.

"What? What's the matter?"

"You're couch. It's-. It's biting me!"

She sat up to reveal a metal spring that had popped through the sofa cushion. She rubbed the sore spot on her rear.

Orion picked himself off the floor to find Diana looking around his apartment, a horrified expression washed over her.

He looked around his apartment, realized it looked more like a dorm room.

"I'm so sorry. I would have cleaned if I knew you were coming. I…"

Her eyes moved from the second hand furniture to the stained walls to the large cracks in the ceiling.

"This place. What happened to it?"

A wave of shame crossed his face. Embarrassed by the poverty of his surroundings, he just wanted to curl up and disappear.

He had little time for that as Diana grabbed his wrist and the bottle of wine.

"Come," she said, "I think we would be much more comfortable at my place."

An elated rush overcame Orion as he found himself being pulled out his door and up the stairs to her apartment. The thick wood door flung open seemingly on its own. He couldn't be sure as everything was connected to holding onto Diana.

At the doorway, she stopped and smiled seductively. An excited glow overcame her face reflecting the glow on his. She forcefully pulled the handsome creature into her darkened apartment, gave no resistance as he took charge, pulling her dangerously close.

Their lips pressed together in fiery intensity as the door closed itself behind them. Keeping his arms around her, he pushed their bodies against the console. He had to have her. He kept one hand balanced on the console while the other moved up her back searching for a button or zipper of some sort that he could unfasten.

She whispered in his ear. "I want you," and immediately heard his breathing quicken. His hand was up and down her back, feeling all over. He was a slow lover, but she knew it would be worth the wait.

*Where's the button!* He thought to himself. Her dress seemed to have no way to open it. He'd happily just rip it off, if it didn't look like it cost a year's salary. Slowly, he pivoted their bodies to allow his free hand access to her side. The hand felt around, but there was no zipper, latch or anything. How to get this stupid dress off!

Every nerve in Diana's body was tingling. She was almost dizzy from blood rushing to her head. She couldn't wait anymore. His teasing was too much. She had to have him, now!

With the strength of a tigress, she squeezed him in her arms and pulled them around so his back was to the console. She firmly took hold of his neck and kneed him in the gut.

Orion keeled over with a whimper. Diana stepped a foot or two away, ready for his response. He was in good shape so it should be lively. But, his response was very different from what she was suspecting. He clutched his stomach, short of breath, and fell onto the console, his hand bumping against the lamp knocking it to one side.

With the movement of the lamp, the table, the sofa, and chairs all transformed into the futuristic console that was Diana's workplace. Orion lost his balance as the furniture turned and spun.

"Whuh?!"

Before he fell to the ground, he spied the cat statue come alive in the form of that freaky green-eyed cat. It leapt across the room toward him firing a laser that just missed his face.

"IO, no!" Diana's voice shot out.

Laid flat on his back, Orion found himself looking up at the cat, its green eyes glowing. He tried to move, but the cat seemed to weigh a ton, as if a lion, not an ordinary housecat, was standing on his chest. It extended its paw to forcefully push his head down.

"IO!"

Diana leaned down, picked the little creature up as if it weighed nothing. Holding it aloft with one hand, she bopped its nose with an extended finger.

"Shame on you! What do you think you're doing?!"

The glow disappeared from the cat's eyes. It squirmed in her grip, discomforted by her stern glare.

"No, you look me in the eye when I'm talking to you! Look at me!"

The cat, uncomfortable, turned its gaze back to its mistresses.

"You will not harm him. Understand?"

The cat twitched again. Diana gave it a slight shake and furled eyebrows.

"Understand?!"

The cat became still, almost limp in her arms, its gaze meeting hers and it ceased resisting.

When its eyes returned to their native yellow, Diana released IO, who leapt to the other side of the room. She looked down at Orion still lying where he had fallen, dazed and confused. She offered him a hand.

"I'm so sorry about IO. He's a bit overprotective."

Orion didn't take her hand. He was too afraid. Diana sensed his reticence.

"Are you okay?"

He slid away from her. Escaping this room seemed like the thing to do.

She followed him. "Where are you going? Orion, are you okay?"

He was not okay; with some effort his shaky legs got him on his feet.

"I-." words were not coming to him, either. He must make it to the door. "Who... what are you?"

"Orion?" she moved to touch him, a concerned look on her face.

He motioned for her to come no closer. "What is all this?"

She was confused by the question.

"It's my office. It goes wherever I work."

Orion had never seen any office like this.

Studying his face she slowly realized that the man before her was utterly confused. Everything he was seeing was beyond his understanding. Could it be that he really didn't know what was happening? She had to find out.

"How long have you been on this planet?"

She could see he didn't understand the question. She spoke again slowly and clearly, as one would to a child.

"I have been on this planet for three Earth weeks. When did you arrive on this planet?"

Orion backed up to the door. He fumbled for the door knob, gave it a turn to make sure it wasn't locked. This gave him a sense of security. He shouted back, defiant.

"What are you talking about? Who are you!?"

"I-."

"I thought you were a real estate agent!"

"I am. I facilitate the sale of properties like large celestial bodies and smaller nebulae."

Orion almost had to suppress a laugh at the ridiculousness of the statement. Was she pulling his leg or was she crazy? The small cat she called IO, walked up to her side and took a seat, its gaze never wavering from him.

"Yeah, right. I'm supposed to believe that. What's really going on here?"

"I will show you." Diana reached over and pressed a button on the console. To his stunned disbelief, the room's ceiling turned to a starry alien night sky and the walls disappeared, to become a rocky landscape.

Orion found himself standing on the alien landscape, with blue soil and purple mountains in the far distance. A soft breeze blew across his face. He no longer felt the doorknob in his hand. It was gone as was the room they'd been standing in just seconds ago.

IO leapt into Diana's arms, she pet it out of habit.

"You're wondering where we are."

She took a few steps towards a metallic protrusion stemming from the ground. Orion hadn't noticed it at first, but the machine, about waist high, had various colored sensor lights. It was also the only manmade thing in sight.

"What you're seeing is the largest asteroid of the Tran Asteroid Belt. Although, it looks and feels like we're on the asteroid's surface, we are actually still in my apartment. This device," he watched her place a hand on the domed top of the silo. "Is an Index Drill. It's been inserted into the planet to maintain constant measurements of this planet's physical status which are transmitted to me on a continual basis. I keep a record of all energy and physical aberrations, fluctuations, etc. These, I'm required to re-transmit to any registered bidders. Another feature of the Index Drill; it can insert us into a virtual approximation of the planet just as it would be if we were standing in it. This is helpful when showing the property to prospective buyers. You see, I'm transacting the sale of this asteroid belt. It's listed as lot #4o83q. I have represented many properties ranging from large celestial bodies to smaller nebulae."

She pushed a button on top of the Index Drill and the landscape surrounding them quickly transformed back into the ceilings, walls, and floors of her apartment.

Orion feeling the knob in his hand pulled the door open.

"I have to go."

He stumbled out the door of the apartment and headed for the stairs. It was too much. He couldn't believe it all, but he had just seen it. But, what had he seen?!

He had just started down the stairs when Diana emerged. She moved towards him, but he raised his hand out to stop her.

"Stay away! Just leave me alone."

He disappeared down the stairs.

# CHAPTER X
## Dark Matters

The voice was painfully shrill but, no matter how grating it might be, the concern was sincere. "O', I'm not saying it's not great to hear from you, but why are you calling? Is everything okay?"

With the phone to his ear, Orion paced back and forth across the hardwood floor of his living room. Through the kitchen window, he saw the Bentley pull up.

"Mom, I'm fine, really."

"We hadn't heard from you in so long. So, when you do call…"

"Everything's okay. Well, I don't know. I've been feeling a little down. Like I've been moving in a direction but it's not the right one, somehow."

"Can you be more specific?"

He eyed a family picture taken when he was eight. It was a typical studio picture - Orion situated between his parents. All had dark hair and brown eyes, except Orion, whose blonde hair was even paler than now.

Their family could easily have been classified as average
middle class. Orion had dutifully followed the plan his parents' had
prescribed for him. He was put on a college track. Once there, he
was pushed to obtain an English or Business degree aimed at him
getting a job that paid enough to afford a car and a house. But, the
farther along he got on the plan the more wrong it felt. It was a truth
that long plagued him, though he had never been able to put it into
words.

His mother spoke patiently as only mothers are able to do.

"Life can be hard. You know we're all trying to figure everything
out."

They spoke some more. His mom filled him in on how the family
was doing. His father then came on the phone and filled Orion
in on how everything was going at his office. Orion related a few
anecdotes from the world of insurance. His dad shared a funny joke
that had been going around. Orion laughed long enough to please his
father. Mission accomplished, his father passed the phone back to his
wife. She pressed Orion for more information.

"Is it a girl?"

"Sort of?"

"Hm. What's she like? Is she pretty?"

"Yes."

"What does she do?"

"She does real estate…stuff. It's complicated."

The conversation trickled out after that. Orion knew there wasn't
much he could tell them about Diana or his situation. Telling them
anymore would require lying to them or telling them the truth which
would sound even worse. There was no one he could tell. This
knowledge gave him an empty feeling as he hung up the phone.

Work became similarly empty. Each day, Stan picked him up as usual and they would go to the office. While there, it was hard for Orion to do anything else but sit and look at his computer screen. Breaks in the day would come when Stan, when he thought Ogleby wasn't looking, would step over and ask his opinion on some aspect of the plan. Orion would answer, detached and cold. The pointlessness of it all could not be denied.

In the midst of the third day at work going through the motions but mostly sitting like a zombie, Orion decided he couldn't take it anymore and begged out of work on the pretense of feeling sick to his stomach.

Without a car, he was forced to use public transportation. He traveled by bus to the old downtown district, the only real pedestrian part of the city. Disembarking, he realized he needed to be surrounded by people, to disappear into the masses that walked up and down the sidewalks. He wanted to feel part of a crowd.

The streets were not very crowded at this time of day. It was too late for the lunch crowd, too early for the close of business rush hour. Except for the occasional pedestrian, he walked alone. Still, it allowed a semblance of escape from his mind's anxieties.

His half-dazed thoughts were suddenly disturbed when he found an attractive, college- aged girl standing in his path. Her broad smile and query, "Do you believe in helping the environment?" distracted him from the clipboard in her hand and the Sierra Club logo emblazoned on her t-shirt.

If Orion had been a regular in the downtown area, he would have undoubtedly waved her off with a "No, thank you" and proceeded on his way. But he was not and quickly found himself trapped by the young lady's cunningly devised question.

"Yes," he answered, less out of any true feelings on the matter than for some morally instigated feeling that this was what he should say.

Once she had him engaged in conversation, she quickly and successively got him to not only divulge his name, but his phone number, e-mail, and mailing address. In exchange, she pressed her hand on his, thanked him profusely, and handed him a brochure, which he pocketed.

The jarring-ness of the encounter made him lose interest in walking. He cut into the park where he found even more volunteers waiting like vultures for passers-by. A quick left on a narrow side path led him to the Natural History Museum. He bought a ticket.

Being Tuesday during working hours, the exhibit halls were sparsely populated. Shortly afterwards, Orion stood in a room alone with an exhibit titled, "Creatures of the Serengeti Plains". It was populated with large African elephants, herds of zebras, and, eerily, off in the distance, a pride of lions deciding on what their dinner would be that evening.

The next hall was titled, "The Evolution of Man". Walking from one end of the room to the other, it began with the first creature to crawl out of the ocean, a fish with tiny legs, and ended with a succession of pulled primates Neanderthal, Australopithecus, and finally, the pinnacle of evolution, the Homo sapiens. Eyeing the final three stages, Orion couldn't help notice that there were not a lot of differences between them. They had two legs, two arms, two eyes, a brain of larger than ordinary size for their body type, and an aversion to personal grooming.

Most importantly, they were all born on a planet that encompassed all they knew.  For them there had been nothing more in the world than the ground beneath their feet and the farthest point their eyes could see. At the rear of the building was the newly installed planetarium. It was included in the price of the ticket, so he ducked through the black hole motif entryway.

Due to the odd hour, he found himself the sole audience member. The show proved to be typical of past visits. He had been dragged to planetariums a couple of times as a kid, so most of it was familiar. It began of course with the Big Bang theory – science's "Greatest Story Ever Told". A God-like narrator related the story of the beginning of the universe, the formation of the Sun, our energy source, and consequently the solar system - the home of Earth.

But, then the film went on, revealing the universe like a reverse Russian doll. Our solar system was part of the Milky Way, a galaxy composed of 400 billion stars; the Milky Way was part of the Local Group which contained 54 galaxies, including our closest, the Andromeda system; the Local Group was part of Virgo, a super cluster containing 100 galaxies; the Virgo Super cluster was just one tiny part of the Pisces-Cetus Super cluster Complex – 60 super clusters at 1.0 billion light years long and 150 million light years wide. And this super cluster complex was just one part of the "visible" universe which contained at least 10 million super clusters equaling 350 billion galaxy groups.

The incomprehensibly large numbers were voiced by the narrator as splendid renderings of the increasingly large celestial masses appeared on the screen above him. Orion had vaguely heard some of these facts before, but never had they hit him with such resonance. The enormity of it all both took his breath away and made him feel unbearably insignificant. The final projection was a rendering of what the known universe looked like - a vast spider web of light clusters – the depiction of 30 billion trillion stars - the known universe.

Later, as he stepped out of the museum, he looked to the night sky. The stars above: he'd seen them so many times before, but never felt their majesty, never imagined their import. All his life he had been going through the motions; running out the clock. This was no way to live.

Five more days before the show and the list of potential bidders was short, very short. This distressing fact brought Diana, once again, to the small orb which hovered before her. In it was a list of hundreds of thousands of entities with a history of buying real estate. Blinking her weary eyes, she carefully ran her finger over the names, desperately trying to identify someone who might be willing to buy an asteroid field with no significant cosmological or mineral value, i.e., lot #4o83q.

Finding any bidders at all had only been possible because the third largest asteroid – q6 - contained an abundance of low grade ilithium, just enough to lure in the bidders. But was it enough to get them to meet that annoyingly high reserve? Diana determined that she would just have to use all the old tricks of getting a bid high because the very last thing she wanted to do was have to take Apollo up on his offer.

Out of the corner of her eye she spotted a blinking light on the console. Turning to investigate, she saw that a fissure had formed on asteroid q6. She leaned in to make sure she was reading the data correctly. It was a rather small one, not large enough to compromise the integrity of the mass. Still it was something to monitor further because it was q6.

Without thinking about it, her sights moved to the little screen on the console showing the RIB time left for her to sell the last two properties. Ribula's moon had completed eight-ninths of a complete revolution.

It was all too much. Closing her eyes, she leaned back in her chair. Weary of this stressful problem, her mind turned to another – Orion. What if, she pondered, he had been left on this planet as a child and raised here, thinking he was one of the natives? Would it be possible? Theoretically, yes, if he were really young. Wouldn't he know, if only subconsciously, that he was not living with his own kind?

A knock at the door triggered IO to stand at attention. Diana touched the console and it converted back into the living space as she went to answer the door.

It was Orion. She fought to suppress her joy. She hadn't realized until that moment how much she had missed him.

His head hung low as his eyes looked up from the ground to meet hers.

"Can I come in?"

Diana's heart swelled as she opened the door wide.

# CHAPTER XI
## Dining Out

Twenty minutes after the alarms had gone off, the employees of Polymer Mutual found themselves in the parking lot waiting for the fire trucks to arrive. Rumors quickly spread that someone had overcooked some popcorn in the break room.

Stan squinted, shielding his eyes from the sun. He saw Lorraine. She spotted him and was making her way towards him. Where was Orion? They were supposed to work on the presentation this afternoon. He started to scan the crowd again, but, the distant sounds of approaching fire trucks distracted him and the rest of the employees.

Diana's console alerted her to an incoming communication. She smiled when she saw it was Orion.

"Hello, Muscles."

"Hey, are you home?"

"I'm at the apartment."

"Great. We're going to go out to eat."

"I don't have time."

The line went dead.

"Reconnect," she told the console.

IO leapt into attack mode, eyes turning and pointing at the front door.

"Come in," she shouted.

A belated knock came at the door as Orion barged in holding a large wicker basket.

"Why do I bother knocking? You ready to go?"

"I don't have time." she protested, "I've got a lot of work to do."

He danced a few steps across the room, pulled her out of her chair and kissed her on the hand.

"Nonsense! You told me this morning everything was all set for the bidding tomorrow. So, as your teammate, I've decided it's time for a little R&R. Now get yourself ready. I'm not taking no as an answer."

Before she knew it, Diana found herself sitting on a piece of cloth laid on the ground in the backyard of the Atlas Building. She watched in wonder as her lunchtime companion pulled a smorgasbord of edibles from the wicker basket and laid the contents out before them.

Picking up one of the containers, she read the word "balo-g-na", looked up to him queryingly.

"What is all this?"

"It's called a picnic. It's when two perfectly lovely people get out of their stuffy apartment building and sit outside in nature, eating and talking about something, anything besides work."

"Oh, I see..."

She looked around, unsure of the sensibility of eating in the wilderness. Despite the blanket he had thrown down, she could still feel the ground underneath, with little patches of lumpiness. There was also an odd vulnerable feeling sitting in such a low station. This was not a position she was used to.

He began making a sandwich.

"Isn't this great? I hope we're not too close to this shed."

Orion looked at it as if for the first time.

"It's weird. Is this shed new? I don't ever remember seeing it before." He became transfixed by it, "I wonder what's inside."

He reached toward the door, his hand almost to the latch when Diana realized what he was about to do.

Thinking fast, she pulled on his shirt as hard as she could.

He clumsily fell back on her, then turned and wrapped his arms around her.

"What was that for?"

"You're supposed to be feeding me!"

"Oh?"

"Yes, do your job." She ordered teasingly poking a finger at his chest.

"I have a better idea." He moved his leg over hers and moved in to kiss her. She turned her face away so his lips fell on her ear.

"No!" she shouted. "That's not your job!"

She playfully tried to fight him off. He rolled them over so she was on her back, kissing her all over her face, neck and hair. Eventually, she relaxed and let her lips lock with his. Let his arms squeeze in around her. He felt so strong around her. She felt herself sinking. A funny little tingling reached her toes and they bent in a little. No one had ever made her feel like he did. She was ready for him then and there, but it wouldn't be fair to him. Not with him not knowing everything. She pulled back.

"You're not feeding me."

He gave up. They sat back up and he finished making the second sandwich.

"I have turkey and ham. Which do you want?"

She did not seem to understand the question. He realized his mistake.

"Oh, are you a vegetarian?"

She shook her head and decided to just pick one of these sandwiches. How bad could it be? Well, there were those mussels.

Taking the one she didn't, he took a bite. In the corner of his eye he spied her watching how he was eating. It dawned on him that she may never have eaten a sandwich before.

"Are you okay?"

She nodded weakly.

He held up his sandwich. "You eat it with your hands. You don't need utensils."

She lifted the sandwich to her mouth and took a bite. She chewed slowly until she was sure it wasn't going to kill her.

He watched, amused.

"Say, what kind of food do you eat on your planet?"

She gave a distasteful look, "Nothing like this."

She put the sandwich down deciding it would be better to go hungry.

She gave a distasteful look, "Nothing like this."

She put the sandwich down deciding it would be better to go

hungry.

He pressed on.

"Well, what kind of food do you eat there?"

"Nothing interesting."

"You know, in that office of yours, you've shown me planets, neutron stars, binary systems and things I couldn't even describe, but never once where you're from. Why is that? What's the deep, dark secret you're keeping?"

She turned serious. "My planet is a backwater place not much thought of by the main systems. They say nothing good ever comes from there and they're right. It wasn't easy, but I scraped and struggled and made it out of there. The one thing I knew was that I'd never go back. At least not until I'd made it."

He reached over and gave her a hard slap on the arm.

"Ow! Booger down! Why did you do that?"

"Sorry. You had a mosquito on your arm." He reversed his palm to show her the mosquito remnants. "They eat blood and spread diseases. That's why I killed it."

Looking down, Orion noticed a small trail of ants had found their way to the basket. He wiped them off.

"I guess it's time to go back."

"Booger down. That was on me?!"

She immediately began checking every inch of her body for anything else.

Yes," he wiped it off on the blanket. "What does Booger down mean?"

"Booger down?"

"Yeah, you just said that. You say a lot of odd sayings. Like 'Bees and Sweetness.'"

A smile of realization came to her.

"Oh, that's the translanguor."

"The what?"

"The translanguor – it's what translates our speech. That's how we can understand each other."

"Oh?" he thought about this.

"But what's a Booger down?"

"Certain things aren't really translatable. So, it inserts fillers. It's doing the best it can. You should hear some of the conversations from my side. Like your frequent use of 'hockswiffler' when you get angry."

"I see. So, if you say a word or a sentence that doesn't make sense or sounds bizarre, then it's probably because the translator – translanguor – can't translate it."

She nodded. "That's pretty much it."

The number of ants leading to the picnic basket had swelled. He eyed them for a moment, thinking about what he had just learned, then brushed them off as best he could as they returned inside.

Back inside her apartment, Diana opened up her console and went back to work. Orion had taken a seat in his favorite chair, but soon got the message, their lunch was over.

He glanced at his watch. He really should be heading back to the office. He could only take advantage of a fire drill for so long.

# CHAPTER XII

## Cracks in the Surface

"I don't believe it. What were you thinking?!"

Diana listened, eyes directed to the floor of the Bentley as Apollo sat next to her, shaking his head in disbelief.

She started to respond but her flustered seatmate continued.

"You get a report of a tremor on a property you're about to bid out and you don't immediately investigate it?!"

"It doesn't look-."

"They never do until they just blow up!"

His nostrils flared as he waved a hand in the air. His voice had expanded until one could almost feel the walls vibrate.

"It's a fissure on the only valuable asteroid in lot #4o83q. Without the trace amounts of ilithium on that rock, you might as well be selling a pile of dirt!" His hand balled into a fist that he brought down on the center armrest. "You're the broker, the guarantee the property is stable. When something is amiss, you go out and investigate in person! Drenods! Any fool would know that? I thought ready to play the big game! The only thing you seem ready for is to scavenge dead..."

He caught sight of Diana's mortified expression. Pushed back in the far corner, her whole frame was on the verge of trembling. Her chin stuck out in defiance, though everything else about her was like a scolded child. The shock of seeing her in this state stopped him cold. He slumped back into his seat looking forward, looking a little lost.

The doors opened and the dimly lit, rocky terrain of asteroid q6 appeared before them.

The pair exited the transport and Diana, after clearing her throat, pointed to a large hill, made up, like the rest of the surface, of reddish-brown rock.

"We should get the best view of the fissure from up there."

Apollo's bushy red eyebrows lowered as he focused on the faraway hill.

"Then we'd best get going."

She took the lead as they walked, purposely facing forward, determined not to let him see how he had hurt her. This lasted only a few moments before Apollo broke the silence.

"Wait."

She kept walking. Not cognizant at first that he had spoken.

"Diana, please…"

Reluctantly, she came to a stop.

She looked to him. His eyes were averted, his stance unsure. He started, voice awkward.

Now, it was she who cut him off.

"You have a lot vested in this deal. I have everything. Let's go and inspect the fissure and confirm that it's as negligible as the readings show. Then we can return to setting up the bid. Right?"

His eyes met hers and he signaled his agreement.

After the incident in the car, Apollo's tone and manners had changed dramatically. The walk to the hill was long enough to allow some conversation. Rather than the usual pontifications on all things Apollo, he spoke sparingly in a tone that was gentle with long stretches of silence in-between. Occasionally, while walking along the rocky terrain, she would catch him eyeing her. When her gaze met his, he abruptly looked away.

She pointed to a nearby hill made up of the same red jagged rocks as the rest of the surface.

"The center of the fissure line is up there. Shall we go?"

Apollo's head pulled back in surprise.

"You think you can make that climb?"

"Only, if you don't slow me down."

She gave him a cocksure nod and started towards the hill.

The walk up the incline proved more difficult than it had looked from a distance. Her heels, though short, were not the best for climbing the jagged rocks. A look back at Apollo revealed he was having a harder time of it than she. His face was flushed, his steps unsteady.

"Come on, old man! I think too much time luxuriating in your transport and sipping cocktails has made you soft."

Hearing this, he clenched his jaw and clambered up the rocks with increased vigor. So much so, that he was right behind her when they reached the top.

At the edge of a steep drop, she put her hands on her hips and took in the view. Below her, the valley they had started from looked almost black, the only illumination came from a very distant sun at the center of the system. In the sky a dwarf planet floated by. Being lit from the other side, it appeared to them as a dark blob floating past that blacked out any stars that in its path.

"It's rather a nice view from up here." she observed.

Apollo, whose face had become as red as his hair, caught his breath.

"Yes, it is." he said, though it was not the landscape he was looking at but her.

Suspecting his wordplay, she purposely did not meet his gaze.

"So, what goes through the great Apollo's mind when he looks across this rugged, harsh terrain?"

"How quickly we can dispose ourselves of this collection of rocks with no determinable value."

"Really? That's all?"

He nodded. "To be honest, I never look at assets; they're all the same, it's just valuations that differ."

"So it's profit that excites you?"

"My sights," he took a step closer to her, "are always on the heavens. I never stop looking at the starscape; studying it, visualizing how I might alter, rearrange the pieces."

He reached into his coat and pulled out a forest green metal ball just a tad smaller than the width of his eye and held it up between thumb and forefinger. It lit up producing a dot on the night sky much like a laser pointer directed at a wall. Diana watched as he carefully moved the dot along the sky until he found his target, a barely perceptible star. Fixing the pointer on it, the star became magnified as if it were the largest object in the sky.

"See that? The Jearium system. That's where I made my first big sale. It was a nebula that we condensed. It's now home to five trillion inhabitants."

He directed the pointer west to a black space.

"And over there. That point, you can just make it out, used to be a trinary system, all but worthless. We bought it for nothing then broke up the three suns relocating them to key locations."

His thumb and forefinger delicately turned the ball moving the green dot across sky, stopping at each spot.

"There, there, and…there. We were then able to sell each individually for twenty times the original buying price."

Placing her hand on her heart, Diana followed the point of light as it darted back and forth across the galaxy. The old volume returned to his voice as he spoke, not quite bragging, but definitely proud. Like a child showing off his new toys. At that moment, she too felt like a child and all the stars were their playthings.

His royal blue eyes followed the moving point of light. A tinge of wistfulness came through in his speech.

"There's one thing I've never been able to get."

He paused to take a slow breath.

She cocked her head, curiosity piqued.

The green dot hovered over another dark area until a black hole was magnified into view.

Her face twisted up in confusion.

"A gravity hole?"

He nodded. "I've never been able to buy, sell, or broker a deal for a gravity hole."

She let her hand fall to her side.

"But, you can't. It's not allowed."

"I know. No one has ever been allowed to own one."

"And what would that get you?"

He turned to her, his lips curling into a grim smile.

"I don't know if you know this, you probably do. I know you researched me. Unlike you, I grew up at the top of the tree. My father was a broker, too. Some say he was one of the best. In his day, he worked deals that were legendary. As you can imagine, I idolized him; reveled in his history making deals always knowing that, one day it would be me doing that. When I completed my first deal, I made sure to tell him before anyone else. He didn't say much, just looked over the reports of the transaction and pointed out the mistakes. It wasn't good enough. He said I should have consulted him before trying a real deal. With Jearium, it was the same. His comments were 'you could have made more money' and 'you could have leveraged the equity better.' He just couldn't ever let me forget that whatever I did, he had already done it before, bigger and better."

His head hung low. Diana put her hand on his arm.

"I understand."

"It was in his final years, he formed a group to try to buy the Infini 2 gravity hole. He assumed he could get around the rules. But, it turned out he couldn't. Even with all his connections and talent the Titans stopped him at every turn. They felt he was going too far. He struggled against them and wasted a lot of his fortune trying, but he died before he was ever able to get Infini 2."

Diana leaned her head to the left, studying the man before her who suddenly seemed less the indomitable captain of industry and more a frail creature of flesh and bone.

"But, you'll get it." She was confident. "You'll somehow find a way to get the Infini 2."

He lifted his shoulders and gave her a firm nod of agreement.

"He would have liked you. He made his fortune from nothing,

too. A fact which he reminded me of frequently."

She shook her head.

"I haven't made a fortune."

He flashed a warm smile.

"You will."

She turned crimson.

"Okay, enough of that. We need to look at the fissure center."

She proceeded towards the other end of the hill. The rocky indentation they were following narrowed until they were forced to walk single file. Eventually, they came across a four-foot high boulder. Putting finger to chin she strategized how to climb over it.

Apollo tapped her on the shoulder.

"Let me."

Stepping up to the boulder, he placed both hands against it and pushed.

Diana covered her mouth to hide a grin as she watched her companion struggle to push the boulder out their way. His feet kept slipping on the rocky ground and his cape got in the way a few times, but to her surprise, he was eventually able to pry it out of the crevice and throw it off the side of the hill. Being a porous rock on a low gravity body, it did not land with a heavy thud; rather it bounced a few times before coming to rest.

Purposely she waited for him to look back and put her hands to her face, eyes as big as saucers. "Slipthroats and Drenods! I didn't think any one person could have moved that rock! It was sooo enormous!"

Her companion's chest swelled with pride. After a second-take glance at her exaggerated expression, he ashamedly realized she was having her fun with him. Despite herself, this only made her laugh.

Looking thoroughly piqued, he pushed aside his cape and walked past her without saying a word. As she hurried to catch up with him, she noted beyond the edge of hill there was a bluish fog. Craning her neck she tried to make out what it was. The lighting was dim so it hard to see. Once nearer she could see that it was actually a fine blue mist, like rain, but flowing up and outwards. Her steps quickened, she passed Apollo and looked over the edge, her eyes widening in horror.

Fine blue dust was being expelled from a crack in the ground about a quarter mile wide. From this center, narrower lines stretched as far as the eye could see in both directions.

"The ilithium," she turned to Apollo, "it's all pouring out!"

Hand over mouth he beheld the spectacle. He lowered his hand. "We have to stop it!"

Before she could agree, the ground shook. It was followed by another tremor. The fissure widened and the spray of ilithium fanned out until they were faced with a wall of blue.

He grabbed her wrist.

"We have to go!"

She resisted, but as the tremors grew, relented.

Racing through the narrow path they had come in on, Diana struggled to stay on her feet. The shaking ground kicked up dust, filling the air. Several pebbles flew past them. At times, she couldn't see where they were heading. She felt the sting of a rock as it hit her leg. Apollo kept his grip on her wrist, pulling her ever forward.

The ground fell out from under her feet. Stumbling, she realized they were going downhill. Apollo's hand kept pulling her forward.

Towards the bottom of the hill the dust cleared and she saw the starry night and Apollo. On his face were white, luminescent glasses.

The dust clouded over them and all became dark. Beneath her feet, the hard rocky ground vibrated as she struggled to keep balance. She kept faith with Apollo, holding onto his arm as he held onto hers.

How long they ran, she did not know. They stopped abruptly. She felt herself pushed against the cold steel of Apollo's transport. Seeing the interior light come on, she felt her way into the back seat. He followed her in, the door closing behind them.

An orb appeared before Apollo. He selected a spot and Diana could feel the transport gently roll forward. When the vibrating ceased she knew they had left the surface.

A second orb appeared before them. It unrolled to become a screen showing the asteroid field lot #4o83q. Directing the screen with his middle and index fingers pressed together, Apollo zoomed in on the asteroid they had just left. Diana sunk in her seat at the sight of asteroid q6 breaking into three different pieces. The ilithium was gone.

With both hands Apollo's cupped his head; his face contorted from disbelief at what he had just seen. Slowly, he turned to her with a lost look, shaking his head in incredulity.

"I knew it should be monitored. I…I just didn't expect it to implode."

Diana eyes darted back and forth in thought.

"But how? There were no indications in the readings."

Clenching her jaw, she looked him straight in the eye.

"The lot will have to be reassessed. A new list of potential bidders will have to be made. There's very little time. It must be started right away."

Incredulous, he grabbed her wrist.

"Diana, it's over. Any value lot #4o83q had just crumbled before our eyes. You must accept this."

His words did nothing to change the faraway look in her eyes.

"It's not over." She spoke more to herself than to him. "When the final bidding occurs and I make or don't make the minimum reserve, only then is it over.

His chin lowered in sympathy as he let go of her wrist.

"Let's get you home."

Few words were exchanged between Apollo and Diana on the way back from lot #4o83q. The shock of the destruction of asteroid q6 was only really starting to sink in as the Bentley pulled in front of the Atlas Building.

She turned to Apollo whose head was tilted down in meditation.

"I'm going to start a list of new bidders."

"There's nothing to sell!"

His finger was agitatedly stroking the end of one of his red, bushy eyebrows.

"Lot #4o83q has no value to anyone."

"I will let you know when I have something."

She placed a foot outside the car to exit.

"Is your offer still in the air?"

He eyed her quizzically.

"Offer?"

"To buy the last two lots at the minimum reserve price?"

A pained look overcame Apollo. Eventually, he unenthusiastically signaled the affirmative.

"Very well," she slid out of the car, "I'll contact you soon."

"What are you going to do?"

"Anything I can, I guess."

As the last words came out of her mouth, she heard the screeching of rubber on cement, followed by an aborted yelp.

Peeking over the roof of Apollo's vehicle, she saw a yellow car speeding off. In its wake was a black and white, four-legged animal sprawled on the edge of the road, blood coming out of its side.

Apollo eyed her from his seat inside the car.

"What is the matter?"

She bent down to address him.

"A creature was hit by a vehicle. It looks hurt."

He leaned towards her.

"It's not blocking my transport, is it?"

She shook her head, no.

"Well, then good. The fewer animals on this rock the better for my tastes."

Diana gave a short laugh.

Before she could say anything, her attention was diverted by the appearance of the small, brown four-wheel transport that Orion traveled in. It pulled up behind the Bentley.

Shifting into park, Stan grimaced a little as he eyed the dog. It was the Great Dane-Saint Bernard mix, the same one that had run in front of his car before. Its massive frame twitched a little trying to rise, but was too hurt.

The front door of the Atlas building slammed open. Orion emerged, running full-tilt down the walk. He rushed past Diana and made a bee-line for the wounded animal.

Apollo frowned as he observed how Diana was transfixed by the dashing young man who ran like an Olympian.

"On second thought," he slid across the seat to step out. "I'll go up with you."

She looked surprised as he took her by the arm and walked her to her building.

"We can work on your next possible steps."

She let herself be led along but couldn't help but keep an eye on the action taking place on the street.

Orion crouched down to examine the animal lying on its side. It let out a whimper as blood came out of its back right leg. He removed his tie and pressed it against the creatures open wound. He looked to the yard and spotted his landlord who was cutting the hedges.

"Uri! Uri, come down here!"

The old man, with garden clippers in hand was watching the scene from the side bushes. He processed the words then, carefully set the clippers down and waddled over to Orion's side.

Orion watched blood slowly soak into his tie. He motioned Uri closer.

"Here, hold this."

Uri hesitate, a look of horror crossed his face.

"Orion, I don't know about-."

Orion's tone of voice would brook no debate.

"Hold this."

The old man fell to one knee. Orion took the man's hand and placed it where his had been on the tie.

"Keep pressing firmly.  We can't let the dog bleed to death. And you can't put a tourniquet on an animal.

Orion maneuvered around to the dog's side.

"Where do you want it?"

Stan involuntarily shook his head.

"In someone else's car?"

Orion was shouting now.

"This is serious. Back seat or trunk?"

Stan held up his hands.

"I don't know! Just, just put it in the backseat. Heaven forbid we ever get to work on time."

Orion held the dog with one hand, opened the door with the other. He looked to Uri.

"You got it?"

The gray-haired man nodded, a bit unsure, as they slid the limp animal onto the backseat. He had to slide in too, so as not to lose his grip tie.

Orion moved to close the door, but hesitated, eyeing his landlord.

"Can you stay in the backseat with the dog or do you want me to do it?"

The elderly gentleman looked unsure, but then stuck his chin out defiantly.

"I can do it, O."

"Good."

Uri slid in next to the dog. Orion jumped in the front passenger seat. The car sped off.

Diana watched it through the glass of the building's outer door. It turned the corner and disappeared from view.

Apollo had already started climbing the stairs.

"Diana?" his words were tinged with annoyance. "Are you coming? There's work to be done."

# CHAPTER XIII
## Monopoly

Apollo, to Diana's slight annoyance, had become way too comfortable in her apartment. Out of the corner of her eye she saw him sitting in what had become his favorite armchair; his muscular, but elegant hand contentedly swirling a drink he had presumptively fixed from her private stock. His wide shoulders pressed firmly in the back of the chair, legs stretched out to achieve maximum comfort.

"Comfortable?" she asked.

He either did not or chose not to notice her tone of voice, "Yes, I'm fine, thank you. Please continue."

Diana bit her lip.

"Very well. I've deleted all the potential bidders who will have no interest in bidding on lot #4o83q leaving me with…"

"With?"

"With none."

Apollo harrumphed and took a sip from his glass, a bit of the purple smoke escaped up his nostrils as well.

With a downward wave of her hand all the names disappeared.

Apollo jostled the glass in his hand, exciting the vaporous concoction within.

"And how long are you going to waste your time – and mine – looking for a party willing to buy a bunch of rocks for millions more than they're worth? It's time to be realistic. No one will come even close to meeting the bid."

"Except you?"

Her eyes stared pointedly at him until he turned to her. She immediately turned back to the console, held up a fist to the screen and twisted her wrist ninety degrees. An orb appeared.

"There is one name." With pinky extended, she directed the orb to float to Apollo's side. Once near enough, he could just make out a name. He separated his thumb and forefinger to expand the orb until the name was clear.

"Hephaestus? You don't mean the-?"

She nodded her head.

"Below is a list of assets contained in lot #4o83q. Notice the highlighted one?"

He straightened up in his chair as he read over the list.

"Ammonium acetate? What would that do?"

"Hephaestus' manufacturing company has recently acquired a solar energy farm located over… here in the Twenta System. This system used to have copious amounts of ammonium acetate, a key ingredient in the maintenance of solar rocks, but after centuries of solar farming, the systems' supply is depleting and will become critically low in less than fifty ribs. Hephaestus might not even realize it, yet. But once it's pointed out to him, the wisdom of getting his hands on it now will make sense."

Apollo pondered the supposition for a moment.

"Yes," he struggled to say. "That is quite an ingenious pitch to make to Hephaestus. But, he doesn't actually need it right this minute. He doesn't even know he needs it."

"That's where we come in. We'll do him the favor of telling him about his new acquisition's flaw, while simultaneously giving him the solution. A best case scenario."

Her companion fell silent. Diana had never seen him not get the last word on a matter and she took it as a compliment.

Feeling her eyelids droop, she took advantage of the lull in conversation to summon a vaporous drink which rose from the center of the console. Inhaling deeply, the gaseous vapors floated across the console and into her nostrils.

Observing this, Apollo crooked a disapproving browing.

"How many of those have you had?"

"Just this one. You have to admit it's been a long day that looks like it might get a lot longer. Do you want one?"

He shook his head.

"I'll stay with normal lubricants that don't have potentially lethal side-effects."

"Seriously, Apollo, it's just one. I need energy to solve this new wrinkle in the deal. Sure you don't want one?"

He shook his head.

"I'm not trying to accomplishment the impossible in an impossibly short amount of time."

Laying his glass down on the side table next to him, he absent-mindedly picked up a postcard laying there.

"Sierra Club. What is this about?"

Diana jumped, realizing she had left Orion's brochure out in plain sight.

"I don't know. It's some sort of organization."

He raised an eyebrow as he read it.

"Promoting a green and peaceful future." He looked up to her. "You're concerning yourself with the locals, now?"

"It's not mine. Someone left it here."

"You mean your little native friend." He sneered.

"He's not a native. I believe he was left here as a child not knowing what he was."

"What?"

"He was raised as the middle child of some native family. I doubt they knew his origins."

Apollo held it in as long as he could. But, when he could hold it no longer, he laughed long and loud.

Diana failed to comprehend the humor of the situation.

His laughter died down.

"Thank you. That was one of the best laughs I've had in a long time."

"I feel I'm missing something."

"Missing something? Where did you get this incredible story? Did he tell it to you?"

"No, I surmised it."

"That or maybe you were pulled into its orbit by the attractive, sympathetic young man who wants you to believe it."

"That's silly. He doesn't have a deceptive bone in his body. He's almost like a child in many ways, with all the things he doesn't know about the world."

"A child? He looks like a full grown man to me, a very healthy and virile one at that, judging by the way he was running across the front yard and picking up large animals, just now."

Diana suddenly realized she had divulged more than she had intended and abruptly turned back to her console. "I have to get back to work."

"Oh, of course. But, let me just get this story straight." He leaned forward rising enough to pull out the vents of his jacket.

"He told you, no sorry, he has led you through subtle inferences to believe that as a child, unawares, he was inexplicably dropped off on this planet and inserted into a family of naïve Earthlings. They unwittingly raised him without noticing his extra strength, different growing patterns and a host of other disparities."

"Apollo, please."

"I'm almost done. As an adult, he achieves some sort of gainful employment and, by the craziest of luck, ends up taking residence in the very same building you are staying at?"

"Are you finished?"

He leaned back in his chair. "And finally, despite the astronomical odds against it, he runs into you and strikes up a grand friendship. The perfect end to the fairy myth!"

Diana didn't say anything, just pressed her face closer to the console.

Apollo's index finger shot up, "Yes, I see what you mean. That version sounds a lot more plausible than, let's say, he was planted here by one of the potential bidders to try and get inside information on the property."

She rolled her eyes. "You can believe whatever you want."

Pondering the thought, her companion shifted in his chair enough to pull out the tails of the pearl suit coat that had bunched up underneath him, then rested his chin on his hand. "If this spy has already been able to gain the trust and confidence of the realtor, then I'm sure he has become privy to all the key details. This would be bad, not just for the competition, but for everyone involved."

Her face darkened.

"Apollo, no."

He jerked back. Regaining his composure, he stood and took a few steps towards her.

Menace filled her voice. "You will leave him alone."

"You can't keep him around. If it turns out he's working for one of the bidders and you've given him confidential information, that will destroy the whole bid. It will destroy your career. I've put it together; don't you think the other bidders will, too? There's no question. He has to disappear."

She swiveled to face him. "What are you talking about?"

"He's blinded you. You don't see the big picture."

"What I see is how eager you are to get rid of him."

"Yes, I'm eager. Eager to make sure this bidding is not messed up. You know what I have invested in it. Now, I won't make him disappear permanently, just until the bidding process is completed."

She jabbed a finger at him. "You will in no way harm, abduct, or even touch Orion. Is that clear?"

He started to say something. She crooked an eyebrow.

"Promise me."

He raised hands in surrender. "You don't need to make any sort of grand promise. Don't worry, I will not touch a hair on his head."

"Okay." Still visibly riled up, she returned to her seat. Though facing the console screen, her eyes looked off into space as she pondered Apollo's theories.

Apollo too, retreated to his corner. If Diana had been observing him, she would have seen him slumped back into his chair, his left index finger slowly brushing over his eyebrow as he fell deep into thought.

A half-an-hour later, he left without saying a word.

A satisfied smile flashed across Orion's face as he opened the door to his apartment at the end of the workday. Looking around, he saw that the credit card he'd maxed out redoing his apartment and wardrobe was paying off.

Stepping past his state of the art entertainment center, he flung his recently purchased calf-skin leather briefcase onto his new couch and removed his black, patent leather, dress shoes. After collapsing into the matching recliner that was part of the "modern living" deal at the furniture store, he leaned back to admire his castle.

After five minutes of "Orion" time had elapsed, he stretched out his arms then got up to begin the next part of his after-work ritual, changing out of his clothes and into the outfit Diana had given him. Upon gifting him the set of exotic clothes, she had assured him they were the height of fashion in all respectable parts of the galaxy and marveled at how magnificent he would look in them. Getting the hint, Orion put them on each day before heading up to her place.

First he pulled on the tight fitting - in the worst way – bright silver pants. He slipped on the ivory collared, sleeveless shirt and then the metallic jacket, the color of hematite, with elbow length sleeves. Dressing in front of a mirror was never an option. He might see what he looked like.

The last item of Diana's gift was the most unsettling to him. A pair of hairy puke pink slippers that constricted and tightened until they fit like perfectly made foot gloves. More disturbingly, they would give his feet little squeezes from time to time. Not both feet at the same time, just one foot or the other. It felt like having living teddy bears on his feet.

Properly dressed, he stepped out of his cramped bedroom into the slightly larger adjoining room that was both kitchen and living room. He noticed a film of white dust had formed on the floor in front of his recliner. Looking up, he saw that the ever growing bulge in the ceiling protruded an inch more than before. The bulge was directly beneath where Diana's console rested on the floor above.

He would tell Uri about it later. But now he had to go to Diana's, which invoked mixed feelings. It was not that he didn't enjoy her apartment. In fact, with each visit, he'd gotten a little more used to the odd and strange things he would see there. The projected images flying around the room, short little lessons on what the different machines did, cosmographical lessons where she highlighted some distinct, peculiar, or particularly beautiful system that might be of interest to him. Not just by showing it to him on one of her projected star maps; no, the walls, ceilings, and floors of her apartment would transform into the place. But, then the talk would always end up being about her big, larger than life ventures. Whenever he even mentioned his job, she would brush it off. Intellectually, he understood; she was under tremendous pressure with her "big" deal. Having someone to talk to about the ups and downs of his day would be nice, but how could his small little travails ever compete with her galactic enterprises?

His thoughts were interrupted by a knock on the door. Had Diana come down to him? He hadn't been able to get her to come down here since the incident when his couch stabbed her. Now he'd be able to show her his new furniture. Perfect timing, too. He'd just cleaned up the place the day before.

When he opened the door, he gasped. Standing before him was not Diana but a dour faced, middle-aged man who looked like he had received a summons from the IRS. At the man's side was a woman of similar age, every line on her face pointing down – his mother and father.

As they eyed their son's outlandish outfit their jaws dropped.

Orion's heart stopped. "Mom, Dad. What are you doing here?"

His mother was looking through the door past him, "We were in the neighborhood. You going to invite us in?"

"In the neighborhood? You live fifty miles away."

She started pushing her way in. Orion raised his hands in surrender.

"Of course, come in."

He waved his father in. The wary looking man ran his hand through finger-length salt and pepper hair as he took in the surroundings. After glancing at the room, he casually pointed to the ceiling and said in the same Midwestern accent as his wife. "You're ceiling's cracking."

"Yeah, look at that." Orion feigned surprise as if it were the first time he'd ever noticed it.

His mother studied the place. She didn't seem displeased as much as not quite satisfied.

"By golly, you've got new furniture. That's nice."

"Yeah, just got it. Have a seat and try it out."

His parents both took a seat, his dad on the recliner, his mother on the couch. She carefully rested her head on the back of the seat so as not to mess up her hair, still black, as she was not brave enough, yet, to let it go gray. Like an appraiser she ran her olive skinned hand over the furniture.

"How much did these cost? They look expensive."

Orion crossed to the refrigerator and opened it, "Would you guys like a drink?"

His father perked up. "Thanks, son, I'll have a Coke."

"Just water for me," his mom said, her hand straightening out her floral print dress.

Orion handed out the drinks.

His father couldn't hold his tongue any longer. "Son, that's an interesting outfit you're wearing."

Orion remembered how he was dressed.

"Oh, yeah... I was about to go up and meet someone."

"Dressed like that?!" His father wrinkled his face.

"Oh, Bill." his mother chimed in. "What your father wants to say is that we support whatever kind of lifestyle you wish to live."

Bill nodded. "That's right, that's right. We'll support the life you want to live no matter how perverted and hedonistic."

"We just want you to be happy."

"No," Orion shook his head, "it's nothing like that. There's a girl upstairs. She gave me this outfit. I was just going to see her."

His parents exchanged delighted glances.

"Heavens! Who is this young lady?" His mother rose from her chair. "Are you two going together?"

How on Earth could he explain Diana to them? "She's...."

He stopped short, a bit put off by the way his parents leaned in with anticipation.

"Well?" His mother's neck craned forward, a hopeful glint in her eyes.

Before Orion could finish, a loud crack sounded above them and a pile of white dust and plaster flakes unloaded onto his father. The ceiling had given way.

"Oh, my god!" Orion ran to get a towel.

"Bill!" his mother rushed to his side. "Are you okay?"

Bill's eyes opened, peering out through a white mask of plaster dust.

"I'm okay! I'm okay!" He coughed a couple of times and clumsily tried to wipe the thick layers of dust from his face.

Orion handed him a wet towel.

"Dad, I'm so sorry about this."

His father began toweling himself off.

His mother looked to the ceiling.

"Good lord!"

Orion's eyes shot up to behold the spot where the plaster had fallen. His hand went to his chest. The part of the ceiling that fell on his father was where the bulge had been. Thankfully, a layer of wood lath strips still separated them from Diana's apartment above so they couldn't see her place. But what if that collapsed? He had to stop Diana from continuing whatever she was doing up there.

With eyes more on the ceiling than on the two people he was speaking to, he grabbed the doorknob.

"I'm going now."

His mother looked panicked. "Where are you going!?"

"I'll be right back."

He slipped out the front door and ran up the stairs to Diana's apartment. Stopping outside her door, took a deep breath before knocking and sticking his head in.

The air quickly expelled from his lungs as he found himself looking not at Diana's apartment, but at an expansive pocked outcropping above a vast, pale white plain. Twenty yards away, Diana sat at her console back-dropped by a crescent gem blue planet that hung in the starry sky. Orion instantly knew he was looking at the Earth from the Moon's surface.

She gave a broad wave. Her voice was clear and crisp despite the distance and the lack of atmosphere. "Don't worry, I'm almost done here. Then I'm yours for the rest of the night." She gave an awkward wink, not quite having got that custom down, yet.

Orion smiled back, he was going to tell her about the ceiling, but his eye had caught site of IO who was standing not far from her. Playfully, the feline batted a two feet in diameter moon rock into the air and vaulted after it. After a few giant leaps and bounds the feline landed near a white flag on a six foot pole. Apparently tired of chasing after the rock, it settled on blasting it out of the sky with its mouth laser.

The white flag seemed very familiar to Orion. The cloth was stiff, rigged so that it stood out at a right angle, and mounted on a gold flagpole that was inserted into the dirt surface. As he focused on the flag, he intuitively deduced that though the original red, white, and blue coloring was gone, it was the American flag. Logically, it made sense that the colors would fade due to the decades of extreme conditions it had endured. But, he felt a pang of remorse at finding the symbol of man's first steps here, a moment immortalized by this simple piece of cloth, faded so as to be non-identifiable.

IO's head darted back and forth. With its laser eyes, it melted a two-foot diameter boulder thirty yards away. Still frisky, it reached out and playfully pushed its paw against the flagpole which began to bend and then fell over. Emboldened by a swell of patriotism, Orion pushed the apartment door open a little wider, ready to go and right his country's flag.

He placed a slippered foot onto the moon's surface. To his horror, the fuzzy pink slipper emitted a grunt as soon as it touched the moon's surface. It then contracted, squeezing his foot. Orion cringed. It felt like a guinea pig was making love to his foot. He pulled the foot back out and the slipper slowly relaxed back to its usual state.

His actions caught IO's attention. The feline robot leaped over to its mistress's side clearing the forty yards in one bound

This further discombobulated Orion who, despite what his eyes were telling him and the weird behavior of the slipper, had to remind himself that he was not looking at the moon, but at Diana's apartment. He cleared his throat.

"Dear, there's a problem."

"A problem?" Diana interjected. "You're not trying to get out of being with me tonight, are you?" She dipped her head down and stuck her lower lip out in exaggerated disappointment. IO's eyes turned green as it jumped a few feet forward landing in an attack stance. The moon dust it kicked up rose and fell in perfect parabolic arcs due to the lack of atmosphere.

Orion's observation of this may be why he failed to hear the footsteps coming up the stairs behind him.

"It's my ceiling. It's… falling apart. I don't know what you're doing up here, but-."

He stopped, feeling something jab his back, and spun around to find his parents barely an arm's length away.

"Mom, Dad, what are you doing here?!"

He lodged himself in the doorway to block their view of Diana's apartment.

His father's head and shoulders were mostly free of white dust. His mother stretched her neck trying to see over his shoulder. "You know, son. If you keep asking that, we're going to think you don't want us around. We were just curious to see your lady friend."

Orion started to close the door but was confounded when Diana's voice called out from the other side of the door. "Your parents? Invite them in!"

He peeked inside to find Diana's place magically transformed back into her apartment, her console into living room furniture, and IO stretched out lazily on the black onyx side table as if ready to take a nap.

"Really?" Orion asked, not sure if Diana just felt the need to be polite. "Are you sure? I know you're busy. I wouldn't want to-."

"Don't be ridiculous. Invite them in."

"Oh… okay." he pushed the door open enough to let them in. "Mom, Dad, this is Diana."

Diana rose to her feet and gave a slight bow. Orion's father's jaw dropped when he saw her ensemble: a full-length silver silk coat with high fur trimmed collar draped around a cream colored evening dress. Her head was adorned with tiny beads of sea blue pearls tied through her swept back hair.

Orion's mother was similarly awestruck. She hesitantly stepped up, looking more at her shoes than the person she was addressing. "My name's Mary."

She stuck out her hand to Diana who looked at it perplexed. His mother, feeling awkward, finally let her hand fall.

Orion rushed over.

"Mom, Dad. I think Diana's kind of busy."

Diana pretended not to hear Orion. "And this good looking man must be your father?"

The squat, large jowled man eased up a little at being called "good looking" and got over his initial bedazzlement enough to speak.

"Bill's the name. Nice to meet you Miss… Sorry, do you have a last name?"

"Diana's fine."

"Diana."

He took another look up and down at her outfit.

"So, what do you do? Are you in fashion or something?"

Diana shot Orion a querying look.

"Well…" she slowly brushed back a light brown strand of hair over her ear. "I am in real estate."

"Oh, I've got a friend in commercial real estate. What kind do you do?"

Orion put a hand on his parents' backs. "Come on, let's let Diana get back to work. Real estate's a tough business."

He moved to steer his parents to the door but his mother resisted.

"What a pushy son I have!" She sidestepped her son's hand and addressed Diana with a broad smile and a dead on gaze. "We just want to say what a pleasure it is to meet one of our son's lady friends."

"Why thank you." Diana waved Orion down. "You know, I'm not sooo busy. And it would be illuminating to meet the two lovely people who raised such a fine son. I'm dying to find out all about the family history."

"What?" Orion didn't understand what was happening or why Diana was laying on the charm.

She motioned them to the Danish style cream colored couch.

They took their seats as Orion shot Diana a what- are-you-doing look. She flashed a wide smile as she waved a hand over the table stand next to her seat. Her guests' eyes widened and Orion cringed when a panel slid aside and four smoky concoctions in martini glasses emerged on a rising platform.

Diana distributed the not quite liquid refreshments to her guests. Orion's father looked a bit frightened as he took his glass. Orion's mother, however, never took her eyes off her hostess – whom she studied like a tiger eyeing the weakest member of a zebra herd.

Orion took his glass, contemplated drinking it, then set it back down. This was definitely not the time, he decided, to be experiencing new and exotic drinks.

His father observed IO who had just leapt to the windowsill by his chair.

"Hey, kitty. You're a cutie, aren't you?"

With the smile of a five-year old child spotting a new toy, the middle-aged man got up and went over to IO.

Orion panicked.

"Dad, I wouldn't-."

With one swift motion, his father picked IO up and cradled it in his arms.

Orion shot up to his feet expecting all hell to break loose. Instead, IO stayed relaxed, contentment filled its face as his father took a seat back in the chair, gently stroking the feline along the head and back.

Diana found the intense stare of Orion's mother relentless, two dark brown eyes squinting ever so slightly as if in accusation. But, she would not turn away, she decided. The faster she got to the truth, the better.

Orion sat back down in the single seat, his eyes never wavering from IO and his father as he spoke.

"Wow, it's great having you all together." He spoke with the conviction of a captain of a sinking ship telling the passengers not to panic when the water was already to their knees.

Not knowing what was appropriate; Diana shifted her gaze away from Orion's mother and took a long sip of her drink.

Bill eyed his glass which bubbled gently and still smoked, where he had set it down on the side table, furled his eyebrows, then happily went back to petting IO.

Mary held hers but never imbibed it. Her eagle eyes stayed fixed on Diana.

"So, Diana, whereabouts do you come from? You don't seem to be from around here."

Diana waved the question off. "Oh, I'm from little out of the way place you've never heard of. You won't even find it on the map."his arms.

Orion shot up to his feet expecting all hell to break loose. Instead, IO stayed relaxed, contentment filled its face as his father took a seat back in the chair, gently stroking the feline along the head and back.

Diana found the intense stare of Orion's mother relentless, two dark brown eyes squinting ever so slightly as if in accusation. But, she would not turn away, she decided. The faster she got to the truth, the better.

Orion sat back down in the single seat, his eyes never wavering from IO and his father as he spoke.

"Wow, it's great having you all together." He spoke with the conviction of a captain of a sinking ship telling the passengers not to panic when the water was already to their knees.

Not knowing what was appropriate; Diana shifted her gaze away from Orion's mother and took a long sip of her drink.

Bill eyed his glass which bubbled gently and still smoked, where he had set it down on the side table, furled his eyebrows, then happily went back to petting IO.

Mary held hers but never imbibed it. Her eagle eyes stayed fixed on Diana.

"So, Diana, whereabouts do you come from? You don't seem to be from around here."

Diana waved the question off. "Oh, I'm from little out of the way place you've never heard of. You won't even find it on the map."

"I might have heard of it. Try me."

Orion broke off from his sentinel watch of his father to interject. "I've got to say, Mom, Dad, it's just so great having you guys here. When was the last time you visited?"

Before they could say anything, Diana's face hardened and she began directing all her statements at the mother.

"Yes, it's good to have family. Is this the whole family? Does Orion have any siblings?"

The mother looked down. "No, Orion is our only child."

"Yes," added Orion, "I'm the only one. But, from what they tell me, I was such a handful that I was more than enough. Right, Mom?"

"That's right, son." She reached over and patted him on the knee. Leaning in towards the woman across from her, Diana's tone shifted from congenial hostess to that of a lawyer interrogating a witness, "You must have felt blessed when a son like Orion was given to you."

The father nodded absent-mindedly as he stroked IO behind the ears.

The mother, however, shifted a little uneasily in her seat. Diana's almond eyes tightened as she pressed on.

"Being able to have a son must be such a gift, a beautiful little child to call your own to hold and take care of. I can imagine one would do anything to have that dream. Most anything."

Mary's visage grew dark as the two women again locked eyes.

Orion became too distracted worrying about his father and IO to keep track of the conversation. He anxiously sat on the edge of his seat watching his father gently pulling on IO's front paw while the feline spiritedly batted his hand with its free paw. The little creature bit the old man's fingers. Orion was ready to lunge to his aid, but saw his father smile as IO playfully gnawed on his hand and fingers. The old man couldn't have looked happier. IO eventually played out, stretched out on the gentleman's lap and closed its eyes.

Mary broke from Diana's stare and finished her drink in one fell swoop.

"Father, drink up. We don't want to overstay our welcome."

Bill reluctantly picked up his drink and sniffed it warily.

"There's no liquid in it." He protested, "It's just full of smoke."

"Just drink it. You know they're always coming out with newfangled drinks."

Circumspect, the old man tipped it up. The vapors disappeared into his mouth. Lowering the glass, he looked like a kid who had just unintentionally swallowed his gum.

Orion's mother rose to her feet and motioned for him to give her his glass. She took her son's unfinished drink then announced, "Gentleman, we ladies are going to wash the dishes. You two just catch up."

She motioned for Diana to follow her to the kitchen. Caught off guard, Diana shot Orion a *what do I do* look, but he was too preoccupied by his father and IO to notice.

Diana followed the formidable creature into the room she had just learned was called, "the kitchen". Mary set the glasses in the sink. Diana, who had no clue why they were in there or what "wash the dishes" meant, leaned forward to see what the strange being was doing.

"I thought we could have some time alone together." Mary said, turning on the faucet.

Diana jumped back when water came out. A look of horror crossed her face.

"Bee stars! It's broken!"

"Broken? No, it's working fine."

The mother seemed to think nothing was out of order so Diana composed herself and watched in wonder as the Earthling placed each glass under the running water.

"Do you have any soap?" Mary asked.

Diana looked around as if she had any idea what the woman was talking about.

"I…"

"Don't worry about it. These glasses don't even look dirty. Kind of like your kitchen. Like you've never set foot in it. But you wouldn't need to, would you?"

Diana's mouth opened slightly. She froze, not knowing how to answer. Her eyes studied the creature before her trying to ascertain what she knew and didn't know.

The elderly woman set the last glass on the counter.

"Surprised? I knew you weren't one of us from the minute I laid eyes on you."

"I don't know what you're-."

"You don't have to lie to me. You're from up there." Mary

pointed to the ceiling. "It's as plain as day. The way you dress. Giving us drinks full of smoke. And the biggest giveaway is the way you keep looking at us like we're exhibits at the zoo. You going to deny it?"

Letting out a long exhale, Diana responded, "No."

"Good." She lifted two of the glasses. "Now, where do you put these?"

Diana shrugged. "Put them…?"

A sardonic smile crossed Mary's lips. "No, I guess you don't put anything anywhere. Everything is done for you. Here I am doing your dishes and they probably don't even get dirty."

With a weary laugh she set the glasses down.

Diana arched her back. "When you are done laughing I have some questions I'd like to ask you."

Mary jabbed an accusatorial finger at Diana. "You wanna ask questions?! Well, I got some questions for you. Like why you and your kind come into our world never giving a damn about how you wreck lives. And why is it always someone else who has to clean up the messes you make? Poor Orion!"

"Don't try to put this on me and my kind. I'm not the one in the wrong here. What you've done-."

"I knew it! You've been giving me the evil eye, judging me since you first laid eyes on me like I'm the bad guy. What do you know?!"

"What do I know?" Diana's faced reddened. "There's a man in the next room that I've grown very fond of. As far as I can tell, his whole life has been a lie. He was raised by two organisms who convinced him they were his parents and that his home was on this primeval planet where the inhabitants live like animals spending most of their time thinking of new ways to kill each other. For reasons I cannot fathom they conspired to deprive him of a real life with-."

"We didn't deprive him of nothing! Bill and I gave our boy everything we could. Now, it was obvious we couldn't replace everything, because we couldn't. And, he would never be like the other kids. But, we did our best, that's all we could do. Right? I mean...what more could we have done?" Overcome with emotion, her eyes began to well up. She put her head in her hand.

Diana stiffened, unsure of the appropriate response. How do you handle Earthlings in these matters? She settled on what came naturally to her; reaching out and giving the woman's arm a gentle squeeze.

Diana spoke honestly. "I can only imagine what you've gone through."

Mary smiled in appreciation and wiped her eyes. "I'm sorry. I've never talked about it before. Just bottled it up for so long. I couldn't tell anyone."

"Not your husband?"

"He was away, in the service. I couldn't tell anyone, not even him. I had to keep my boy safe. No one could know, I couldn't tell his teachers, friends, no one. Thank god he never got seriously sick or hurt. That was my biggest fear. The doctor would find out or wouldn't be able to help him because he was different. After the first year, I'd grown so attached to him that -. He was super smart. You could tell it from the beginning. And so beautiful, his eyes, like little oceans looking up at me." A smile of remembrance grew on her lips. "I would hold him in my arms; wipe off the tears when he cried. He was my baby. Do you understand? If anything'd ever happened to him I...I..."

Diana put her hand on her heart. Emotions overwhelmed her. The love this woman felt for the man she called her son.

"I understand." Diana did.

The woman wiped her eyes. Her face was blotchy. "Where do you keep the paper towels?" She opened the cupboard next to the counter and found it empty. Her head dropped. "Oh, yeah. It's not a real kitchen."

Diana shook her head.

Mary wiped her face with her sleeve. "God, this day really turned out different than I thought it would. I knew something was wrong with O' when we'd last talked. Never thought it would be something like this."

Diana gave her arm a pat. "So, how did you end up with him?"

Mary hesitated until Diana crooked an eyebrow.

Mary shook her head. "That-. That's not important."

"But it is. How did you end up with Orion?" Diana grabbed her by the arm, firmly this time.

Mary struggled. "All I can say is that Orion was left here to die. I couldn't allow that to happen."

"Someone abandoned their own child?"

"Mary!" Bill chimed in from the other room. "MARY!"

Mary put the last glass down on the counter and pulled loose from Diana.

"I'm coming, Bill." She pushed through the swinging door.

"Oh, my God!"

Diana rushed out to find Mary's hands covering her mouth as she looked at Bill holding a limp IO up in the air.

From the opposite side of the room, Orion excitedly waved his hands.

"Dad, just put him down."

Bill's mouth was agape. "I don't know what happened. I thought he was sleeping, but he's just all limp!"

The veins were bulging on the side of Orion's head.

"Look at me, Dad. Just put him down very, very carefully."

Mary rushed to her husband. "My goodness, Bill, what are you doing?"

Bill saw Diana. "I'm so sorry. I don't know what happened. I didn't do anything. I swear."

He gently placed the limp gray mass down on the white armchair as if placing a baby in its crib. When he turned around to the others they could see tears welling in his eyes.

Diana raised her eyebrows in wonderment at the exaggerated reactions of these Earthlings. She crossed the room and slipped her hand under IO's chin feeling around until she found the right spot.

The limp feline sprang to life and jumped out of the chair landing halfway across the room and scurried back to Diana's side. All the other occupants in the apartment let out collective gasps. Bill's face went from shock to slow relief. Mary visibly sighed. Orion clutched his chest and took a seat on the arm of the couch; all the energy had drained from his legs.

The feline robot jumped up into its mistress's arms and nuzzled her face. Diana whispered just loud enough for IO to hear. "Don't worry, little buddy. It's alright. You just let yourself get turned off. Next time you'll be more careful, won't you? Hmm?"

The faintest hint of a smile crossed Diana's lips as she bemusedly observed the condition of her guests.

"My cat is a heavy sleeper." With a touch of whimsy she declared, "It looks like everyone's ready for another drink."

Taking their lack of response as an affirmative, she waved her hand palm up and another four smoky concoctions rose from out of the side table.

As his parents took their drinks Orion edged up to Diana.

"I'm gonna take my parents back to my place. I don't know how much more of having all of you together I can take!"

She shook her head. "No, let them stay a little longer. These are the ones who raised you."

"They're my parents, yes."

"Then I would like to observe them a little longer."

Orion's head crooked uneasily to the side.

"Observe them…?"

"What do Earthlings usually do at events like this?"

"I don't know. We talk."

"What else?"

"Play games, sometimes."

"That sounds perfect! Would they be comfortable playing some of my games?"

"Do your games involve using the console or teleporting contestants to other planets?"

"Yeah, that's a no go." Orion sighed. "I think I might have a Monopoly board downstairs. I'll go get it."

The board was set up quickly. As Diana had never played before, it was agreed she would team with Orion. This proved pointless as she had acquired a complete grasp of the real estate game within minutes and spent the next thirty-three of them leading their team to victory with gentle admonitions like, "Don't buy the violet lot! Look where it's placed on the board! There's only a two point six percent chance of landing on it!" and "Why are you throwing money away!?

Save the money for the orange and the red properties! Those are the properties that will crush our enemies when fully developed!"

About a quarter of the way into the game Orion surrendered his dice rolling duties after Diana had repeatedly remonstrated him for not throwing them right. He found her rolls highly suspicious, though, as they inevitably resulted in either doubles or numbers that magically let their little race car pass over all properties owned by opposing players.

His parents proved good sports, though neither seemed overly absorbed by the game. Bill kept looking over at IO, as if trying to reassure himself that the yellow-eyed feline was in fact okay. Mary's attention was on Orion and Diana, her eyes darting back and forth between the two of them. Her forehead wrinkled as she noticed her son looking despondent at having been pushed out of the game by his partner. He stepped back from the game and took a seat on the couch as this woman from another planet rolled her second doubles and quickly moved the race car the allotted spaces.

It seemed the rest of the game would go on like this, but then Diana, on what would be her last turn of the game, looked round and noticed Orion wasn't next to her.

"Hey, what are you doing back there?" She held the dice out to him. "I need you to roll."

He shrugged. "No, you're doing fine. Haven't you won, yet?"

She extended her arm out a little farther.

He shook his head. "You don't need me. You're the monopoly master."

"I don't want to win without you." She made a pouty face. "It wouldn't be any fun."

Orion took the dice and rolled. Diana repositioned herself so she would be at his side rubbing her hand up and down his back as he moved the racecar four spaces.

As Mary watched this last interaction, the wrinkles on her forehead smoothed, the tightness in her shoulders eased.

The game ended shortly thereafter and was packed back into its box. Mary waved a hand to her husband.

"Come on, Bill. We've imposed ourselves long enough on this nice lady."

Diana's head jerked up in surprise. "You're leaving?"

Bill nodded. "It's past our bedtimes."

"But, it's only…" Diana had to stop herself. She had no idea what the local Earth time was.

Eyes bleary, Orion nodded. "They've still got to drive home." He pulled open the door.

"Very well," Diana relented and addressed the couple. "Then I will bid even's end to you. As they say where I'm from:

> May gravity never slow you,
> May luck be always in your grasp,
> And if far from loved ones you do roam,
> May your star's light guide you back to home."

Bill smiled as he joined Orion in the hall.

"That was just beautiful."

Mary shut the door behind them to be alone with Diana. She tenderly took Diana's hand in hers.

"Before I go, I just wanted to say that seeing Orion with you, the way you two care for each other; that put my heart at ease. I know he's with his own kind. You'll give him what I couldn't."

She gave Diana's hand a squeeze as a tear trickled down her face. "I'm afraid you're going to take him away. But, I can live with that so long as I know you'll do what's best for him. Do you understand?"

Diana nodded and gave the earnest woman's hand a squeeze back. Mary left.

Alone, Diana found her questions had been replaced by an uneasy feeling about what she was going to do next.

# CHAPTER XIV
## The Impossible

As he reached for Diana's door, Orion's hand brushed against his tie. He froze realizing he'd forgotten to change into the outfit. A quick glance at his watch told him there was no time to go back to his room.

With a sigh, he turned the knob which was never locked and pushed on the door. A scent akin to burnt orange peels invaded his nose. Poking his head in he jumped, suddenly realizing why Diana had no need for locks.

Through the darkness, her cat stared at him with its green luminescent eyes. The ambient light streaming through the window was just enough for Orion to see the feline's belyingly delicate frame perched on the fireplace mantel. Diana's console was gone and there was no sign of her. He immediately felt the hairs on his back stand up with the revelation that he was alone with IO.

"Hey, kitty."

He slowly gave a half wave.

"Um, I'm going to leave, now."

He took a step back.

"Please don't kill me, okay?"

He was about to take another step when he heard the faint trace of a voice. With raised brow, he eyed the feline, which hadn't moved.

The whisper of a voice came again. This time, however, it had a feminine ring to it.

Orion crooked his head to the side. Was IO a female robot cat?

"What are you saying? Are you speaking?"

Tentatively, he took a step back in. The cat remained still. But, he heard the voice again. This time it was a male voice too low to make out.

"Are you trying to tell me something?"

Another step brought Orion almost to the center of the living room. The closer to the cat he moved the more coherent the voices became. There were two voices in conversation: a man's, which he didn't recognize, and Diana's.
Her voice, though, sounded unusually pitched. Perhaps to match the exasperated male she was conversing with.

Orion, still trying to ascertain the source of the voices, took another step towards IO. The cat, to his relief, had remained sitting, but its gleaming eyes, never blinking, followed him. With each step, the voices grew louder and clearer. Tempting fate even more, he took yet another step closer to the room's guardian.

His foot bumped against something. Something hard. Looking down, he saw nothing. Kicking lightly, he found he was hitting an an invisible object. Tapping his foot in a few other places, he deduced that the invisible object held the same place and dimensions as Diana's console.

He pulled back, wary of touching something wrong. IO, sitting unmoved, was a blank slate. Tentatively, he looked away from the cat and down to the unseen console. Moving as close as he felt comfortable, he leaned in to hear, trying to make out what the voices were saying. Diana's voice came through, even higher pitched than before as if she were being forced to do something against her will.

"But the ammonium acetate is plentiful in most all of the asteroids."

The male voice came in:

"And what good does that do if they blow up, too?"

"Q6 was an anomaly. The other properties are stable."

"Surveys have been done to verify this?!"

Orion heard no response from Diana. The other voice broke the silence.

"Exactly, and so how is Hephaestus to know if the rest of his new acquisition might not go, too?"

"There have been no signs of that happening."

"Like, you tell us, there were no signs of q6 going white. You would have us promise a large amount of money for-."

"It's not a large amount at all! Just bid the reserve price. Then you'll be getting the ammonium acetate for half its real value."

"I would hardly say that. Ammonium acetate is not exactly ilithia. We could get a better price."

"But, not all at one place. With lot #4o83q you would have it all in one place."

A short silence ensued. Orion leaned in a little further wondering if the connection was lost. The male voice sounded:

"We will agree to your arrangement on two conditions."

"Yes?"

"Firstly, you contact no more any parties to enter the bid. You do not have to stop bidders, but you must not solicit any further parties."

"That is acceptable."

"The second is that you run a survey over the entire asteroid field to ensure its safety."

Another short silence followed. It was eventually broken by Diana.

"But there's not enough time to-."

"Adnaeum! These are our conditions!"

"I-."

"Do you agree?"

A weak, "Yes," came in reply.

"Adnaeum."

Orion heard no more. Straightening up, he eyed IO whose eyes had reverted to yellow, the glowing gone.

A rushing wind sound filled the room as if pressure was being release from a large valve. Orion twirled around but couldn't locate the source of the noise. Turning around again, he gave a gasp. Diana and her console were sitting at their place. Her face masked in a ghostly pallor.

Orion couldn't contain himself. He rushed to her side.

She nodded weakly, flashing the biggest smile she could muster.

"Hello, Muscles."

Accepting that it really was her, he grabbed her by the arms.

"What just happened? Where were you?"

Slumped down in her chair her brown eyes studied the floor as if trying to comprehend what he was referring to. Her head wobbled forward and back as her eyelids drooped. Fearing she might faint, Orion rubbed up and down on her back. He had never seen her in such a weakened state before.

"Are you okay? Do you need to rest?"

She put her hand on his.

"There's no time."

Her headpiece was a little off balance. He straightened it for her.

"What are you talking about?"

"Lot #4o83q. I have to start surveying."

She swiveled her chair to face the console, placed her hands on the dashboard, adjusted a knob, then fell completely limp. Catching her, Orion righted her back up in her chair.

"You're not in any condition to go anywhere. What's happening? How did you get like this?"

She used his arm to pull herself up and thought about the question before answering.

"Lot #4o83q. I just made a deal."

"You and your deals."

She closed her eyes until she had enough energy to continue.

"I made a deal with Hephaestus."

"Who?"

"Large factory owner. Believed to have killed several people. He has agreed to meet the reserve."

"That's... great?"

Eyes still closed, she shook her head.

"They're demanding a survey be done on all the asteroids."

"Well, you can get to it after you've rested."

She opened her eyes.

"I must start, now."

"I know you're a toughie and all, but you don't look up to it."

"It doesn't matter. The bid is in two days. The survey has to be completed in four di-ribs."

Orion mouthed the calculations.

"Six hours. That's not much time."

"No."

With a hint of desperation, she reached for the console. Two orbs pulled up, characters of information streaming across them. With concern, Orion watched as she began what he deduced was the asteroid survey.

A 3D image of an asteroid appeared in the left orb. Extremely life-like, it looked as if it were the real artifact placed in glass in a museum. Characters in whites and yellows streamed across the second orb. Orion was experienced enough now to recognize that it was geological information about the pictured asteroid.

The slender finger Diana pointed at the orb shook from fatigue.

"Identify and catalogue for geological make-up."

The orb turned a dull green for half a second before reverting to its original color. The findings registered on the left orb.

Bleary-eyed, she read through the report.

"Now, record and certify."

Both orbs turned gray for a second then reverted back to their original states.

Orion leaned forward, interested by the process.

"How many more asteroids are there to survey?"

She made a hook motion with her finger.

"One million two hundred six thousand twelve."

"What?! You'll never make that in six hours."

"I have no choice."

Weakly, she raised a hand.

"Q2. Identify and catalogue for geological make-up."

He placed his hand on her arm.

"This is ridiculous. Let me help."

She continued as if he had said nothing.

"Identify and catalo-. I mean... record and certify."

Her head drooped a bit before it jerked upright. She eyed the orb, blinking.

"Diana." He brushed her leg. "Diana, you're too tired. Look at you, you're half passed out."

She shook her head in exaggerated back and forth motions.

"I have to do this!"

"Why? Why do you have to do this?"

"Because this is what I was meant to do. If I lose this I have nothing. I will have to go back home... a failure."

"That's crazy. You're amazing."

She looked at him pityingly. Making a push up motion with her hand, a vial containing smoky ingredients rose out from the console. She inhaled deeply, the smoke traveled the three feet between the

"That's crazy. You're amazing."

She looked at him pityingly. Making a push up motion with her hand, a vial containing smoky ingredients rose out from the console. She inhaled deeply, the smoke traveled the three feet between the container and her nostrils where it disappeared.

Immediately, her eyes widened and a refreshed alertness came over her.

"I'm sorry for my display, just now." Her words were clearer. "I... I have to get to back to this. You don't have to stay. This is my problem."

Orion was studying her. Her voice had regained most of its strength but was slightly raspy. Her eyes were almost unnaturally wide open, but with definite signs of fatigue around the edges. He bowed slightly and stepped back to the chair where he took a seat.

Examining the orb, she deduced what step she had left off at.

"R3. Identify and catalog for geological make-up."

The orbs turned green again, then bright yellow.

She bit her lip.

"Examine anomalies."

The three-dimensional image of the asteroid rotated and four blue specks lit up.

"Clorime filter."

The orb with the asteroid darkened to an aqua blue for a second, then reverted back to original projection of asteroid R3. The blue specks were gone.

"Record and certify."

The two orbs turned gray.

Orion watched the process for the next couple of hours until he, too began to have to fight the effects of weariness. His companion would slip occasionally or make a mistake but would catch herself and continue. Feeling the pointlessness of staying awake, he finally until he, too began to have to fight the effects of weariness. His companion would slip occasionally or make a mistake but would catch herself and continue. Feeling the pointlessness of staying awake, he finally let himself doze off.

For Diana, the succession of asteroids became one long blur. She stopped at one point, unsure if she had recorded and certified a specific asteroid a few numbers back. Had she completed it? No asteroid could be missed or the report would show the survey as incomplete.  She struggled for a second to remember the name of it. What was it?

Finally, it came to her.

"R243254."

The asteroid and its corresponding data appeared on the orbs. Having trouble reading the characters, she rubbed her eyes. Pushing her face closer, she studied them realizing this asteroid had been recorded and certified. Why hadn't she remembered that? She was wasting time!

An ache in her back announced itself as she sat straight in her chair. She remembered the stimulant. But, she had taken too much in too short a time already. If she took it, it could kill her. A sinking feeling came over her. There wasn't enough time, she felt so drained. What asteroid was next? Her mind had stopped working.

With no more strength to hold it up her head slowly dropped down until she lay facedown on the console, blackness overtaking her.

A beep from the console brought her back from the brink. Her head jerked up a few inches from the console. She looked and saw that she had only been asleep a second. With a quick pward motion of her hand, another vial of the smoky concoction emerged from the console. She inhaled. The smoke was pulled from the vial and headed for her nostrils.

At the last moment, she realized the danger of what she was doing and turned her head away. The smoke blew across the side of her face but not into her system. Her muscles tightened in horror at the danger she almost put herself in. As they loosened again, she felt the last vestige of consciousness seep out of her. Somewhere in the back of her mind a cry sounded that she must continue the survey. Everything she had worked for would be lost. This voice was subsumed with all other thoughts as she unavoidably surrendered to the world that dreams inhabit.

# CHAPTER XV
## To See

Daylight streamed through the window forcing Diana to squint. As she rolled over to the other side of the bed to escape the glare, she felt the folds of her dress twist around her legs and realized she was still in her day outfit. How and when she had ended up in bed was a mystery. Before she could reflect on it further, she heard someone talking in the next room.

"Record and certify."

Her mind flashed on the survey. Getting out of bed she scurried to the living room. To her bewilderment, she found Orion in his work clothes at the console, surrounded by eight survey orbs suspended at eye level.

He spotted her in the doorway.

"Good morning."

Hurrying to his side she eyed the orbs with an appearance of dread.

"What are you doing?!"

He straightened up, proud.

"Finishing the survey. I only have three more to do."

"What?!" She sounded horrified. "But you don't know how to…"

"I watched you do it for two hours last night. It's not rocket science."

She stuck her lips out, not understanding.

"Rocket science?"

"I mean, it was easy for me to do. And obviously two orbs weren't going to get the job done fast enough, so I pulled up some more."

She shooed him away replacing him in the seat.

"Why didn't you wake me?"

"When I got up you were sprawled out all over the console. You were so out of it I wasn't even sure if you were alive at first."

She looked over the readings on the console.

"You actually are on asteroid q1206010?"

He nodded matter of factly.

She still looked incredulous.

"All the others before have been surveyed?"

"Yes. Like I said, there's only three to go.

She took a deep breath.

"We might just make it."

With two crooked fingers, she directed a pair of orbs to her.

"Q1206011. Identify and catalog for geological make-up."

With two crooked fingers, she pulled another set of orbs towards her.

"Q1206012. Identify and catalog for geological make-up."

While standing in observance, Orion's legs felt weak from fatigue so he took a seat as she finished the survey.

Pointing the four fingers of her left hand at the console, she twisted it counterclockwise. The eight orbs disappeared.

"Sent!"

She spun around to face him.

Orion looked to his watch and smiled.

"You mean?"

To his surprise, she sprang from her chair and fell on his lap. Laughing with glee, she planted a flurry of kisses on his face.

"Yes! Yes! The survey results are traveling across the cosmos to that horrible, murderous Hephaestus. He and his rodent of a representative with his stupid 'adnaeums' thought they were asking the impossible, but we did it!"

Another flurry of kisses caught Orion off-guard. He had never seen her so wild. She rolled back and forth, her sharp elbows and knees jabbing him in sensitive areas.

"Ow! Ah!"

To save himself, he held her in his arms to keep her still. Pressed against her body, he inhaled deeply, savoring her scent, her soft, smooth skin.

Restrained, she fell quiet as her head came to rest on his shoulder. In his arms, peace settled in, cocooning her from the cruelty and harms of the world outside.

It was he who broke the silence.

"So, what's your next step, champ?"

"To get back to work, of course."

She pushed herself off of him and moved to return to her console.

But he was too fast.

"Not yet."

He grabbed her by the giant ivory bow that covered her back, pulling her into his arms, nuzzling the back of her neck.

For another blissfull moment she closed her eyes.

"Really? Really? I know you were raised on this wild and primitive planet," she teased. "But don't you ever think of anything else?"

He shifted her around clutching her waist, eyes dancing with passion.

She shook her head disapprovingly.

"Well I, Mr. Earthman come from a civilized planet where people get to know each other before they start doing things like that." She pulled away, but not very hard.

He pressed his face closer to hers.

"Then let's get to know each other, right now."

His lips met her turned cheek. She pulled her head farther back.

"There'll be time for that. When this deal is finished."

She reached behind her back then made a move to escape.

He grasped for her.

"Where do you think you're going?" He grabbed her bow again, but found she had disconnected it from her outfit. He had the bow but no Diana.

She took her seat and looked at the readings on the console.

He got up to follow but met her pointed finger.

"Back in the chair, muscles!"

His face knotted up in frustration eyeing the lithe arm directing him to sit.

"Hey, I don't come around everyday just to have you order me around."

"I know exactly why you come around."

She unsuccessfully tried to repress a smirk as she pulled up a blue orb from the console.

"And you might have gotten farther had you been wearing the outfit I gave you."

He rolled his eyes.

"Honestly, I can't wear it every night. At the very least I need to wash it once in a while."

"Wash it?"

"Get the dirt off."

Confused, she tilted her head a little, eyes darting around trying to understand what he meant.

"Why would you clean it? It doesn't stain."

"The outfit doesn't get dirty or smell?"

She chuckled to herself at the ridiculousness of the question.

"If your clothes didn't stay clean, then what good would they be?"

Defeated by her peculiar sense of logic, he gave an exasperated sigh and took a seat.

"So, really, what's your plan from here?"

Her eyes looked skyward, tongue pushing out on the side of her mouth as she pondered the question.

"The survey is complete. The show will be very small and simple, so really, there's nothing more to do for it. I will go back to working on lot #5jie6c."

"Sounds good. What do you need me to do for it?"

"Oh, you're part of my team, now?"

Turning serious, he eyed her.

"I don't know. Can you do it all on your own? You tell me."

With a professorial air, she looked him up and down.

"On one condition."

"What?"

"That you dispose of that silly leash around your neck."

He realized she meant his tie and quickly removed it and unbuttoned his top button.

She motioned him to keep unbuttoning. Once he had gotten to the fourth button down, she nodded her head in approval and began her explanation.

"Let me show you how to cross-reference potential bidders with their cosmographical location."

As she began showing him the process, Orion found it to be rather simple. So much so that he couldn't help himself from drifting off into thought, pondering this amazing woman from another planet who was showing him one of the tools of the intergalactic real estate trade. Why did she move him so? Was it her looks? The way she dressed? Her over the top outfits? The appeal of Diana, he finally decided, was that she knew who she was and exactly what she wanted to be. She had found her place in life, where she fit.

Several minutes passed before she finished the explanation.

Nodding his weary head, Orion noted the morning sun peaking over the rooftops.

"I'll get on it. Should only take me an hour."

She lipped a "thank you" and turned back to her console.

He kept his word and told her when the cross-referencing was complete. Glancing at his watch and found he had run out of time with little less than an hour to get ready for his day job.

"Okay, it's time for me to go."

Diana was wholly engrossed with four multi-colored orbs before her.

"Yes, see you tomorrow."

He gave her a kiss on the cheek.

"Tonight, more accurately."

He started for the door, to make the descent back to his hole of an apartment but stopped, hearing her voice.

"Orion."

He turned around and watched her carefully choose her words.

"You were right earlier... I cannot do it all on my own. It may not seem like it but I-."

Her fingers nervously pulled at the diamond-lined fabric of her dresss.

"There are only so many ribs in a rotation and we've so little time left. What I'm trying to say is that knowing you're coming back each night to help me see through this absurdly impossible task is what's keeping me going. I'm glad you're my my teammate."

In a flurry of emotion, Orion's stomache simultaneously rose and fell at the same time. He felt so incredibly happy that, for a second, his legs began to give out.

"Not as glad as I am."

Desperately seeking to escape the intimacy of the moment she looked away.

His gaze went from her to the orb hovering on his side of the console. Like a futuristic crystal ball, it was projecting index drill readings for the last property to be sold – lot #5jie6c.

"Please, promise me you'll get a little rest, today. For tonight, think of what I can do so you don't have to. Like something for this last property. I think I'm even more eager than you to knock out this whole crazy deal thing."

She gave no response, looking downward now.

Studying the the stream of numbers and figures floating past him he suddenly thought to ask, "How big is it? Lot #5jie6c?"

He could see Diana flinch before she responded. Her tone became almost accusatory.

"What do you mean?"

"Lot #5jie6c, how many miles or kilometers is it? I can't quite tell from looking at the index readings. It looks pretty massive, is there a way I can see all of it?"

There was calculation in her response.

"The index drill allows one to see as much of the property as you want. We can do that sometime…when there's time."

She continued working and he moved to leave. As his hand touched the doorknob, he stopped when he heard her say, "Wait."

She nodded towards a shelf on the far end of the room.

"There's a vision device on that shelf."

He walked over and found a pair of lady's glasses, black with thick, cat eyes frames. The granny glasses look was exacerbated by the line of tiny diamonds running along the top of the frame.

Picking them up, he walked over and presented them to her. Without looking away from the console she told him, "They're for you."

He was perplexed.

She added, "Wear them. They will fix your eye problem."

"What eye problem?"

There was no response. She had already delved back into her work.

That evening, Orion slumped on the couch watching television and eating alone. On the news, a heroic, female reporter stood, flanked by a raging forest fire that had engulfed a quarter of Idaho. Not feeling like getting even more depressed, he reached for the remote. He wasn't looking where his hand was going and it bumped against the glasses that Diana had given him.

He eyed them. They really were ridiculous looking. Why did she give them to him? They weren't even men's glasses, more like the cat eye shaped ones worn by the grumpy granny in the "Maxine" cards. Would they even fit him?

Setting his dinner down on the side table, he picked the glasses up and put them on. Amazingly, they fit perfectly. They were so light and form fitting, it felt like he wasn't even wearing glasses.

Seeing through them though, was quite another thing. The colors on the furniture were more striking but there seemed to be fewer of them. Not only were the walls and ceilings a little dimmer, but everything was much increased in contrast.

Rising from his chair, he walked the room, looking at various objects as if for the first time, intrigued by what each item looked like through the glasses. In most cases, it wasn't a dramatic difference, just enough to be noticeable. The cupboard doors in the kitchenette were a more subdued yellow. The couch was a darker shade of green.

He moved to the window and studied the night sky and streets below. He found them changed. Things not in the path of the streetlights or the residential buildings were almost black. The usual glow from the trees and bushes was absent. The stars in the sky were nearly invisible, with only two or three shining brightly enough to be easily seen.

He pulled down the spectacles to make sure everything just hadn't become different. Sure enough, with glasses off, the view went back to normal. The bushes and the trees produced their aural glows, insects were visibly scurrying through them often pursued by bats, and the night sky teamed with thousands upon thousands of stars.

Satisfied that it was the glasses, not that the world had changed, he put them back on and stepped away from the window. It was getting late, time for bed. Grabbing the remote, he aimed it at the television to turn it off, but froze when he caught sight of the screen.

For the first time ever, the images on the screen were not confused. He could distinguish shapes and forms. He went weak in the knees at this, falling back onto the couch. He was astounded that the box in front of him was depicting shapes, objects and people very similarly to how they would be in real life. It wasn't perfect, but it was so much more real, more vivid than he had ever seen before.

On a hunch, he used the remote to set the screen display back to the default. Amazingly, the picture was even clearer. Like a kid, he flipped through the channels, blown away each time by what he saw. People were competing for prizes, others were solving crimes, and on another channel people were cooking. He had seen all these before as weird distorted images, now he could see them as they were.

An hour of watching the new, improved television passed before he remembered he was wearing Diana's glasses. With a bit of dread, he lowered them and found that without the spectacles, the television screen reverted to its blend of weirdly distorted lights and colors which made people appear as phantasms.

There was no doubt about it. These funny little glasses could change everything.

# CHAPTER XVI
## Bet Your Life

A sinking feeling washed over Stan as he struggled to put together the various pieces of the company saving plan he had promised to deliver three weeks before. The game show idea was sound, but rigging it to entice young and old customers and then linking them together was proving too difficult to make work. The presentation to the president of Polymer Mutual was this afternoon and, as usual, his appointed partner was nowhere to be seen.

He popped over to Lorraine's cubicle.

"Hey, Lorraine."

"Stan? Wow, what brings you to my cubicle? I'd thought you'd forgotten where I sit."

His serious mien told her he wasn't in the mood for jokes.

"Have you seen Bernie?"

"Bernie? He walked by a little earlier with Ogleby. You two are presenting today, right? Can't wait to hear all the amazing stuff you've come up with."

Stan had already rushed off in the direction of Ogleby's office. Through the glass, he could see his boss seated at his desk conversing with someone with long, blonde hair. A few steps closer and he stopped dead in his tracks; it was the company president, Ms. Polymer.

Growing even more anxious, he craned his neck over Bernie's cubicle wall, which was still empty. Checking that the coast was clear he ducked into the cubicle and bumped the mouse to see if the computer was on. When the screen lit up, a PowerPoint slide appeared with large titles reading "Bet Your Life!"

Before he could go further, two people talking came to his attention and Stan quickly departed the cubicle. Desperate and frustrated, he looked out over the wall of cubicles for any sight of his "partner". Seeing none, he returned to his own workspace half-noting Orion hunched over the keyboard next door.

Slumping into his chair, he began to sulk. But the sound of his neighbor's furious typing proved too distracting and he began to reflect on Orion with whom he had barely exchanged a word this morning on the ride in. Orion had been so helpful the other day with drawing up the mechanics of how the game show concept would work and would, if implemented correctly and quickly, really improve revenue and optimize company/customer interaction. But since then, had not broached the subject or shown any visible interest in Stan's affairs. Bereft of any help, Stan had found himself unable to fully write up the concept and smooth out many of the necessary details.

This made Stan's blood boil. Being deserted by Bernie was bad enough, but Orion? As soon as they were in the office this morning, his fair-haired friend had made a beeline for his cubicle commenting that he didn't have time to talk, too many things to do.

How could Orion leave him in the lurch like this? Not have time to help a buddy, a colleague. Really!? He wouldn't even have a job if it wasn't for Stan. And would it have killed him to take an hour or two to help with the plan? Apparently so. But Orion sure had time to make them late every morning. Sure had time to waste chasing after that dame in his building or with whacky escapades like harassing some poor little kid who strayed into his yard.

Stan's attention was drawn back to the incessant typing next door. Just what was Orion typing on, anyway? It better be work related.

Angrily, he pushed his keyboard away and decided he was going to check up on his "friend".

Casually, he rose from his seat, stretching and giving a little yawn - justification as to why he needed to stand.

On tippy-toes, he was high enough to see over Orion's cubicle wall. Unfortunately, his industrious co-worker's back was to him. Whatever was on the computer screen wasn't visible from this angle.

Grabbing his half-filled coffee cup, he slowly walked past Orion's cubicle. Annoyingly, he still couldn't make out what was on the screen.

"Hey O', what's up?" the anger in his voice was thinly veiled at best.

Orion half-turned to him, but remembered himself and turned away. Not quick enough, though, for his friend to miss the eyewear.

"What the…" Stan queried. "Are you wearing glasses? Oh, my god!"

Head still turned away Orion swiftly removed them, flushed with embarrassment.

"Can I help you with something, Stan?"

"I…heard you typing."

"Yeah…I'm working."

Stan pondered asking more questions, but was still confused by the large, ridiculous glasses.

"Okay. I'll go back to work, too… On the presentation I have to give in an hour and a half."

With that, Stan popped out of sight.

Orion waited a beat before turning back to his screen where he surreptitiously replaced the spectacles that Diana had given him and, as if by magic, his computer screen transformed from hazy, hard to read blurs and lines, to the clear and concise rows and columns of a spreadsheet.

Before he always had to print spreadsheets to read them without strain but with these new glasses he could read and work directly on the computer. Making edits and changes became a breeze. And, once he figured out the formulas, he was quickly on his way to working out the kinks in the overall plan.

Scrolling through the spreadsheet he found a problem with column number thirteen thousand one hundred thirty-two, but if he just inserted a formula onto column seventy-nine, row AA, that would clear it up.

He leaned over to insert the formula, but suddenly found his chair being jerked around bringing him face to face with Stan.

"What have you been doing over here?! And why are you wearing those ridiculous granny glasses?!"

Orion's face squinched up, thinking of some logical explanation.

"What do you mean?"

Stan started to say something, but couldn't, his lips tightened to to suppress laughter.

He pointed to the glasses.

"Please. Take those crazy things off. It's hard to take you seriously."

Orion complied.

"Look Stan, I don't under-."

"You've been hiding yourself away all week, lost in some kind of world in your mind. I have less than an hour to present this concept to the president of the company. Could you please just take a few moments so I can run over it with somebody? Bernie's been MIA this whole time, it's just been me working on it."

Orion became aware of his friend's hunched over frame and forlorn expression.

"Okay, I'll listen." Orion softened, "But let me show you what I've been working on first."

He pointed a finger at the spreadsheet on the screen before him.

"Here you go." He stopped for a second to replace the glasses but, catching a glimpse of Stan's horrified reaction at seeing them, removed them again.

"The game show is the candy that lures in new customers and engages our current ones. But, it's the first step. These tables..." he shuffled the screen through the twelve separate spreadsheets that comprised the parts of the plan, "represent our full plan. Inputting the various formulas, I've inserted twenty-three different scenarios and they all work."

"The plan works?"

Stan lips parted and his eyes widened. With this news he exited and returned, rolling his chair in to have a seat.

"You mean you've been sitting here, day after day, working on the plan?"

"Of course. What did you think I'd been doing all week?"

Stan refrained from comment.

Orion waved his hand in front of the screen.

"Think I've worked out all the kinks. Was just finishing up the final details."

"Well," Stan leaned in. "Show me what you've got."

"Here on the first sheet, we have the age ranges of our sample group."

Without his glasses the screen was virtually impossible to read, but he pressed on.

"These are correlated with their respective incomes."

Stan raised a hand.

"Wait, why is the table titled 'GEOGRAPHICAL FACTORS' and I don't see an income column."

"I…"

Orion realized he must have pulled up the wrong table. Reflexively, he moved to grab the glasses, but stopped, remembering Stan's disdain for them. Instead, he took his best guess, selected the tab to the left. The new table pulled up.

"Okay, so here we have the ages of the sample groups."

He heard no question, so he knew this must be the correct table.

"With this page, we've correlated their ages with where they live. As with the other tables, I've incorporated actuarial numbers."

"Actuarial numbers? You've incorporated the tables?

Where?"

Orion squinted hard at the screen, broadly waving his hand in the general direction of the screen.

"Over there. You can see it."

Stan looked more closely.

"No, I don't.  In fact I don't get how this column correlates to that column."

"I, uh…"

Orion couldn't even guess which two columns he was referring to.  Stan pointed to the bottom.

"And this total doesn't even make sense if I'm reading this right."

"Well, um…"

A wan look came over Stan. He shook his head as he looked at the numbers that added up to nothing. The computer clock read half past twelve. In less than thirty minutes he would have to present this incoherent, fantastical plan to the president of the company.

Exasperated, he stood up, a massive headache throbbing in his skull. Before he could say anything, the voice of the manager's administrative assistant sounded on the phone's speaker.

"Attention. All analysts are to report to the main conference room."

"Damn…" Stan hit the cubicle wall with his fist.

Orion jumped a little.

"Stan, let me show you this other spreadsheet."

Stan had already rolled his chair back to his cubicle.


The asteroid tilted away from the sun, leaving Diana and the six bidders in complete blackness.

Not until a pen-tip sized light turned on did she realize the dark state she had left her guests in. The Pount lamp belonged to the second bidder, a gaunt man with a prominent red beard that extended to his knees. As he raised the light to chest level, reflective speckles in his beard twinkled like the stars in the sky above them.

Touching her index fingers together a tiny one-inch orb was summoned. It emerged from the console and flew over the heads of the assemblage where it lit up like a light bulb.

Several of the six beings in attendance reflexively covered their eyes, not being prepared for the sudden illumination. Diana's stomach muscles tightened realizing her blunder.

"Sorry."

Her comment was ignored by most of the attendees who spent their time exchanging ominous, conspiratorial glares. This was certainly a rough lot of people, Diana couldn't help thinking to herself and, the longer they had been kept waiting, the less friendly they had become.

The husky construction miner from Sphericledes gave a loud sigh. He had been the most visibly frustrated at having to wait for the bid that was supposed to start half an hour ago. Constantly in motion, he would break his pacings only long enough to kick stray rock chips off into space.

Diana hoped the group's patience would continue. No one had said anything or complained so there was that. But the one person she desperately needed to be there had yet to arrive. She looked over the console for any sign of their coming.

The man with the red beard began whistling as he took a seat on a rock. This left his beard touching the ground.

The whistling was his way of threatening her, Diana knew. She exhaled, knowing she had to begin. Any longer and the bid would be forfeit. Touching her console, it and the chair on which she sat lifted off the ground.

She raised her arms, addressing the group below.

"The biddi-."

Just then, a crack of light appeared at the far end of the asteroid. It widened as if a door was opening in a darkened room. A robed figure entered, silhouetted by the light of Diana's hallway. He stepped onto the rocky surface pushing her apartment door closed and all was as it was before, just the asteroid and the space beyond it. To Diana's great relief the bidder she had been waiting for had arrived.

She tipped her head to the new arrival. The here-to-fore unseen representative to Hephaestus peaked out from his hood and bowed.

"My apologies. Adnaeum."

He then looked to the others in attendance with eyes of deep purple. None of the other bidders would meet his gaze and a few even brusquely turned away in discomfort.

Diana raised her arms again, fingers splayed.

"As we are all here. The bidding will now begin."

Once the isolation shield came up around her console, she quickly took a seat and watched the bids as they came in. With such a small turn out the process would not last long.

The first number was surprisingly low, but that was often the case. The next two were only slightly more. Still far below the reserve. What seemed like an eon, passed before the next one came.

Diana's heart stopped as she laid her eyes on it. It was drastically too low. Even though she knew it did not matter, she couldn't help feeling apprehensive. No one had even come close to meeting the reserve, but it would be alright as soon as Hephaestus' bid came in. She took her eyes off screen and looked up to Hephaestus's representative. He wasn't moving. The clock was almost up. Why wasn't he bidding?

    Her eyes turned back to the screen. She hunched over countdown screen. She looked up and saw him moving, finally. She looked back down at the screen. The time was ticking away. 4...3...2...

# CHAPTER XVII
## The Presentation

Seated around the conference table the collection of gloomy looking analysts in dark suits denoted the morbid atmosphere that enshrouded Polymer Mutual as the sword of Damocles hung ever lower above its future. More than one of them was making use of the free moment to comb through emails on their phones just in case a reply to any of the dozens of resumes sent out might have miraculously resulted in a job offer. Their bleak faces indicated that this had not occurred.

Orion took a subtle peak at Stan who was seated next to him. From the minute he had taken his chair, Stan had sat with a dour face slumped forward like a banker who's just found out there's been a run on the bank. The direness of his body language seemed to go wholly unnoticed by Lorraine, sitting on Stan's other side, who eyed him like the proudest of mothers, her big blue eyes beaming with pride.

The conference room door opened and Bernie appeared.

Stan bolted upright.

"Bernie, I-."

His words were cut short as Bernie was immediately followed by Ogleby and Ms. Polymer.

Bernie's eyes pointedly never looked in Stan's direction as he took a seat on the furthest end of table.

Ogleby led Ms. Polymer, who stood a full two inches taller than him, to the front of the room.

"Everyone, I don't think I have to introduce you to our president, Ms. Linda Polymer."

An exchange of nods ensued with a sprinkling of half waves.

Standing at the end of the table Ms. Polymer extended her hands, palms up, to them.

"Good afternoon. I've just come from a pre-meeting where I heard a very interesting proposal for a way to reach younger people. I thought the progenitors of the idea should present it to the group, but they've asked that I do the honors."

Ogleby nodded emphatically and motioned for the lights to be turned off. The smart board lit up and the words "Bet Your Life" flashed onto the screen in a bold television font.

Ms. Polymer motioned to the screen as if she were a model on *The Price Is Right*.

"The idea they came up with is for Polymer Mutual to have an on-line game show where contestants can win prizes big and small. Everything from Polymer Mutual pens to a grand prize of a lifetime of free healthcare coverage."

Even in the darkened room, Orion could see Stan's jaw drop.

Lorraine leaned over.

"Stan, I don't understand. Why aren't you up there?"

Ms. Polymer finished up. "And we'll have our marketing section design it to be hip so as to attract young people. This is not exactly the kind of idea I was expecting from the Analysis section, but it is an outside of the box idea that might just work. Any thoughts?"

The group looked back at her in silence many still taking in the idea. Stan was too stunned to say anything. A look of indignation was growing on Lorraine's face.

Ogleby quickly stepped up to the president's side.

"Ms. Polymer, I want to thank you so much for giving your valuable time to be here. I just know this idea will work out."

"Well, you and Bernie really came up with quite a proposal."

Lorraine's face had become as red as her hair at what she was hearing. Raising her hand she blurted out, "What about Stan's ideas?"

All eyes turned to her and Stan.

Ogleby was hurriedly leading Ms. Polymer to the exit. They were just to the door when a loud booming voice shouted, "Let's hear Stan's plan."

The voice was Orion's. Ms. Polymer came to a stop.

"I'm sorry. What was that?"

Lorraine jumped back in.

"Stan has a presentation, too. It's all ready."

A glint of recognition came into the president's eyes as she looked Stan over.

"Yes, I remember. You were one of the two original volunteers." She looked perplexed. "But, I thought…"

Stan stared slack-jawed.

Lorraine nearly jumped out of her seat.

"He's been working on it. Night and day."

Ms. Polymer gave Ogleby an inquisitive look.

Ian Adrian

The small man's shoulders dropped. He reluctantly stepped back into the room and began waving his hands.

"Now, now. The president has a plane she has to catch. We'll send her a report lat-."

Orion interjected.

"Let Stan give his presentation! It might just save the company."

Ogleby's nostrils flared up. "Now that's enough!"

He looked Orion dead in the eyes. "I expected more from you."

He then turned to the president and took her by the arm. "I'm so sorry. I will deal with them. Let's get you to the airport."

The president pulled her arm away.

"Actually, I think I'll stay and listen to the proposal."

"What?!"

Ms. Polymer shot Ogleby a look that cut him down to size. He submissively took a step back. She then pulled out a chair and took a seat.

"Okay, Stan – that was your name, right? I'm listening."

Ogleby, as if he were Stan's best friend, rushed to his side.

"Why don't you go up to the board and share your ideas with the group."

The rapid series of events left Stan looking like he was lost in a fog. Responding to his bosses motioning to the front of the room, he clumsily made his way to the presentation board.

Looking upon his peers, he looked very much like the emperor with no clothes. His hand reached down to calm his shaking leg.

The manager wondered at Stan's silence.

"Well, come on Stan?"

Licking lips that had become too dry, Stan furled his eyebrows.

Lorraine leaned across to Orion.

"He said you helped him with the plan." She whispered. "You should go up and help him now."

Orion's features took a dark turn as he quickly shook his head no.

Stan brushed a stray brown hair behind his ear and finally spoke.

"We were thinking that maybe… It just seemed that the problem is… well, there aren't enough young people getting insurance. This is causing problems. So, we thought that to get them to buy it, they'd have to have a reason. What if they could join in with their parents? You know, combine plans even after they've aged out. This will give them more of an incentive. And, well, boost the numbers."

After this, he ran out of steam. An awkward silence ensued as the audience grasped that this was all he had to say.

Ms. Polymer had a disappointed look.

"Anyone have any thoughts?"

One of the more eager of the young analysts, Yana, raised her hand before speaking.

"This has been looked into before and deemed unprofitable. What data do you have that would support this idea?"

Stan's mouth opened but nothing came out. Helpless, he started flipping through the pack of papers in his hand.

"Yeah… Well… It's complex."

Lorraine's voice had grown a few levels above a whisper as she spoke into Orion's ear.

"He's dying up there. Why aren't you helping him?!"

Orion shook his head and looked down.

A look of disgust came over Lorraine's face.

With a sigh, Orion got up and quietly slipped out the door.

Stan finished his answer.

"…and maybe it wasn't profitable before. But, that was then. Do you get it?"

Yana shook her head in the negative.

Bernie's hand shot up from the far end of the table.

Stan hesitated, unsure what to do. Finally he pointed to the bespectacled co-worker.

"Yes, Bernie?"

Bernie straightened up before speaking, his words tinged with a bit of a gloat.

"Can you point to any example where a plan like this has worked?"

Stan thought a second. "No."

"And you don't have numbers for us that show the plan will work."

Stan had to again shake his head "no".

"Then why should the company go through with it?"

Stan's mouth fell agape at the audacity of the comment. His shoulders sagged as he felt the knife firmly inserted in his back.

Out of the corner of his eye he spotted Loraine waving wildly at him. This distracted him enough from really letting Bernie have it.

"Well, Bernie," Stan bit his tongue, "you've made some excellent points."

A visibly annoyed Ms. Polymer sighed and took a look at her watch. She seemed to be on the edge of saying something when another arm shot up. It was Larry, the bespectacled new guy who wore his clothes one size too tight.

"What's on the spreadsheet?"

"Spreadsheet?"

Stan turned to see that a spreadsheet had pulled up on the smart board. It was one of the ones Orion had been showing him. He let out a gasp.

"Oh, that's not really anything. It's just there for dramatic effect. Don't look at it. Please."

Orion returned a little winded and made his way to Stan's side.

"Stan, I'm so sorry. I had some technical difficulties with the smart board. Your charts are up now."

"Uh, yeah. Thanks. I think I'm done here."

Stan went to make an exit but Orion held up a hand to stop him.

"But everything's up. The tables that demonstrate how the plan works. Not just to save us, but to turn Polymer towards a whole new way of doing business, one that will let it dominate the industry."

Stan shot his friend a quizzical look.

"Uh, yeah. Why don't you show them this part."

Stan stepped out of Orion's way motioning for him to take the spotlight. Orion froze, realizing he was trapped. All eyes were on him, now. He saw Ms. Polymer grow impatient by the minute and Ogleby break into a devilish grin.

Not knowing how to begin, Orion defaulted with a sweeping motion of his hand that had all the characteristics of someone hailing a cab. He then began:

"Within these spreadsheets we've combined actuarial tables with environmental and socio-economic patterns, correlating the age ranges that should be included. As my colleague stated, children will be allowed to join their parents plan at half the rate they would normally pay up until the age of thirty-three. At this point their payment percentage will slowly increase until they reach one hundred percent at age forty-one. The parents, in exchange for joining with their children, would get a ten percent decrease in their plan."

Stan seemed pleasantly shocked at Orion's efficient explanation of the idea even if he didn't fully understand what had just been said.

A collection of hands shot up around the room, but Orion continued.

"To drive the plan as quickly as possible into the public consciousness, we propose that Polymer take a cue from other industries and provide further incentives like frequent flyer miles and other cash incentives for the children and parents who participate in the program. The game show would be another way to distribute the incentives. Stan, back to you."

Stan had shuffled over to the side, as if trying to make an early retreat.

Called out by his co-worker, he managed a series of collective "uhs" before getting out, "Uhm, yeah that's the plan, alright. Any questions?"

Even more hands had shot up in the air. A few of the younger analysts were nearly falling out of their seats.

Stan reluctantly pointed to one of them, a ruddy-faced young man who looked like he had gotten his nose cut off.

"But, a person at thirty-one will cost too much to fit into that plan."

Another voice interjected.

"And how do you cover all the conditions that don't show up until the late twenties?"

Yet another voice chimed in.

"And aren't you just taking away any reason for a young person to get health insurance at the normal rate when they can get it for half?"

More questions poured in on the two presenters.

Overwhelmed, Stan took a step back and tipped his head to Orion to take over. Orion couldn't decide which one to answer first.

But, it was the president, Linda Polymer, who quelled the cacophony of questions by stepping up and waving her slender hands until the room fell silent.

She then turned to the two presenters.

"Gentlemen, this is a lot to take in. It is definitely a much more substantial idea than the game show."

Ogleby and Bernie both cringed a bit at the jab.

"But, I'm not against big ideas… If they work."

She sauntered past Orion to take a place at the smart board, her eyes running up and down the columns.

"Since you're proposing a massive shift in our company's practices, let's take a look at the numbers. Like my grandfather, I'm a numbers cruncher. That's the blood that pumps through the heart of the insurance business."

She pointed to the third column from the left.

"It looks like you correlated morbidity rates to the environment. Is that correct?"

Stan and Orion exchanged looks. Stan took a half step back letting Orion know that he would have to take this one.

"Yeah," Orion explained. "Environmental factors can play a large factor in health needs. The most basic would be in the number of allergy treatments people in different areas might require. Correlating these environmental factors would let us target regions with the least adverse environmental factors. It's been the lack of health causality elements like these and painting with too wide a brush when implementing large-scale plans that has hurt us."

"So, you've been able to work out these factors?"

"Yes, and incorporating these into our plan's roll out would provide significant revenue without conjoined cost payouts. We'd save a fortune."

She brushed her long straw-colored hair back behind her ear as she ran her eyes up and down the fine figure of a man before her. The light from the smart board highlighted his blonde hair while the shadowing on his eyes turned them to dark, steely grey. She would find out now if the insides matched the cover.

"This column. Take me through this, so I can understand where you're going."

She eyed him, daring him to fail.

Orion's confident air evaporated. His eyes squinted as they struggled to read the board.

He turned to Stan for help but was met with agitated *keep on* signal. On the other side Ms. Polymer giving him an, *I'm waiting* look.

Orion played for time.

"Which column are you looking at?"

"None in particular," she replied. "Just walk us through this one so we can see the process."

He looked helplessly at the board, almost pressing his face against it trying to make out the columns and rows. His nose brushed the screen his face was so close to it. But, it wasn't any better.

"I…I guess…"

He gave up trying to read the board, looked up and saw how perturbed the president was beginning to look. Stan looked on the verge of a nervous breakdown.

Orion held a finger up.

"Excuse me."

He reached into his jacket pocket and pulled out the glasses.

Gasps and "oohs" sounded from around the room as he put the cat eyes spectacles on and looked up.

Titters grew when, for the first time, the jewels along the frames lit up, little flashlights in the semi-lit room.

Seeing all this, the color drained from Stan's face. His eyelids drooped. It looked like he would collapse any minute.

Ms. Polymer took the glasses in stride and put her finger to her lips to quiet the room.

Orion eyed the spreadsheet with fresh eyes. With his finger, he adjusted the spreadsheet to the correct position.

"Yes, yes, you picked an excellent place to begin. The numbers on this row correspond to the..." And thus he continued. Energetically he ran Ms. Polymer and the rest of the audience through the calculations. With the glasses on, he was on fire and the story he told with his charts and hundred column spreadsheets was the greatest business success tale ever told. Combinations of formulas equated extreme monetary gains. Factors were included in equations that had never been inserted before. People, who now could not afford it, would be able to finally get the safety net that home and health insurance provided.

Midway through, he asked three of the audience members, including Ms. Polymer, to act in a role-playing exercise to demonstrate how much money different customers could save with the program. After that, he enlisted an unwitting Stan in joining him in performing a shadow puppet show that demonstrated all the money Polymer Mutual would make from the increase of customers in rural areas.

He concluded the two hour presentation by singing a modified

"Happy Days are Here Again" the title lines altered to "Polymer is in the Black Again" and was joined by Stan, the crowd of analysts and a bedazzled president Polymer.

Not since the early years of the modern insurance industry, had such revolutionary ideas been proposed and embraced.

# CHAPTER XVIII
## The Faux Leather Chair

Orion burst into Diana's apartment that night with a giddiness in his step. He was so excited that he failed to notice Diana's not greeting him or that she was not sitting at her console as usual, but in the arm chair by the window. He rushed over to her barely able to contain himself.

"Something amazing happened today."

This broke her out of her meditation.

"Really?"

"Yeah, and it has to do with those glasses you gave me. Stan and I gave our presentation today; the one to the president of the company."

"Oh…" Diana's shoulders fell as a look of disappointment came over her.

He continued. "It went rough at first but, with the help of those glasses you gave me, we were able to really wow 'em. It's so amazing being able to use the computer like everyone else. I looked at the screen for hours today and no headache. I think, somehow, I understand people better with them on. Anyway, after that, the president took us into the manager's office to discuss implementation. Ogleby was ticked off the whole time because his attempt to take over the plan had been busted. It was sooo funny. He played real nice in front of the president though like he was our biggest supporter. You know, if this works right, we might even be getting a promotion."

With one look, he realized Diana's head was leaned back on the chair, a vacant look in her eye. Eventually, she noticed he had stopped speaking.

"That's nice."

As he studied her, his face became flushed, his head throbbed in indignation.

"Why are you doing that?!" he lashed out.

The strength of his voice made her head turn.

He continued, "Whenever the talk is about your big deal, we're all supposed to drop everything and think about nothing else. But, if I dare say one thing about my day at work, you roll your eyes like I'm some batty old aunt."

"What are you talking about?"

"This!" He pointed back and forth between them. "I'm sharing my life with you but your too busy staring at that orb."

"What am I supposed to do?" She shot back. "I'm working on a deal with real implications. I don't have time-." She cut herself short.

His eyes widened.

"Yeah, say it. You don't have time…for me. The deal, always the deal. I don't matter to you unless I can be someone you can talk to about the deal."

She stood up and walked to the console, leaning against it with head hung low.

"Can we talk about this some other time?"

"Why, because you have to work?"

She hit the console with her fists.

"Drenods! Why are you being like this?! Don't you see what I'm going through, how hard I have to work?"

"I'm just tired of being ignored. I'm realizing that whatever I do, you don't care. I get some success and all you want to talk about is the only thing you ever talk about. The stupid deal."

She shook her head in disbelief.

"I have spent so many hours with you, teaching, training you. I've shown you planets, stars, black holes, nebulae, yet you still persist in wasting your time on tiny, insignificant little endeavors. What is it you do exactly at this company? Sell insurance to people who are too dumb to drive their transports around without crashing into each other?"

"Very funny. I do a job that helps people when they're in trouble. That's what the insurance business is about."

"You're feeling ignored, is that it? I'm not giving you enough attention."

Diana cocked an eyebrow.

He pursed his lips.

"The company's in trouble; will probably go under in a year."

"And why do you care so much? You don't even like your job."

Orion reflected on this for a moment.

"I'm a lousy analyst, yes. I have no business working at Polymer Mutual. They should have let me go twenty-times over. The others, though, are different. They love what they do. They may gripe and complain sometimes, but at the end of the day they get a real sense of satisfaction from getting to work a job they like as part of a team.

They have each other." He stammered for the next words, "a place where they fit in."

Diana's features softened as she heard the pain in his voice. Her hand fell on her heart as she stepped around to his side of the console.

Sullen, his eyes turned downward.

"But, now they're gonna lose all that: their jobs, their incomes, getting to be part of something. Everyday, I see them, how sad they are, but there was nothing I could do... until today."

His eyes rose up to meet hers.

"That's what I've been trying to tell you. These glasses changed everything. I could read the spreadsheets, I could figure out the formulas to fix the problems the company's having. I stood up and gave a kick-ass presentation. I helped. I made a difference."

Diana sighed as she looked upon this fully grown man standing proud with the glint of a child who had walked himself to school for the first time. Despite herself, she couldn't help but be affected. The ends of her mouth curled upwards as her anger washed away, replaced by a warm rush that filled her chest.

She placed her hands around his cranium shaking it with playful frustration as she pressed her face to his.

"What am I going to do with you?"

She kissed him.

His eyes widened; confused, but not displeased.

"Um, I hate to ask this, but Stan and some of the others wanted to meet up tonight to celebrate. I think I should go."

She nodded in agreement.

His shoulders fell in relief.

"Are you sure it's okay? Stan's just so excited. It means a lot to him. Why don't you come out with us. You've never met Stan or any of the people from work."

She shook her head.

"Thank you, no. I-. I'm not up for too much fun tonight. I'm sorry."

"That's okay."

He gave her a kiss.

"I'll go out tonight, but tomorrow, we'll get back to working on deal. I'll even work extra hard."

He gave her another kiss on the cheek and departed leaving Diana alone. With him gone, the harsh reality flooded back in. The vicious truth she had found herself too ashamed to admit to him. There was nothing to work on. Hephaestus' bid had not met the reserve. Her three property deal had failed.


Orion had become known around the office as the "spreadsheet man" and, for the first time ever, colleagues would stop by to ask him advice about their projects. Eventually, people would stop by just to say "hi." Where before he could hardly have named more than one or two of his coworkers, he now knew everyone's name plus details about their lives like how many children they had or what part of town they lived in.

In the weeks that followed the big presentation, he and Stan submitted three more proposals all falling in line with the initial big idea.

The last of these proposals went into further detail covering the specifics of when the company linked insurance coverage of sensors with their children under thirty-two years of age. The benefits to the customers would be fantastic and the company would benefit from having locked in new customers with a very small likelihood of actually needing to make a claim who more often than not lived at home with their parents, anyway.

Marketing produced a rushed but effective advertising campaign and the programs were initiated. Almost immediately a slew of new customers began pouring in. At the end of two months, enrollment was up twenty-two percent. The company's new clients equaled increased market share. Consequently, the company's credit rating in all the major indexes rose. That would help them with the bridge loan they would need to cover the interim period.

For Stan it was personal. Looking around the open office space he sighed contentedly. He took no small pride in being partly responsible for the newly hired analysts that were sitting in cubicles that had been empty for months.

He had just sat back down in his chair when he spotted Lorraine walk past his cubicle door. But, she didn't stop and talk like usual or, at the very least, give a flirty wave. Shortly afterwards, he heard her talking to his cubicle mate.

"Hey O'. Wanna do lunch?"

"Uh. Hi, Lorraine. Okay."

Stan rose, fast enough not to miss the moment. Lorraine spotted him immediately.

"Oh, hi, Stan. I was just asking Orion if he'd join me for lunch. I made too much for myself and had enough for two."

Orion's smile matched the upward pointing tips of his cat-eyes glasses.

"Wow, Lorraine, that's so nice of you."

"No, problem, Sugar."

She reached over and gave Orion's arm a squeeze. "Golly, I never realized those arms were all muscle."

Stan emerged from his cubicle and stepped next to Lorraine.

"Lunch sounds good."

Lorraine batted her lashes. "Oh, Stan, would you like to eat with us?"

"Well, I…"

"Of, course you're welcome to. I'd have asked you but, after all these years, you've never suggested we eat lunch together."

Before the slight rebuke had found its mark, she motioned the two of them to follow and soon they were walking along a row of cubicles towards the back of the office where the kitchen was.

As soon as he could, Stan inserted himself between Orion and Lorraine as the three walked in single file. He pointed to his friend's ridiculous cat eyes spectacles which were now worn openly around the office.

Being used to his friends disdain for the glasses, Orion removed them.

Lorraine opened the door to the darkened room and quickly jumped to the side, followed by Stan. The lights came on and he found himself surrounded by his coworkers.

"SURPRISE!"

Shouts of "Happy Birthday, Orion!" filled the room. All the analysts were there, including several managers. But, most touching of all, they were all wearing plastic cat eyes glasses. Some of the more inventive people had even glued on fake jewels along the frames to better capture the look of Orion's pair.

Lorraine was the first to give Orion a big hug; Stan did not look happy about that, but then she tossed him a pair of plastic cat eyes glasses. He put them on and gave Orion a slap on the back. "Happy Birthday, buddy!"

They all sang "Happy Birthday" and people motioned to Orion to put his glasses back on. He did, sporting a Cheshire Cat grin. Cake was served, "Happy Birthday" was sung once more, and Orion looked around at all his co-workers, friends really, whose names only a short while before he had barely known if at all. Kwesi from accounting who would often confess to wanting to grow dreds but didn't think his boss –the wife - would let him. The girl with the dark bangs whose name, Orion had learned was Priscilla. She was debating following her boyfriend to California. Already eating her second piece of cake was Margaret from HR, who wore too much make-up and was openly resentful that her sister had married a solar power tycoon. Even Bernie was there, looking dejected, leaning against the wall in the back corner of the room drinking soda pop out of a red plastic cup.

Holly, the five-foot two admin assistant rose to her feet.

"Does the birthday boy want to say anything?"

Orion felt a hand push him forward.

A chorus of voices erupted. "SPEECH! SPEECH!"

Stan waved them down.

"Let the guy speak, already!"

The calls faded out and all eyes were on Orion. He cleared his throat as his eyes turned downward. His hand fumbled with his tie.

"Hey, everyone. I-I, just want to thank you. This…" He cleared his throat again. "This means a lot to me. I know that when I came here, I was a little… awkward. I didn't talk to anyone and I know that no one thought much of me."

A few mumbles of denial sounded.

"No, no, I knew. And, I didn't care. It sounds weird, now. But, I didn't. I had gotten used to going through life alone. Like I didn't need anyone. And that makes me so sorry that I lived like that, because now that I've gotten to know you, all of you. I realize what a great gang you all are. And…" He blinked his eyes, took a deep sigh. "And it makes me sad, that all that time I was sitting at my desk, I was missing out on the chance to know you and be a part of this great team. I'll never forget this. Thank you."

A stream of "yeahs" erupted and people stepped forward to give Orion big hugs and slap him on the back. Lorraine's mascara was running and even Stan's eyes were a little watery.

Soon the conversations turned to various funny stories about life at Polymer Mutual, a company that had pulled itself from the brink to become a team once more. Management had allowed the party to go on for an hour, forty-five minutes longer than the norm for such events. Eventually, everyone was gently directed back to their workstations.

Ogleby, a slight scowl on his face, pulled Stan and Orion aside. "You two come with me."

The two followed their boss as his small stout frame marched across the rows of cubicles that made up the open office area.

Reaching the far end of the room, he pulled out a key to unlock a wooden door then pushed it open revealing a large office. Stan's mouth fell half open in shock. Three times the size of an analyst's cubicle, the office had solid drywalls versus the cloth-lined cubicle walls of their old offices. There was no window, but the metal desk with a wood top and high back faux leather chair more than made up for that.

With a wave of his hand, their manager ushered them in, following and closing the door behind them.

The lights were off. Orion and Stan tensed as they realized they were alone with him in the dark room. In the shadowy room they could make out the menacing scowl that was still on his marine sergeant-like face.

He held out two sets of keys.

"Here."

Orion and Stan hesitated.

"Take 'em!"

They quickly complied.

Ogleby waved his hand around in quick, jerky motions as he spoke.

"You decide between the two of you who gets which one. E-mail me when you've made a decision and I'll alert Tharpe."

Ogleby pulled open the door to leave. Light flooded in.

Stan spoke.

"Wait, what is this about?"

Ogleby gave a deep sigh and slowly turned back around, his face in dark shadows.

"What do you think it means, Mr. Terrance?"

Stan looked to an equally confused Orion then answered with a shrug.

Pained and exasperated beyond relief, Ogleby's nostrils flared as he spoke.

"I just gave you the keys to two senior analyst's offices. What the he-!" He caught himself. "You figure it out!"

With that he exited, slamming the door behind him.

Stan and Orion, in the dark, exchanged looks of shock.

"You don't think?"

"I don't know!"

A real sense of accomplishment overcame Orion as he stepped out of Stan's car and looked up at the Atlas Building.

His friend leaned over to talk through the passenger side window.

"Well, Mr. Senior Analyst Orion, I guess I'll see you tomorrow."

"Most definitely, fellow Senior Analyst Stan. Tomorrow, we'll come up with ways to make even more money for Polymer."

Stan gave a thumbs up, "And find out how big our raise is," then drove off.

Orion saw Diana's lights on. He had not quite admitted it to himself but it was all for her. The long hours. The drive to succeed at work. He was amazed by her and inspired to become something, to be somebody.

After their fight the night before, he made sure to stop at his place and change before sprinting up to Diana's apartment. Entering, he found her working at the console. IO stood in battle position, eyes glowing green, pointed at Orion.

He set his bag down to give her a kiss.

"How was your day?" he asked.

"Not so-."

In his ebullience, he cut her off.

"My day was great." He stuck his chest out in pride. "You are now talking to a Senior Analyst with his own office. I can afford a car, now. We'll be able to take trips out of town. Isn't that great?"

"That's nice." Her reaction was even less excited than he'd

anticipated.

"Things will be different, now. Work is going really great. But, don't worry. I haven't forgotten the big deal. Now we're on on lot #5jie6c, right? So just tell me what you need me to do."

She took her eye off the console for a second.

"Nothing."

His eyebrows lowered, not understanding.

She swiveled the chair around to face him.

"I couldn't get myself to tell to you last night. Too ashamed, maybe. Lot #4o83q, it failed to meet the reserve."

"What? But I thought-."

"I did, too. It's my fault. I thought Hephaestus would bid reserve as agreed, but he didn't and I honestly have no idea why."

Orion got a good look at her face, anguished, eyes red, lips tightly pursed. Her shoulders were hunched forward, as if great weight lay upon them.

"What can we do?"

"Nothing. The owner won't lower the reserve. I can see no way out of this."

"That sounds a bit hard to believe. It can't possibly be that bad."

"You don't understand." She said testily. "That was the deal. All three lots have to meet the reserve or no commission. I'm finished. No one will ever trust me with their properties."

He put his hands on her arms.

"Let me help. We'll put our heads together to see what we can figure out. Like a team."

"I appreciate the offer but-. It's just that there's only one person who might be able to help, now. I've contacted them and they're on their way here."

Before Orion could ask who, he spotted her glance at the front window. He immediately knew what he would see before he had fully turned around to spy Apollo's Bentley pulling in front of the building. He looked back to Diana, her face contorted with distress and guilt.

"He's an expert - the master of the game." She declared, "I have to use him however I can and consider myself lucky to have his aid and council. If anyone can get me through to Hephaestus, it's Apollo."

Orion couldn't hide his displeasure, eyebrows furled and his lips tightened.

Her hand caressed the side of his face.

"You understand, right?"

He didn't quite nod, but he didn't shake his head, either. This was the best he could do.

"You go and do what you have to do."

She gathered up her purse and headed for the door.

"Oh, and don't come back to the apartment when I'm not here. I don't trust IO not to try to eradicate you. I'll let you know when I get back."

Once he had made it back to his place, Orion could see through his kitchen window that the Bentley was already gone. Diana had left him. A creeping suspicion had entered his mind. Was this how it was all going to end?

# CHAPTER XIX
## In the Depths

Once the Bentley left the curb, Apollo began the conversation.

"Tell me the situation. Include everything you can think of that might be relevant; pretend I know nothing of the deal."

Diana tried her best to do as directed.

"As you know, lot #4o83q is an asteroid field roughly twenty thousand yearlings long."

Apollo raised his eyebrows. "Yes, quite large."

"With the ilithium gone, the only thing of value it had was the ammonium acetate. But, I calculated that I could probably interest the industrialist Hephaestus in it."

"Yes, that was a surprisingly keen idea. Hephaestus," Apollo pondered the name, "made his fortune through the enormous factories he owns which produce all sorts of goods throughout the galaxy. I've sent feelers out to him before, but I've never been able to hook him. I'm sorry, go on."

She continued. "So, I had made a dark side of the moon deal

with him to bid the low reserve in exchange for my not soliciting any more bidders. Even, though I clearly articulated the price and he knew the reserve. When it came to the final bid, he beat out the other bidders, but was still below the reserve."

Apollo smiled to himself, nodded knowingly.

"He knows that he's the only real bidder so he's forcing the owner down on the price. Hephaestus is very rich for a reason."

"He's got me under the hammer. His bid was official. Once the last official offer has been made, there's no changing it."

Apollo raised a finger.

"With the reserve not met, the owner will have to rebid the property. Undoubtedly with a lower reserve which will let Hephaestus buy the lot #4o83q at the price he likes."

"But, how did he know that no one else would meet the reserve?"

"Welcome to the master's game. The other bidders have been bribed or bullied. Hephaestus is the only real contender and he wants the property for as cheap as he can get it."

"And me?"

"You're collateral damage."

Specks of light began filtering through the windows of the Bentley. By the time the vehicle had slowed to a stop, the planet Globulus could be seen through the window.

The two of them exited the vehicle. The field before them was filled with knee high balsam grass. Just beyond was a rock formation into which doors and windows had been carved.

Diana's forehead wrinkled as she pondered the task that lay ahead. The crude rock structure looked primitive and foreboding. Even the idea of walking across the field became daunting.

Apollo grabbed her by the arm.

You've already failed."

Diana's jaw dropped, caught off-guard.

His wide, steely-gray eyes stared into hers.

"I see it in your eyes, your posture. Everything about you says you've given up before the game is over."

She cleared her throat.

"I admit I don't see what chance we have here."

"What's important in the game is how you play it. If you lose it's because you didn't play it correctly."

She furled her brows.

"The rules of bidding are very strict on-."

"Ignore the rules!"

He tightened his grip on her arm just short of causing pain.

"Rules are an artifice, a tool our opponents use to trap us. Rules do not apply to people like us unless we want them to. That's how you win the game. Got it?"

Diana nodded, a little unsure of what she was getting.

He released his grip on her arm.

"The bid was put in by one of Hephaestus's representatives. We'll just consider that offer null and void. We bypass the representative and talk with the source."

"The source?"

"The bidder of course."

The only way to the rocky structure was through the tall grass. Diana's shimmering dress kept getting tangled in the stiff but bendable grasses. Apollo's long overcoat did not fare much better. By the time they had traversed the field, the bottom half of Apollo's overcoat was covered in seedlings that apparently could cling to anything. The blemish on his appearance would have highly perturbed him were he not on a mission.

As they cleared the field of grass, two figures emerged from the main opening of the rocky structure. Diana instantly knew the taller of the two as he had been Hephaestus' representative at the bidding. He still cut quite the figure; with dark hair pulled back, adorning a black and plum robe, and looking at them with deep purple eyes. The second one stood a step behind, wearing a black robe but never identified himself.

The former stepped up. "We are honored by your visit. Is it the great Apollo who accompanies you, Diana?"

She nodded. "We have come to give words to Hephaestus."

The representative bowed slightly. "Apologies. Hephaestus can speak to no one. You may address me with any questions, problems, concerns, adnaueum."

Diana could see no physical way around the two so she made her pitch.

"It's about the bid for the Alaeon Asteroid field – lot #4o83q. It was not enough to meet the reserve."

The representative retorted quickly. "We submitted our bid. All rules were followed."

"Yes, but you didn't meet the reserve. If you raise your offer by twenty percent you could-."

"The rules of commerce do not allow an amendment on a final offer once it's been submitted."

"Yes, that is the rule but-."

"Then there's no more discussion. We have followed the rules. Conclusion!"

Apollo cut in. "You are a representative, right?"

"Of course. This is most understood."

"We don't believe it."

"Believe? What do you mean?"

"We have been told by reliable sources that you are not Hephaestus's representative."

"This is ridiculous. Everyone knows I'm his appointed representative. Fact."

"And how are we supposed to know that?"

"I…"

"We demand proof. Now."

"Ridiculous. You have no right."

"Right? We have the right the moment you make bids on property we represent without proper authorization."

The representative's face reddened.

"I have the authorization! Go now!"

Apollo's voice never fluctuated. It just stayed steady as he pushed on.

"Then give us proof. Because with our suspicions, we are not only going to dismiss your bid, but we will have to not allow you to make a bid on any successive offers."

"What!?"

"That's just the way it has to be."

Diana nodded. "Believe me, we don't enjoy doing this. But ensuring proper procedures are followed is my responsibility as agent. Rules are important."

"I've had enough of this! You will leave now! Adneaum!"

"What?!" Apollo stepped forward. "Are you accusing us of trying to swindle you!?"

"I-. I said no such thing."

Diana could just detect the slight hint of a smile on Apollo's lips.

"Oh, now you're implying that we haven't been up front with you."

"I didn't say that!"

Apollo pointed his finger at the flustered man.

"And there's nothing we're hiding about the asteroids. They're containing prisonium is just a rumor started by our enemies who are trying to sabotage the deal!"

The representative's ears perked up.

"Prisonium? We'd not heard about that!"

"That's because there's nothing to hear. Prisonium is just a rumor."

Apollo's hands cut through the air to press the point.

The representative became quite befuddled. He looked to his assistant.

"Please leave, now." His voice was almost pleading. "You insult me and there will be no more of it."

The representative pointed to Apollo's Bentley.

Apollo motioned for Diana to follow as he turned to head back to the car. The two had made it four or five steps when a large popping noise emanated from the rock wall structure.

Apollo stopped, grabbed Diana by the wrist.

"We're in." he whispered to her as they turned back to face the representative and his assistant who had also turned to face the structure.

What appeared to be rock faded into a door twice as tall as a person in height.

The representative held his hand to his ear and nodded reverentially as he listened to the incoming voice audible only to him.

With a final nod, the representative looked to Apollo and Diana. Resentment in his voice, he motioned to the doorway.

"Hephaestus will see you, now."

Diana and Apollo moved forward. The representative held up his hand.

"Just the agent! She is the only one to enter."

Apollo whispered to Diana, "It's you from now on. Be careful. Not everyone makes it out of there in the same shape they went in."

She understood and entered alone through the door into Hephaestus's lair.

The passageway was long, a mineshaft really, walls made of carved stone. Bits of phosphorescent rocks strewn across the walls and ceilings illuminated the cavernous hallway.

She walked to the end of the hall, to the front of a large vault. Massive and solid, the door was probably even more impregnable than it looked. She could hear the tumblers and mechanisms turn.

The vault doors opened in layers, many of them, too many to count. Diana kept moving forward until she was walking through the tunnel as door after door pulled away from her path.

Finally the widest, thickest door, slid out of the way revealing a splendidly ornate chamber, large, speckled with vivid green Dinium furniture and illustrations along the walls of workers forging tools and building machines and equipment.

The fantastic murals depicted the legendary story of how Hephaestus built his empire with the machines and factories that built the tools of civilization. The murals were a testament to the greatness of the owner. Unlike most shrines, there were no pictures of the man responsible. The reclusiveness of Hephaestus was legendary, but even in his own abode, his visage was nowhere to be seen.

Once in the room, Diana heard the distant sound of tumblers turning. Spinning around, she saw the doors close behind her. Each one descended and sealed shut in the reverse order of how they had opened. As the last and thickest door slid down, she realized how isolated she was.

"Hello?" her eyes darted around the palatial chamber.

"Is anyone here?"

Nothing. Even the air didn't move. She was standing in a hermetically sealed room. Was this a trick? Was she being disposed of? A punishment for her questioning the representative's orders? Yes, she thought to herself, this was retribution for her impertinent behavior. But, then why was Apollo not in here with her? Maybe, because he was too powerful, he would be missed by intergalactic friends who would come to his aid.

These were conjectures, but her mind raced wildly through all of them, turning them over, weighing them against reason.

A creaking noise made her jump. It repeated a few times, coming from the farthest and lowest corner of the room, slightly obscured by a black marble support column.

"What do you want?" a voice, old and gravely shouted from the same shadowy corner.

Diana could just make out, in the darkness, the form of a figure. Just the outline.

She had to catch her breath before she could speak.

"I am Diana, the broker handling lot -."

"I know who you are. You complain about my bid," the voice, low, seemed to come from all around. Despite this, Diana firmly addressed the shadowy figure.

"You didn't meet the reserve. I just wanted to give you the chance to raise your bid. You'll be able to make the reserve and take possession of the property."

"I've put in what I consider a fair offer. With the ilithium gone, what makes this property worth more than that?"

"You know what. The property has more ammonium acetate in one location than any other mass in the quadrant."

Her words were met with silence.

"Ammonium acetate," she added, "Is what makes your factories run. You need this very much. But so would some of the other miners. If they were able to get hold of it, then you would have to go to them in the future to restock your supplies."

Defiant anger filled his voice.

"You tell me what I already know. It's too late. I will not debate with you. The final bid has been made. You, I mean, your client can't afford to turn down the offer. The owner needs to liquidate immediately. He can't afford to hold out for the current reserve."

Diana just laughed; a forced laugh, but hopefully convincing enough.

"He can't afford not to. The reserve won't change. And, next time, there will be new, different bidders, especially after we have contacted the other miners."

She turned away from him to return to the vault door.

"Wait!" he called out.

She continued walking to the vault door.

He stepped out of the shadows. "Come back!"

Slowly, she stopped and turned around, gasped at the sight she beheld. Hephaestus had stepped out enough into the light to reveal a face torn with deep scars. His exposed arms, sinewy and dark, were equally covered with scars from endless years of burns and lacerations.

Seeing his ravaged form, she suddenly understood his reason for solitude.

He realized that he had stepped too far out. But, it was too late. He had already been seen.

"Yes, this is what I look like. This was the price of working my way out of the hell they call the Lycaeum mines. That's where I was sent as an infant. Sent there because I was deemed physically and mentally unfit."

He took a step closer, coming out of the shadows even more, letting Diana see every scar, laceration, and burn. Almost no spot was left unblemished.

"Do I frighten you?"

She gave no response. Her calf muscles began to quiver and weaken. She took a long, deep breath to contain herself lest her whole body begin shaking, too.

He gave her a grim smile.

"My own parents cast me into the darkest part of the Lycaeum mines, ostensibly to work. But, really, to die, disappear and never be thought of again. I paid dearly for every meter I moved up. For most, their scars are on the inside, hidden away. Mine can't be hidden nor can they be forgotten. They remind me every day of how I earned the position I have, today."

He stood a full foot taller than her, maybe more if he hadn't been leaning down to address her. As he spoke, he had moved nearer to her, until he was so close she could hear his raspy breathing. She stood firm, a rock face in a windstorm. The deal had to be saved.

Hephaestus let out a long exhale. A whiff of hot air touched Diana's cheeks. His eyebrows furled, abruptly rising.

Seeing his visitor had not flinched, he relaxed his stance. His voice softened to a more moderate tone.

"You are playing a game with nothing in your hand. Yes, I could meet the reserve price, but it's too late. I have already submitted the final bid."

She corrected him. "You mean your unauthorized representative submitted a bid."

"He was authorized!"

"That's what you say."

"You must be in jest! I warn you, if the bid is redone, the result will be the same. I will bid the same and no one will bid higher."

"Can you be sure of that?" She looked him directly in the eye. "How long can you keep the others out of the bid? How much did you have to pay them for staying out this time? What did you have to promise them?"

"I have unlimited wealth. What does it matter to me?"

"How much more will you have to promise them not to bid the next time? It is you who must understand. The reserve will be the same, only you'll have had to pay out even more money keeping out the competition. It seems that you will be paying a rather high price for lot #4o83q. That's not good business."

Hephaestus let out a howling roar and swung his arm just inches from Diana's face, slamming his fist against a column and cracking it.

It had grown uncomfortable for Apollo, left outside with the surly representative and his silent assistant. He considered returning to the comfort of his transport parked on the other side of the field of grass, but decided he should stay close to keep an eye on things. A worried feeling had begun to grow; guilt, too, for having let Diana go inside by herself.

He began pacing back and forth debating how much longer he should wait before doing something. The question was what could he do? Hephaestus' lair was legendary for its impregnability. An army with inversion guns couldn't even begin to penetrate it. And now, Diana was trapped in there by herself with a man known for making enemies disappear.

His increased pacing drew the attention of the other two.

The representative's voice took on a sardonic tone.

"Haven't you figured it out? You went too far. Now, she will be taken care of. Finished!"

Apollo did not condescend to respond to this sniveling man, a man not even of his station.

The representative took the lack of response as weakness and pushed on.

"Why don't you just leave now? You have lost."

Before Apollo could decide whether to cut this sniveling creature down to size, the three of them heard the vault doors opening from inside the rocky structure. They stepped back and waited as a protracted series of whirrs, clicks and sliding noises sounded.

Five minutes later, the wall opened up and Diana emerged. She gave a respectful bow to the representative and flashed a victory smile to Apollo.

The representative seemed equally as shocked at seeing her come out smiling as he was at seeing her come out at all.

She let Apollo take her by the arm as they traversed the field back to the car.

Once seated comfortably in the back, Apollo listened to her story.

"So, then he smashed a column. I don't know, but I think it was one last test to see if he could break me. I told him that if he kept breaking support columns, he would crush both of us. He then smiled and offered me a drink."

"A drink? I thought Hephaestus never drank. He was too pure for that kind of stuff."

"Well, apparently, he makes exceptions. So, we drank, or at least he did. I didn't trust the stuff, so I lipped it, pouring bits of it out when he wasn't looking."

"That was smart. I've done the same thing myself when conducting business."

"So, more relaxed, he listened to my case, which hadn't changed one bit since we arrived and finally relented, agreeing to bid the reserve. Knowing you were outside, undoubtedly kept him from trying anything else."

Apollo nodded at this, not seeming to realize that she had thrown the last part in to give his ego a stroke.

"I will arrange to have to have the bid ammended."

"You certainly have connections, Apollo."

"That is only way to make it in this game."

He poured them a drink.

"To a job well done."

They tapped their glasses.

"I couldn't have done it without you."

He smiled. "I know."

# CHAPTER XX
## The Heart of the Matter

Orion had successfully elevated himself about three or four feet off the ground. Now, to propel himself across the room. Shifting the two large marble sized orbs in his right hand, ever so slightly, he veered to the right a few feet. Leveling the orbs, he stopped the rightward movement. Heart racing, he again was relatively still. Most unnerving was the swaying of his feet back and forth as the two balls only exerted their power on his midriff leaving his lower half dangling.

Out of the corner of his eye, he peeked to see if Diana was watching. Alas, as usual, she was totally absorbed in her console. This annoyed him. What was the point of flying if no one could see? But, he would change that!

Carefully, shifting the two orbs, he veered left then, with a bending of the wrist, lurched forward. But, it was too fast! He was heading towards the window. He immediately unbent his wrist and jerked to a stop, legs swinging forward. He peeked at Diana, glad she hadn't seen that.

His hand manipulated the two orbs, rotating him to face her. Feeling a little more confident with his piloting prowess, he bent his wrist down, propelling himself towards his target who was still engrossed in her work.

With subtle steering he maneuvered around her.

"Hey, I think I've mastered these balls. I'm master of the balls!"

He began circling around her. "I'm master of the balls!"

She did not bother looking up.

"I'm glad you're enjoying your new toy."

"This isn't a toy. It's amazing!"

"Flyballs are what we give to small children."

He was increasingly annoyed that she had still not looked up at him. Feeling that he truly was the master of the balls, he shouted out to her. "Hey, watch this!"

Flying to one side of the room, he hovered there until finally, eventually she looked up. Carefully, bending his wrist down, he lurched forward, then rolled the orbs over each other, turning his torso clockwise until his feet swung over his head. Once, twice, he spun around while flying across the room. There was only supposed to be two spins, but the momentum spun him around for a third spin. He shifted the orbs in the reverse direction, but it wasn't strong enough to stop the spin and hurling him into the far corner wall.

"Aaaahh!"

After the thud, Diana turned back to her displays and metrics.

It took a bit for Orion to clean up the mess – a side table had been broken beyond repair -but once done with that, he retrieved the flyballs that had rolled across the floor and was aloft once more. Taking it easy this time, he flew up behind Diana.

"So, what're you up to?"

She answered without looking up from the screen.

"Looking over a list of potential bidders."

"Hmm." He rolled his eyes. "But, this is the weekend, a time for fun!"

Flying in circles around her head, he asked, "Are you hungry?"

"Yes. But I've no time to go out. We'll have to get it delivered."

"I could fly there."

He put on his cat eyes glasses, which he now wore whenever he went out.

She shook her head.

"And then you could explain to the authorities how you're able to defy gravity and fly without a license."

"You've got a point there... You need a license to fly."

With his free hand, he pulled the phone from his pocket and ordered Moo Goo Gai Pan and Crab Rangoon.

The person on the other line asked how he would be paying.

"Oh, wait, I left my wallet in my apartment."

She handed him her blank silver card. He tapped it on his phone's mouth piece.

"Thank you," said the person on the other side.

He confirmed the order and thanked the lady on the other end of the line.

"Food'll be here in about twenty minutes."

"Good."

He placed her card back on the tabletop where she kept it.

"Wish I could just fly over and get it."

"But, I like my food in one piece," she quipped.

"Funny. So, what are you up to now? Anything I can help with?"

In response, she flicked a finger up and a virtual list of names materialized before them.

"These are the persons who have registered to be bidders."

"Yeah, I know. They've all been vetted to see if they can actually pay."

"Yes, Apollo was nice enough to allow me access to his database. It's amazingly detailed. The tools he has at his command are simply amazing."

The mention of Apollo caused Orion to roll his eyes. Diana was too busy lecturing to notice.

"Good. Now inserted in lot #4o83q was an index drill."

Another flick of her fingers triggered the screen to switch to an image of the index drill, a cone jutting out of the ground, with a dome top and adorned with display panels.

"There is also one in lot "5jie6c, as there would be for any property on the market. Let's take a look."

She hesitated a second before pulling out a pen-sized stick which pointed in the air causing three new orbs to appear.

He raised his hand to stop her.

"Wait, you're going to give me a big lesson, aren't you. I don't get it. Why do you keep trying to give me the whole giant picture on everything? Just set me up on tasks and I'll do them."

"If you understand the complete system then you can determine what tasks to do yourself."

"We don't have time for you to teach me how to fish. I don't need to understand every little thing."

"Teach you to fish? Why would I-? I really don't understand you sometimes. Please, could you just listen. Would that be so hard?"

She returned to the orbs which each had an individual color: one was yellowish, the second blue, the third red.

"As per tradition, when the final bidding ceremony happens, each registered bidder or their representative must be there in person in order to bid with witnesses present. All potential bidders will be watching the readings from the index drill – the 'meat thermometer' as you called it – inserted into the lot. You know what an index drill does, but now we're going to go over how to understand its readings."

With a flick of her finger, the three orbs enlarged.

"As you can see, the property is stable. The third sphere has a reddish tint. Once you become familiar with this, you'll be able to read the colors. You'll be able to detect change and be able to decipher what direction it's heading in."

"They all look the same to me."

"Remove your glasses."

He pulled off his cat eyes glasses and could suddenly see the orbs each had a distinctive color.

"Oh, I see it now. What's that pen in your hand?"

"It's a control stick. It remotely controls the index drill, a sort of a key/remote control for the sensor."

She handed it to him.

"Go ahead, put your finger on the head and lower the pen slowly."

"Sounds a little kinky." He gave her a wink.

"How many times must I say it? No bad jokes! Just do it."

He did and the middle orb enlarged.

"What is it that I'm looking at?"

"This sphere is a display of the physical materials that make up the property. Squeeze the key."

He complied and the sphere changed to a light blue.

He complied and the sphere changed to a light blue.

She pointed to it. "This is aluminum. The property has a large amount of it. You can tell by the color and darkness how abundant it is. Now, squeeze the key again."

He obeyed and the orb changed to a very pale aqua marine.

"This is what you would call lyceum. There is very little of it represented in this property. You will learn to read the index and know it like the tops of your shoes."

He smiled at this.

"Like the tops of my shoe, huh? Well, it doesn't seem too complicated."

"It's not rocket science." She winked.

"You really think I need to know all this?"

She nodded emphatically. He was more right than he could have known, she thought to herself. But, he had to be prepared. She had to bring him into her world as soon as possible. Time was running out.

Dinner had been an education for Diana who had patiently let Orion instruct her on the art of using chopsticks. She was able to get the hang of them but did not see the point. Most of the modes of eating on this planet seemed rather impractical to her. But, it made him happy being able to teach her this new skill. With each bite she took from the chopsticks, she would see him beam with pride.

There was something else there, something beyond that. It dawned on her, for perhaps the first time that this man had known nothing but life on this world and was limited by being raised by locals. She couldn't help but feel a swell of delight at the thought of his being in love with her. But, quickly, her mind dismissed the affair. It was very simple. She was the first woman of his kind he had known; their intimacy, the vast new world that she had introduced him to. It would almost be surprising if he hadn't developed some sort of romantic feelings towards her.

If pressed, she would have had to admit that she had grown incredibly fond of him. His looks were extremely nice. There wasn't much that could be improved there. Handsomeness in a man was nice, but hardly a basis to build an emotional bond, much less a future together.

Maybe it was the situation they were in that stirred her feelings for him; knowing that he needed her to watch out and take care of him even when he didn't know it himself. There was something about his innocence that made her want to hold and protect him. She had never felt this way about anyone before. His mannerisms, which could be both off-putting and incredibly sweet at the same time, tugged at her heartstrings. But this could never be a real relationship. They were too much apart. No, she was simply preparing him for what was to come.

A paper insert had come in the Chinese restaurant delivery bag with a promotional offer. He caught her eyeing the slip of paper he had strategically left at the corner of the table.

He answered the question he presumed she was asking.

"It's a Valentine's Day meal offer."

She pointed to the shape printed above the letters. "Does this design have a special significance? I've seen it before."

"It's a heart. That's our symbol for love."

"A heart? Is it spelled the same as the organ that pumps the blood throughout your circulatory system?"

"We consider them the same thing. People in the old days used to believe that the heart was where love came from."

"Love comes from inside here?" She reached over and placed her hand on his chest.

He nodded.

"What an odd idea," she commented. "The stomach would have made more sense. And this Valentine's Day?"

"It's a holiday devoted to love."

"A holiday for love. How sweet."

"Well, it's really a holiday fabricated by the postcard companies to sell greeting cards."

"How do people celebrate this love holiday?"

"With cards, dinner, maybe even a gift."

Diana's mind was taken by the concept. Logic and sense flew out the window. Her face became flushed, her eyes took on a sparkle as a swelling of emotions rose up inside her. Her grin was mischievous as she laid her hand on his.

"That sounds fun. Let's do it!"

"You mean?"

"Yes."

As the import of the idea sunk in, Orion too, glowed. Grinning from ear to ear, he pulled her in and gave her a giant kiss.

Unprepared for his reaction, Diana had to catch her breath when the kiss finally ended.

"Bees and butterflies!"

He pressed his nose to hers.

"This will be the best Valentine's Day ever."

"I agree." She beamed and gave him another kiss, running her hands along his muscular chest, losing herself in the warmth of his arms.

"I want to do everything." She declared. "The whole works."

He gave a firm nod. "You got it."

"What was it you said, cards, dinner, a gift?"

"Yes, we'll do it all, cards, dinner and gifts."

Her eyes gleamed as she contemplated it.

"A celebration of love."

"Valentine's Day."

Suddenly, her look of bliss disappeared, her eyes narrowed and lips puckered in a look of concern.

"About the gift, I'm not sure…"

"Not sure?"

"If I give you a gift does it have to be…" Her face scrunched up with a look of distaste.

"Yes?"

"Do we have to-? I mean I guess I could find one if it's required. It would just be so…"

"What?!"

"Do we really have to give each other a heart?"

Orion's chuckle quickly escalated into full-blown laughter. Still laughing, he gave her a bear hug. This miffed Diana, though, as it didn't answer her question.

# CHAPTER XXI
## The Gift

All his lingering doubts and fears faded once Orion stepped inside the strip mall jewelry store. Looking over the shiny baubles on display, a warm, happy feeling swiftly settled in and he knew this was definitely the place to get his lady love her Valentine's Day gift.

Seeing an interested customer, an attractive-enough brunette sales associate quickly buttoned her suit coat and stepped up to the counter.

"Good afternoon. Please let me know if there's anything you'd like to take a look at."

She waved her hand over the engagement ring section.

Orion shook his head.

"Not at that stage, yet. Looking for a Valentine's Day gift."

"Oh, getting an early start. Good for you. Anything in particular you were thinking of?"

"Well, I-."

"We have a special Valentine's Day collection over here."

He followed her to the section labeled, "For a Love that Will Last 'til the End of Time."

There was a selection of sparkling rings, necklaces, and earrings all of which incorporated red rubies along with diamonds designs to inject a Valentine's Day mood.

The sales associate, whose name tag read, "Emily", observed the overwhelmed look on her customer's face. She pointed to the glass.

"These Half-Heart earrings are very popular."

Each earring was a ruby on white gold in the shape of half of a heart that would be whole if were put together. He inspected them, his head rocking side-to-side as he vacillated.

The associate asked. "What kind of person is she?"

"Very classy."

"Rich classy?"

"Let's just say… she wants for very little."

"Hm, that can be tough." She bit her lip and walked over to a display case in the far corner.

"I had a boyfriend once who was super rich. He was a little mean and not much to look at but he was always getting me things. The problem was I never knew what to get him. I mean, anything I got he could have just bought himself. What can you do?"

Orion nodded in agreement.

"What did you get him?"

"I got him something very special - a dog."

"How'd it go?"

"Well, he started being mean to the dog, yelling at it and hitting it. He'd be nice to it for a while and then, out of nowhere would start hitting it with a rolled up newspaper."

Orion looked aghast.

"Is he still doing this?"

"I saw this and realized, hey, that's how he's treating me! I wasn't going to put up with that, so I left him. I took the dog, too."

She ended with a definitive nod.

Orion gave her a thumbs up.

As they talked, she led him to the final display case tucked in the back corner of the showroom.

"This is where we keep the odds and ends pieces. Maybe you'll see something she doesn't already have."

Tucked away in the display case, amongst odd items like a diamond encrusted bookmark and an owl head hatpin was a diamond tennis bracelet. Set on white gold, its clear stones glistened in the halogen lights.

Orion pointed to the bracelet.

"That one."

She placed her hand over it. He smiled.

"No question about it. How much is it?"

She removed it from the case, revealing the tag to Orion, then draped it over her own wrist so he could see how it would look.

It looked gorgeous.

Taking her cue from Orion's face, she started to replace the item.

He held out a hand, "Wait. Let me see it."

She laid it gently in his hand.

The weight of the piece was substantial compared to its size and elegance.

"Have any sales coming up?"

With a *sorry* look, she shook her head no.

He calculated the math in his head. With the promotion he was making more now. But it wasn't anywhere near enough to cover this.

Slowly, he extended his hand to return the bracelet.

The associate ceremoniously took it, placed it back in the display.

"You know," she threw in, "We also have a bracelet in our synthetic diamonds collection. I can show you the catalog."

Orion gave a why not look.

She pulled out a two-inch thick catalog and began flipping through it.

"They cost less since they're not real diamonds. Let's see, the tennis bracelet was in our Apollo line, if I recall."

Hearing the name, Orion gave a slight snort.

"I'll take it."

She looked up.

"Sorry?"

"I'll take the one you just showed me in the case."

He was as surprised as she was by this pronouncement. The tennis bracelet was set back on the felt pad, the two of them looking at it.

"Yes," he said with finality. "This is the one I want."

At the register, Orion took out five credit cards but was still unable to cobble together enough to make the purchase. One look at the bracelet, all the lustrous diamonds adorning it, and Orion knew it was the only thing in this store worthy of Diana.

"Do you have layaway?"

The associate nodded, "yes."

The paper hearts taped to the windows may have canceled out the classiness of the single rose in the crystal petal vase placed on the window, but Orion didn't care. It was Valentine's Day and he had just been able to pay off the diamond tennis bracelet. For five dollars extra they had gift wrapped it for him. Why they didn't do it for free was what he wanted to know. But, now he had it and would give it to the woman he loved.

Diana had declared that she couldn't go a day without working. So, a Valentine's Day dinner at her place was agreed upon.

It was a Saturday; he had plenty of time to prepare a nice, home-cooked meal. This was not something that came easy to him. Fortunately, with frozen dinners, one only had to remember to remove the clear plastic cover before microwaving.

It took him three trips up the stairs to bring the sumptuous feast made for the love of his life. Setting the last plate on the table, he chided her.

"Stop working. Come to the table and eat."

Chastened, Diana commanded the console to convert to the living room with a wave of her hand then joined him at the table. Looking it over, she realized he had set a formal meal for two. This gave her a warm, tingly feeling in her stomach.

After letting him get her chair, she watched in interested delight as he carefully dolloped various foods onto her plate and filled her glass with a red liquid.

He took his seat.

"Bon appetite."

She tipped her head.

"Merci, monsieur. Tu as assemble une belle table."

"Of course you know French." he stated, not a bit surprised.

"I hope the food's okay. I'm not the world's best cook."

Diana found the repast laid before her was actually quite pleasant, moving even. The dish called "lasagna" was a bit chewy. The "Brussels sprouts" were soggy in the mouth. The "wine" was okay, but did not taste nearly so good as the champagne.

"This is so nice."

Her words made him beam with pride though he suspected she was not being totally genuine.

After a dessert of ice cream with hot fudge sauce, the couple moved to the couch.

From a bag he had brought with him he pulled out the gift.

"For you. I saw it and thought of you."

She took the little paper box tied with ribbon and bow, admiringly running her hand along its shiny surface.

"It's very pretty. I like this little bow. And the colors, very tasteful."

After another second of watching her caress the gift box he felt compelled to say:

"You-. You unwrap it."

"What?"

"Tear the paper off."

He reached over and tore into the wrapper for show.

Her mouth dropped in shock at the desecration of her gift.

He took her hand.

"Like that. It's wrapping paper. The gift is inside."

"Oooh. I see."

She bit her lower lip as she carefully and cautiously tore the paper off, struggling with the ribbon and bow until a felt-lined jeweler's box was revealed.

Diana smiled wildly.

"Thank you!"

Before she could exclaim what an attractive blue box it was, he gently told her:

"It's a box. You open it. The gift's inside."

She nodded, comprehending, fingering the box until she was able to pry it open.

Orion's heart skipped a beat as the bracelet almost slipped out onto the floor, but Diana caught it, held it in her hand, admiring it.

"It's lovely. Thanks so much."

She raised it up and shook it a little.

Watching her with her new gift, he swelled with pride.

"You're welcome. I thought of you when I saw it."

"Bees and butterflies," she admired it for a few seconds. "I know just the place to hang it."

She rose moving to the window.

"Yes, right here. That's perfect!"

Orion's eyebrows furled. He got up and joined her at the window.

"No, you don't hang it up."

"It's not a sun catcher?"

"No, no. It's a bracelet. You put it on your wrist. I'll show you."

He gently lifted her wrist and slipped it on.

"There you go."

She smiled again, but seemed to be waiting for something more.

He put his arm around her.

"So, you like it?"

"Of course, I do! How do you work it?"

"What do you mean?"

"Well, how do I operate it? What does it do?"

"It doesn't do anything. You wear it. To look beautiful. It's a fashion accessory."

"Oh…?"

He could feel a hint of disappointment cross her face.

She shook her wrist a little watching the bracelet jiggle.

"Yes," she said unconvincingly, "It's very lovely. Now, let's do my present to you."

Grabbing his hand, she led him back to the couch.

Once they were seated, she reached into an invisible pocket in her day dress and pulled out a small square box with a slender string hanging out from where the lid met the lip.

"This is for you, for love day!"

Taking it, he looked at her, touched.

"I didn't know you were going to give me something, too."

"Of course, silly. Open it."

Her eyes widened with excitement.

"I know you'll love it!"

The box was rather weightier than it looked. Though only three inches high and three inches wide, Orion found he had to hold it with two hands, it was so heavy. Worried about dropping it, he set it down on the coffee table with a thump.

"So, I just pull the lid off?" he asked.

She nodded.

The box felt to him like cardboard, but very shiny. He tried to remove the lid but couldn't. It was on too tight.

"How do I get it open?"

"The Tyson string."

She made a pulling motion.

Deciphering her meaning, he picked up the string, pulled it and the lid popped open. He pulled the string up the rest of the way and found a very elaborately colored ball attached at the end. It looked like a luminescent marble.

"Wow... it's beautiful."

Seeing him holding her gift, Diana was almost bursting with excitement.

"It's the first of the twin moons of Cupidos. Since their inception, they have spun around each other while rotating around their mother planet. Countless love poems have been written about them."

It was quite a sight he had to admit. And it really looked genuine. The detailing was exquisite.

"I've never seen anything like it. How's it made?"

"Made? How is any moon made?"

He drew his eye right up to it.

"I mean, the detailing is so intricate. I can see a little ecosystem. The clouds almost look like they're moving."

"They are moving."

"That's awesome. I'd love to get this model under a microscope to see just how detailed it is."

Diana suspected that he didn't fully grasp what he was looking at.

"This is no model. This is the first moon of the twin moons of Cupidos."

"I don't get it."

"I'm giving you the moon. You're holding it in your hand."

He struggled to keep up.

"You mean I'm seeing the moon like looking through a telescope?"

"No, this *is* the moon. I bought it for you. It's been compressed inside a tantric field. The field protects what's in it. Nothing on the surface has been hurt. Its properties are the same as they were before, just smaller. Light enough to carry around."

Orion fought the shaking of his hand only for fear of dropping the entire celestial body that was on the other end of the string. Was there life on it? It looked like it had a whole ecosystem. It took all his strength to carefully set the moon back down on its box. Never had so much been in his hands.

Beaming, Diana leaned over and gave him a big kiss. He was too overcome to return it. She pulled away from him. He was still speechless; eyes locked upon her Valentine's Day gift.

# CHAPTER XXII
## The Beginning of the End

As he entered the first floor elevator, Stan marveled to himself at how things had changed at Polymer Mutual.

Not since mandatory car insurance laws came into effect had the insurance company seen such a turnaround in its fortunes. Through a recent series of changes, a whole new way of providing health insurance was revolutionizing the industry. Joint ventures with other insurance and finance companies were supporting new customer expansion while dividing the risks. The number of policy holders had shot up twenty-fold. Analysts were predicting Polymer Mutual's stock valuation would rise twenty percent by the end of the year. And, as a symbolic victory, the number of people playing "Bet Your Life!" each day was higher than the ratings count for "Wheel of Fortune".

Lost in these meditations, Stan stepped out of the elevator and into the Analysis Section. There was jauntiness in his step as he sauntered past cubicles, most of which were now occupied by busy employees. One of the new analysts passed by and he gave her a confident nod in return. He paused a moment outside his office door that had a brass plaque on it reading: "Stan Terrance".

Seeing his name on the office door still made him smile; affirmation that his life plan was right on schedule.

Throwing his bag next to his faux-leather chair, he spotted the date on his wall calendar marked and underlined, "Teleconference with president!"

His stomach tightened when he realized there were only two days more before they had to pitch their ideas. The majority of Polymer's new clients were young women, perhaps, because they were the main participants in the "Bet Your Life!" game. The president was unhappy about this and had ordered her "dynamic duo" to develop ways to bring in a broader list of clients.

"Hey O'," he cracked open Orion's office door.

To his chagrin, he found his fair-haired colleague slumped over his desk, head in his hands. The cat's eyes glasses sat on the keyboard that had been pushed to the side.

Stan closed the door behind him.

"Another hard night working on new ways we can make Polymer the largest insurer in the world?" he asked, hopefully.

There was no answer. He parked himself on the edge of the desk and put his hand on his buddy's shoulder.

"I'm tryin' to think up ways about how we could incentivize under thirty-five year old males to sign up for life insurance. Any ideas?"

Orion looked up and quipped, "Give them a subscription to Playboy when they sign up."

"No go." Stan retorted. "No one reads magazines anymore. Not when you can get it free online. C'mon, we've only got two days before we have to pitch to Polymer. Don't let me down, now. I've just started feeling like that office next door is really, actually mine."

Orion's attention had drifted. His features reverted back to the dark look they had when Stan had entered.

"I'm not good for much of anything today."

"Why, what's the matter?"

"Diana."

Stan suppressed an eye roll.

"Okay." He sighed. "Tell me about it."

"We celebrated Valentine's Day and, you know, I had saved up to get her a really nice bracelet."

"Yeah, you showed it to me like twenty-five times."

"Well, we exchanged gifts and she gave me something that was a thousand times bigger than what I gave her. I can't even tell you what it was, but it was beyond belief. It horrifies me a little even. But, it made my gift look like nothing."

"Don't be stupid. Your little bracelet looked great. Any normal girl would be crazy for it."

"Normal? That's the problem. She has everything she could ever want at her fingertips. And in her world, I don't know where, hell, how I could ever fit in."

"Yeah, it's hard dating a chick that makes more than you. But, that's what the modern world has given us."

"She knows it, too. I see it in how she talks to me. I'm not her equal. I'm a child who she likes, but pity's a little. In her eyes, that's all I'll ever be - a sort of project."

Stan felt bad for his friend, but was also calculating how to get him back to the task at hand.

"You know, they say one of the cures for these things is to just throw yourself into your work. You know, just dig right in and figure out how to get males under thirty-five to-."

"I'm serious, Stan. This is eating me up. She's the most incredible thing that ever happened to me. I met her and everything else in my life just fell in place. Look at me. For the first time, everything is going right in my life. I got a promotion and a raise. I'm popular. I finally fit in. Every day is all the more sweeter because I know she'll be there when I stop by her place each night. But what kills me is that with or without me she would be just fine. She has her work, her high-powered friends. She'll go on and me… She'll leave. When her work here is finished she'll leave. What have I got to make her want to stay? I don't know."

Stan stood up. His workmate was obviously not going to be good for much today.

Orion had slowly slumped back over his desk. Stan gave him a gentle pat on the back.

Oblivious, Orion gazed at the windowsill.

"I can't take it anymore. I'm going to break up with her."

Stepping out of Apollo's Bentley, which had pulled up to her curb, Diana turned around and handed Apollo a light card.

"Almost forgot."

"What's this?" he eyed the translucent card, "An invitation to the bidding. So, you've set a date?"

"Time and place," She beamed with pride. "It's all on the card."

"Will he be there?"

"Who?"

"That person you specially invited. You know that special guest."

"Person I invited?" Diana's eyes darted back and forth trying to think to whom he was referring.

Apollo elaborated.

"You know, the odd, diminutive man. What's his name? Oh, yes, that's right. My mortal enemy - Boibemad."

This knocked the wind out of Diana. Apollo dropped this on her too quickly for her to feign ignorance. Somehow, he had found out about Boibemad. Worse, that she had invited him.

The shock of it dried her throat. After seemingly interminable silence, she was able to speak.

"You're upset."

"About Boibemad, the only person who would or could outbid me being invited to bid? Or that he was personally invited by you?"

"Apollo, I…I just needed to get the highest amount possible for the property. It seemed like the most logical way to bring the price up. I didn't have a choice."

Fists clenched, brows furled. Apollo was visibly suppressing his rage.

"You weren't going to get a high enough price as is?! Burnt dinosaur! I thought we were in this together. You slit my ankle! If you had just come to me, I could have come up with a way to get you a higher price for the deal."

"How?!" her voice surged. "Yours was going to be the highest bid. Would you have raised your bid on your own?"

His eyes dropped down. The answer, of course, was no. The great Apollo would never spend more on a property than he had to.

Her heart beat faster, afraid that he might just leave that minute and never come back;  abandoning her when she still needed him.

But his breathing, which had become quick, slowed back to normal. He was about to speak when Stan's worn down Honda, engine sputtering, pulled into its usual spot behind the Bentley.

Apollo rolled his eyes.

"Of course!"

His eyes squinted menacingly, "We're not done with this."

Despite having parked behind Apollo's Bentley innumerable times, Stan looked through the windshield, in the light of the setting sun, unsure of what he was looking at. It looked like Orion's girlfriend. His friend's hangdog expression confirmed it.

Stan watched, with a look of sympathy, as Orion stepped out of the car.

Though Diana pretended not to notice Orion's arrival, Apollo appeared displeased with the interruption and outraged that Orion would approach them.

"Here comes your little pet."

She shot him a stern look.

Orion had never approached Diana when she was with Apollo. Before, it was because he was intimidated by Apollo and didn't want to get in the way of her business transactions. Today, though, he didn't care.

"What happens," Apollo asked, "When he finds out what you're really selling?" He didn't wait for her answer or Orion's arrival but slipped into the back of the Bentley.

Its doors abruptly closed before pulling off leaving Diana standing by herself.

Orion stepped up to her.

"Did I disturb anything?"

"No, we were just talking about business."

He said nothing. She slipped her arm through his and they sauntered up the front walk. Just outside the entry door, she held her hand out, palm up, and a light card materialized.

Orion stared blankly at her hand.

"Take your glasses off," she said.

He removed them and his eyes suddenly widened as he saw the light card.

"What's this?"

"Everything is set." She informed him, beaming with pride. "The bidding is set for next week, here in our building."

His voice lacked the enthusiasm of hers.

"That's nice."

"Lot 5jie6c is the last deal of the trifecta. Some of the most important people around the galaxy will be there to put in bids. There's so much to do."

She put her hand on his arm.

"I'm going to be a bit difficult in this period and I know I haven't been much fun. But, I just want you to know that no matter what happens, I don't think I could do it without you. This will be our moment of triumph."

She kissed him on the cheek as he opened the front door for them.

Orion forced a smile. He knew he wouldn't leave her now. Not with so much on the line. He'd wait until after the show. He owed her that.

# CHAPTER XXIII
## The Lie

RSVPs trickled in at first, but after a few days, came in waves. Diana posted the ever growing list of responses on a light board projected at the far end of the room. Little points of light showed responses coming from the far ends of the universe.

Sitting comfortably in his usual seat, Orion watched as she sent out the latest status information for lot #5jie6c to the potential bidders. The last week had been a blur. She had worked even more feverishly than before, which he wouldn't have guessed possible. In the morning, on waking, he would ascend to the third floor and find her already working on the console before the sun was up. At night, he would return to his apartment and empty bed leaving her still at work at the luminescent console surrounded by glowing, translucent orbs streaming countless bits of data. He wondered when she slept. Maybe people on her world didn't need sleep. Come to think on it, he didn't know if she was human or humanoid. He shivered. No, nothing non-human could make him feel the way she did.

Information was constantly streaming in on the bidder's profiles,
their economics; the likelihood that they could offer a legitimate bid
and how much. Further information on lot #5jie6c came in, as well,
with analysis on minor physical and atmospheric changes. To Orion
it was all dizzying beyond imagination. But, to Diana, it was pure
manna and making sense of it all is what she lived for.

He couldn't say when exactly it happened or what triggered it,
but one day as he watched his lover working at an extra frenetic pace,
a question dawned on him for the first time.

"What is lot #5jie6c?"

Diana didn't respond. Her gaze on the console numbers
intensified as she crooked up two fingers to begin a call transmission.
A minute later, she was conversing with a bizarre looking woman
from some oddly named place he couldn't quite make out. It
would be another hour, in which time Diana had made a series of
transmissions, before there was a lull in which Orion had a chance to
repeat the question.

"Dear."

"Yes?"

"What is lot #5jie6c?"

"Oh. It's the property we're to going to put up for bid."

"But, what is it, exactly? An asteroid field? A star?"

"Oh, no, it's not a star. That's funny." She spoke more to herself
than to him. "It's the final piece of a three property deal. I have to
sell all three or else I don't get a commission from any of them.
Crazy, huh? But, I didn't have a choice. This was my one shot." Her
voice trailed off then she turned to him, "You understand, right?"

"Yes." He answered. He understood that she had not directly
answered his question.

"I'm sorry," she said, "let me get back to this analysis. I haven't vetted all the new bidders, yet."

With that, she turned back round to the console. A nod of her head triggered a series of screens to pull up and a large energy orb to form around her.

Effectively cut off from any more conversation, Orion paced the room a while until he found himself by the window that overlooked the backyard. Standing close, he noticed something odd – two little holes in the glass. He ran his fingers over the glass, could feel a slight breeze running through them. They were holes, slanted downward and set apart from each other at exactly the same distance as a cat's eyes.

Orion slept in his apartment that night. He was anxious so it had taken a few hours to get to sleep. When he was awakened by sunlight peering through the shades the gnawing questions in his mind had still not been put to rest. The two holes in the window had etched themselves into his thoughts.

He got up and started making himself breakfast. But then he saw something that almost made him choke on his cereal. It was that crazy man-boy in the white suit and spiky blonde hair that he had met a while ago. The one who had spoken about burning ant's eyes and other crazy stuff in a booming god-like voice. What was him name? Boy be mud? It didn't matter.

He watched the little man-boy walk through the front yard and disappear around the corner of the building.

In a flash, Orion ran to the hallway and looked out the window down on the backyard. There, he saw Diana and the kid. They were entering the shed.

Somehow, he knew the shed shouldn't be there, but could think of no reason for this feeling. His phone rang and he pulled it out of his pocket.

"Hello."

It was Stan.

"Hey, I'm out front. Where are you?"

"Uh, yeah… Something's come up. I'll be down."

"WHY ARE YOU ALWAYS LATE?!"

Pocketing the phone, Orion found himself staring at the shed through the window, wondering what Diana and the boy were doing in there for so long. Deciding to investigate, he rushed down the flight of stairs, skipping every other one. Emerging onto the front stoop he ran into Uri. The old man didn't budge from his spot at the top of the front stoop.

"O', good to see you."

Orion came to a sudden halt, his way blocked by his gentle landlord.

"Uri. Just stepping out."

"I see. Your friend, he's out there in the car. He always seems upset. Maybe he should get off the coffee."

Uri pointed to Stan.

Orion took the opportunity to step past him.

"Yeah, I'll tell him."

Orion virtually jumped down the front steps.

Uri called after him, "You know, I was wondering. Have you ever seen the aurora borealis? I'm putting the telescope up on the roof, tonight. We should be able to see it."

"Sorry, Uri. Busy."

Orion pointedly didn't look at Stan even when he heard the honking. Nothing was going to stop him from getting to the backyard.

But, then he saw Boibemad, not in the back but on the front sidewalk walking away from the Atlas Building. There was no doubt it was him with that unmistakable white suit and theatrical, skyscraper hair. He was almost to the far corner.

"Orion, you okay?!" Uri called out.

He ignored his landlord and rushed around to the back of the house looking for Diana. There was nothing but the shed.

Ignoring his fears, he stepped up to it. The doors were closed with a standard key securing them. Cautiously, he reached out to pull open the door. At the last second, he stopped, thinking better of it.

The shed was an anomaly. What was it doing here? It was a standard wood-framed gardening shed. It's presence in the backyard should be the most natural thing, but every fiber in Orion's body told him that it wasn't supposed to be here and that the last thing he should do is touch it. This was a piece of puzzle that had been running through his head these last few weeks. Now the pieces were coming together, but he was still missing a few.

Maybe, he could still catch the little kid. That might be the piece that solved everything.

Breaking into a sprint, he dashed back around to the front of the house. His target had almost made it to the corner.

Before Stan knew what hit him, Orion had jumped into the passenger seat.

"Follow that boy in the white suit!"

"What?!"

"That kid! The one with the hair!"

Boibemad took a right at the end of the block and disappeared out of sight.

Orion slapped Stan on the arm.

"Now, he's getting away! Go, go!"

His friend seemed so crazy that Stan gave up, started the car, and drove after the three and a half foot tall pedestrian.

"Take a right here!"

Stan complied. They rounded the corner just in time to see Boibemad step inside a construction tent standing in the middle of the street, the kind put over manholes during repairs. Two very large construction workers, adorned with yellow construction helmets and red vests stood guard outside the tent.

Weirded out, Stan stopped the car about ten feet away.

"What are we doing?"

Without answering, Orion jumped out of the car and rushed over to the tent.

The two giant construction workers did nothing, said nothing to acknowledge his presence.

He addressed them.

"I want to see Boibemad. The little kid – man - who just stepped inside the tent."

The two centurions had yet to move. Eyes looking forward; just the slightest impression of breathing that indicated they were alive.

This was getting him nowhere. He sized them up. They were each twice his size, but maybe if he was fast enough.

With an abrupt lunge he ran towards the opening fold of the tent. His right hand had made it through, when, quick as light, the two centurions blocked his path with their arms. He shifted to duck below their arms and roll in, but felt an implacable hand grab the back of his shirt and lift him in the air.

"I just want to talk to Boibemad!"

Still seated in the car, Stan watched in disbelief as the two bruisers lifted his friend up as easily as one would a piece of tissue paper. As Orion thrashed, struggling to free himself, one guard grabbed his arm the other his leg. They carried him wordlessly back to Stan's car and unceremoniously dropped him on the hood.

Once, the two unbelievably large construction workers returned to the tent, a petrified Stan rushed out of the car to see if his friend was okay. Orion looked a little disconcerted but not hurt.

Stan called out to the two hulks who had repositioned themselves at the entrance to the construction tent.

"Sorry, about my friend. He's been guzzling too many of those five hour energy drinks."

There was no response.

Orion was half back on his feet by now. He made a move to go back to the tent.

Stan didn't let go of his arm. It wasn't easy; Stan had never realized how strong Orion was.

"Easy O', what you doin'?"

"I've got to see Boibemad."

"You won't get past those two guys. I think they'll really pound you if you go back."

Orion, felt the bruises grow on his arm and leg where they had held him, nodded in agreement. Back in the passenger seat of Stan's car, Orion began deliberating.

"Maybe, if you distract them, get them away from the tent, I can rush inside."

"Are you crazy?!"

Stan, not wanting to drive anywhere near the yellow construction tent, proceeded to make a three point turn.

"What the hell's the matter with you?!" Stan's face was crimson. "You could have gotten yourself killed back there. These weird mood changes you've been having. I'm starting to think you're losing it. Sometimes. I-."

"Take me back to my place."

"Maybe we should go to work. You know, to our jobs."

"Take me back now!"

Orion's voice was dark. Stan shook his head, ready to be done with the whole horrific morning. Instead of going straight, he took the left turn that led to the Atlas Building. Ahead of them, the Bentley pulled off and passed them by, heading in the other direction.

As soon as Stan parked the car, Orion jumped out and headed towards the house.

"What are you doing?! Where are you going?!"

It was no use, Stan realized. His friend was walking, full tilt, around to the back of the house. Stan knew he should just go to work, but couldn't abandon his friend, not in the crazy state he was in.

"Aw, hell…"

He jumped out of his car and raced after Orion. He found his friend in the backyard standing in front of a gardening shed.

Uri, who had witnessed their return, came around to see what all the commotion was about.

"What's with everyone running around like crazy? You gonna scare the tenants."

Orion eyed Uri.

"There's something in this shed. I don't know what it is, but it's very important."

Stan had lost his patience. "There's something in the shed, huh? That's what this is about? Well, there's only one way to solve this mystery."

Shaking his head in annoyance, he stepped up to open the shed.

Orion looked up at Diana's window and saw IO looking down at them, eyes glowing red.

"Stan, no!"

Orion jumped between Stan and the shed.

"Orion, what the hell's the matter with you!"

Orion turned to his landlord.

"Uri, do you know where this shed came from? What's in it?"

Uri, at first didn't seem to comprehend the question. He looked at the shed as if seeing it for the first time.

"Hasn't that always been there?"

For some reason, this wasn't the answer Orion was expecting. Had the shed always been there? Was it he who was imagining everything? What was his mind trying to tell him? Why was he so afraid of it? Just then he saw a pair of glowing green eyes peering out from the bushes. IO had come down to them.

"Don't touch the shed!" he directed them. "Go to the front of the building."

"Orion, I think,-" Stan began.

"Go! Now!"

Stan and Uri exchanged worried glances. Orion's eyes were so determined that the two relented and started backing away.

Keeping an eye on IO, Orion followed them around to the front of the building.

The feline slowly followed, staying relatively out of sight, but never taking its sights off the three of them.

Stopping in the front yard, Uri's complexion had reached a ghostly pallor. Stan was beyond frustrated, his hands at his sides balled up into fists.

Orion spoke to them in the calmest voice he could manage.

"Thanks, Uri. Sorry to give you trouble. Okay, Stan. Why don't we go to work, now."

To emphasize the last sentence he walked over to the car and got in.

Wordlessly, Stan got in after him, started the car and pulled away.

The last thing Orion saw through the passenger window was IO's green, glowing eyes dim before it pulled back into the bushes.

That night at Diana's was a seemingly normal one. She was at her console working, while Orion busied himself with one of the little chores she had given him. This time, it was graphing out points of high methylene on a galactic chart. Usually, engaging in these little jobs was fun for Orion – sort of a cross between a video game and knitting. But, his mind was dwelling on darker matters tonight and they colored everything he did.

Diana had not the slightest idea that anything was different. She hadn't noticed Orion's terseness of speech when they had eaten dinner, nor the slight furling of his brow that often cropped up. She had just thought this a normal night, with everything in place as it should be. That was until Orion began his interrogation.

"You know," he began, in a tone quite innocent, "I saw you this morning."

"Oh, really?" She kept her mind on the console and the task in hand.

"Yeah, you were walking around with a small boy."

"Oh, yes. That's one of the prospective bidders - Boibemad."

"Where's he from?"

"Galactus 7. His full title is Boibemad, the great and mighty ruler of Acreon, Septon, and Deonis, and third son of Alteron."

"That's quite a title. You two were in the backyard. What was there to see inside that shed out there?"

The last question made Diana flinch.

"What do you mean?"

"Into the shed, that's where I saw you take this Boibemad."

She struggled for an answer. Coming up with nothing, she reverted, regretfully to something she had never done in their relationship before. She lied.

"The shed doesn't exist. It's just a temporal transportation device. Make sure not to touch it. It can be dangerous to mortals."

# CHAPTER XXIV
## Love...

Sitting in the relatively luxury of his galaxy traversing limousine, Apollo took note of Diana's rather haggard appearance as she walked from the front porch of the Atlas Building to his vehicle. Why she had picked this place to stay was beyond him.

The door opened itself and she took a seat.

"Apollo."

"Diana. Hm, you don't look so good. Problems with your little Earth pet?"

She was not amused.

"He began asking me questions last night."

"Questions?"

"He asked about the shed behind the building."

"The…"

She nodded.

Crooking an eyebrow, he slowly shook his head.

"I told you that relationing with the locals would be a mistake.

He's bound to find out what you're doing. The show is only a few days from now."

She raised her hand. "I know. I know. But, I hope…I feel that when he finds out everything, he'll understand."

Apollo stayed silent, his raised brow indicated he knew better.

Sitting inside the windowsill, IO watched the Bentley take its mistress away. It stood up and positioned itself to jump to the floor. Orion's head popped up right outside the window. Startled, IO jumped back but couldn't catch itself and fell on the floor.

Looking back, it found Orion still outside the window bobbing up and down a bit.

Orion pulled open the window.

"Here, kitty, kitty."

Transforming to kill mode, the feline attack machine lunged, flying towards him with claws extended, but missed, as Orion shot up in the air.

IO caught one of the vines running up the building. It looked up just in time to see Orion, steering himself with the two flyballs, rise up and disappear over the roof.

Grabbing the vine with all four paws, it took IO a third of a second to scurry up to the roof. There it saw Orion disappear down the chimney.

In one leap, it cleared the thirty feet between the edge of the roof and the chimney. With eyes that could see at any level of light the feline peered down the long chute and saw its prey descend the chimney and exit out the fireplace.

IO hesitated, but not for long, and was soon scaling down the chimney in pursuit, its claws digging into the brick to slow its descent. Almost to the fireplace, the chimney damper closed. With no escape, IO found itself stuck at the bottom.

Covered in soot, Orion burst out the front door of the Atlas building with crowbar in hand. He had no idea how much time he had. That was if his theory was right. If it wasn't, he might be dead in a few minutes, anyway.

Racing around to the backyard, he came upon his target – the mysterious gardening shed. A laser blast startled him. Another followed it. Crumbling bricks bounced along the roof and soared off the roof's edge. That must be IO blasting its way out of the chimney, Orion thought to himself. There was no time for hesitation. With two hands on it, he jammed the crowbar in-between the lock and the shed door. Nothing happened.

Another laser sound erupted along with more crumbling debris.

There was no more time left and nothing to lose. Orion jerked the crowbar, breaking open the lock. Deftly, he swung the shed doors open.

Inside was a fully functioning index drill – or the meat thermometer as he had often referred to it. The silo shaped object lit up with sensor readings. There was no time to reflect on this for IO raced around the side of the building to the front of the shed.

Inside the shed, Orion realized he was trapped as IO's eyes glowed bright green and then fired.

Diana stepped out of the Bentley, the wheels in her mind were spinning. She had lined up everyone for the open house and they would all be there in two days. Her goodbye to Apollo was a mere wave of her hand, none of the usual formalities. She was sure he understood. Back when he was working on the first of his big deals, he must have been similarly dazed and inundated by it all.

The plethora of thoughts filling her mind scattered when she opened her apartment door and found Orion on a chair in the dark. As much as him being there, what startled her more was the dark look in his eyes.

"Orion?"

"What are you hiding in the shed?"

"What?"

"What are you hiding in the shed?"

She thought to lie again, but couldn't do it. Not again. Not to him.

"It's an index drill. Plugged into the Earth."

Her eyes searched the dimly lit room until they came upon IO who was sitting in repose in the far corner of the room. Her little guardian's blank look revealed nothing.

"You're wondering how I was able to find out," he observed.

He jerked upright and walked to the window. In the glass he could see the moonlight filtering through the glass, shining on her face, picking up the strands of gold in her hair.

"Don't blame IO. He more than did his job. I figured he would. That he'd zap me and take my memory of whatever I'd find when I looked into the shed. So, I wrote myself notes about what I was going to do and hid them around in different places. I then set up my phone cam in the bushes to record whatever I did at the shed. You can't imagine what a weird thing seeing yourself getting zapped unconscious by a little cat with laser eyes is. But, that's not what really hurts. It's knowing that you're behind it all."

Diana uttered the only words that came to her, "I'm sorry…"

"You're sorry…? What exactly have you been doing all this time? What's the real reason you're here?!"

"I'm doing my job."

"Your job?! What is that? Are you here to sell the Earth? Is that what I've been helping you with…?"

"In two days, there is the open house."

"How can you sell the Earth?! People live here. I live here. My family lives here."

"You don't understand."

"Understand? What is there to understand?"

She took a deep breath before answering.

"This planet is just a property like anything else. It has an owner. Just like everything in the universe. The owner has decided to sell. It wasn't my idea. I'm just brokering the deal."

"An owner? Who is this owner? Maybe we could convince them not to sell."

"I can't disclose the owner. That wouldn't do you any good, anyway. There's going to be a sale."

"But there're billions of people living here. What's going to happen to them?"

"You don't need to worry about the Earth creatures. Don't you understand?"

"No, I don't understand. How can you not understand? What you're doing is immoral!"

She pursed her lips. There was anger filling up within her.

"Please…leave."

"Don't try to shut me out. I'm going to stop you! Stop all this."
She pointed a finger to the door.

He stomped out, slamming the door behind him.

# CHAPTER XXV
## ...Hurts

Sitting in his office, Orion could barely look at the papers on his desk. Their significance had become nothing in light of all he had seen, all he now knew.

Lost in his meditations, he failed to hear the knocking at the door and didn't even notice the visitor until the stout, curly-haired gentleman was standing in front of his desk calling his name.

"Orion… Orion!"

He awoke from his trance, looked up at the figure before him, bespectacled, with a comb over. This wasn't his manager, but his manager's manager, Barclay.

The senior manager was a bit red in the face.

"I-. We've been getting concerned about your lack of doing… anything."

Touching his face to make sure his own pair of glasses was on, Orion nodded mechanically.

The senior manager, unsatisfied with the reaction he was getting, leaned forward, putting his hand on Orion's desk to stress the point.

"You're not answering your e-mails or your phone for all I know. You missed the teleconference with the president without giving a reason. Son, you seem to just sit here and do nothing. What I've come down to find out is: why?"

The only response Orion could articulate was an anguished sigh. He didn't look at the man before him. What was the point? Everything they did here was pointless. They were just tiny, infinitesimal specks on the cosmic tableau. The rise and fall of Polymer Mutual was inconsequential compared to what was happening in the universe around them. What was going to happen all too soon to the planet they called home.

The senior manager kept on.

"…and we can't have you not doing anything. It's not fair to everyone else."

Again, Orion sighed.

"Look, Son, maybe you should just take the rest of the day off and work out whatever it is that's eating you."

Orion agreed with an absent-minded nod and, shortly after, packed his bags. He hadn't known how much longer he could have stayed at work anyway. He had to get out, escape from the monotony, the meaningless of this ten-by-ten prison cell life.

Through his office door, Stan spied his friend exit through the front door and jumped up to chase after him. He caught him just outside the front door of the building.

"Hey, O'! Wait up. You okay?"

One look reminded Stan that his friend hadn't been okay for a while now.

"Need a ride?"

Orion shrugged.

They had only made it a few blocks in the car before Stan found he couldn't hold his tongue any longer.

"So, anything you want to say?"

No response.

"O, I'm worried about you. You're not talking or doing anything. You just... I don't know."

Orion stayed silent.

"Look, can't you just give me an idea as to what's the matter? This is really hard for me. It's like I don't know you, anymore. You were doing so good. Everyone at Polymer knows you saved us. They'll work with you, whatever's going on. Let's go back. You'll see. It can go back to the way it was."

The park and the Museum of Natural History were coming up ahead of them. Orion saw the trees swaying in the wind, the rippling of the leaves, all beckoning him. The car felt too confining. He struggled to breathe, grabbed the door handle.

"Let me off here."

"What? You're speaking, now?"

"Pull over, now. Let me out!"

Stan relented, pulled the car to the curb. Before his friend closed the door, he called out:

"If you decide you need anything, I'm here, okay?"

The door closed with a thud as Orion made his way into the park. In his rush, he pushed through the dense thicket that ran along the sidewalk and emerged in a wooded area. He steadily pushed forward until he could no longer hear the sounds of the street, the sounds of civilization.

After walking a while, he found a seat on a sawed off tree stump nestled in a cozy clearing. The trees were in full glory, covered in a myriad greens. Sunlight filtered through them and warmed his face while a symphony of bird song and rustling leaves pushed out troubled thoughts. The world was at peace.

But then he heard talking and realized his seat was not so remote as it seemed.

On the other side of the bushes was a walkway where a couple of the ubiquitous clipboard carrying volunteers stationed themselves and began stopping passers-byes to solicit for their cause. This set worked for Greenpeace. As before, their pitch began with, "What have you done to save the planet, today?"

After the sixth time hearing this question asked, he couldn't take the irony, anymore. Grimly he made his way to the park entrance.

They were everywhere. He ran into another one. It was a young, attractive girl-guy couple chatting up any one they could convince to stop. "Excuse me. Hello. Just wanted to ask, what have you done to save the planet, today?"

Again! Words failed him. He wanted to scream. He wanted to tell them to throw their brochures away, to go home and make love because they only had a few days left. He didn't. He passively took the flyer, mumbled thanks, and kept walking almost stumbling down the sidewalk.

The question pressed on his mind like a hammer hitting a bell. The answer was always the same – nothing. What could he do? If he knew, then, whatever it was, he would do it. But, there were too many unknowns. Like, who owned the Earth? What would the new owner do with it? If Diana's stopped, will there just be a new broker brought in? No, he needed to know more. With him and Diana not speaking, he saw no way to find out.

At the end of the block, a silver-grey Bentley Limousine pulled up. He didn't have to ask who it belonged to.

Never before had Orion had such a smooth ride. The windows were tinted so that the world outside was only a glimmer. But, the show was inside the limo, and its star was Apollo.

After inviting Orion for a ride, he proffered an odd, smoky drink which Orion was not brave enough to imbibe, and began speaking about the situation at hand as he saw it.

"There are many bidders for lot #5jie6c – Earth - as you call it. Did you know that's what lot #5jie6c was? Did she tell you that?"

Orion nodded. Apollo looked disappointed by this, but continued.

"Well, there are many bidders, but Boibemad is able and determined to outbid everyone else for the planet. He desperately wants it. As soon as he buys it, he will strip it of all its minerals. The energy from the core will be directed back to his home system where he lives like a king. If Boibemad wins the bid, your Earth will cease to exist. That is fact."

Orion looked askance at him.

"And you, I suppose there's nothing in this for you? Or did you just want to keep me updated on events out of a sense of sharing?"

Apollo's smooth smile reappeared.

"Yes, of course there's a reason. My co-investors and I would undoubtedly be the highest bidders if not thwarted by Boibemad."

"And this would be a happier outcome because…?"

"Because of what we'll do for the Earth. Unlike most of the other investors, we want to make this asset, with its high H2O content and stable environment, into a galaxy class vacation resort. Instead of hurting the planet, we'll install a cleaner, more pleasant atmosphere."

"So, earthlings should rejoice?"

Apollo processed the question for a moment.

"The denizens of this asset will be a part of this, too. There will be functions they can perform."

"I see. I'm sure they'll love that."

"As you're not even one of them, you won't be harmed. You'll be on your new home, wherever that ends up being."

Orion realized just then, that Apollo didn't know he was an Earthling.

"You won't let me stay?"

"You know that isn't possible."

Orion did not know. There was so much Diana hadn't told him! But he wasn't going to let Apollo know that.

"What I still don't get is why you're telling me all this?"

"Some things are meant to be known and some aren't. The key thing is that, as things stand, Boibemad will win the bid on Thursday and the Earth will be decimated. There's still a chance, though. You have influence with Diana."

"Yeah, right. You're the one whose altar she worships at."

"I wish that were true. She always keeps me at arm's length; wants me for my connections and knowledge and influence. In the beginning, I may have had a chance with her. But, you came in to her life and she's given her heart to you." A pained look flashed over his face. "I lost out on Diana, but I will not lose out on lot 5jie6c."

Though Orion hadn't realized it, the vehicle had come to a stop.

Apollo looked him in the eye.

"You seem to care about this planet. If that is true, you'll find a way to convince Diana to make sure I win the bid. That's the only chance your planet has."

Orion was not convinced of this. But, his door pulled ajar and he knew that was the signal for him to exit.

The Atlas Building wasn't located near any bus stops so, if one took the bus, a mile and a half walk followed. The end of this walk was where Orion found himself, the building he called home just coming into view. It was late enough in the day that even though the sun was still out, the moon was clearly visible in the sky just beyond the three story building.

The journey had given him plenty of time to think about his next move. That there were no good ones was clear enough. But something had to be done. On that point, at least, Apollo was right.

Looking down the front walk of the Atlas building, a million ideas raced through his mind. So many things he could do, so many courses of action he could take. But, act he must and act, he would.

With no more thought, he swiveled left and began marching to the corner. His pace picking up as he rounded the corner and saw, several blocks down, the silhouette of the manhole construction tent, the temporary abode of Boibemad.

The same two large construction workers were standing guard at either side of the tent's entrance. They loomed even larger than Orion had remembered. The worst part was he still had massive welts on his leg and arm when they had picked him up like yesterday's trash and deposited him on the hood of Stan's car. The memory of the last time guided him as he stepped around the large, diamond shaped "Men at Work" sign. He straightened up a bit and tried looking super confident as he approached the first burly construction worker who must have looked like an oversized Greek statue beneath the construction outfit.

"I need to talk to Boibemad. His highness, Boibemad. About lot #5jie6c."

The guard's face grew expressive as he raised up a pipe wrench. Orion flinched, thinking he was going to be brained. But, then, to his surprise, the construction worker stepped to the side and with a slight bow, waved him in.

Orion could not have said what he'd expected to find inside the tent, but it was definitely not the Spartan bareness he found. The furnishings were nothing more than two plastic chairs around an open manhole. The floor was the street, the walls and ceiling the white tent. An ice-fishing shack would be more elaborately decorated.

Boibemad, still dressed in his white three-piece suit, was seated in one of the two chairs. He vigorously motioned for Orion to take a seat in the other. Once seated, Orion waited for Boibemad to say something, anything. But, all he got was a sly grin from his host who looked at him with unflinching, deep-set, hazel eyes.

Five minutes of this passed. Orion decided to initiate the conversation.

"I need to talk to you about the Earth."

The boy across the manhole did not seem to understand the question.

Orion continued, "I mean lot 5jie6c."

This elicited a note of comprehension.

"Good stuff!  I'll cook my soup in that bitch!"

The little man jabbed his fists in the air, in quick punching motions. He then took on a victorious air, sticking his chest out triumphantly.

"What I wanted to talk to you about was your plans for it."

"Lot 5jie6c? I will disembowel it!"

"But, this is the home to billions of people. They were born here, they live here. If you go through with your plans you'll kill them all. I beg of you, your highness. Think of the people of this world."

The boy straightened his white tie, bent over in his chair, and reached down to a small nail that had been inserted in the street next to the manhole. Twine had been tied to the nail which then ran down into the open manhole cover. The little man pulled up on the twine vigorously until a large can attached to the other end came out.

He held the oversized can, easily as big as his head, to his mouth and drank the liquid inside. From the look and smell, Orion guessed it was sewer water and felt a little nauseated at the sight of the person across from him noisily guzzling it down.

Boibemad lustily drank down the contents of the can, at least what didn't end up on his suit. Then tossed it back into the manhole and raised a tiny fist in the air.

"The weak are pity fools. You a pity fool!"

He shot up and paced excitedly back and forth across the tent.

Orion struggled to pivot his chair to face the boy.

"I'm not trying to stop you. I just wanted to try to say that there's a middle way."

Boibemad's pacing increased until he was circling the inside of the tent. Orion, frustrated with trying to keep his eyes on his talking companion, stood up, too.

This action immediately incited a look of horror and indignation on the face of the blonde-haired lad who held up his hands defensively.

"What are you doing?!"

Before the confused Orion could answer, two of the burly construction workers rushed in and picked him up like a cheap rag doll.

He struggled against them to no effect.

"Wait, I just want to make a deal!"

Boibemad stormed over to him, pointed a finger accusatorially.

"I will disembowel lot #5jie6c to smithereens!"

The guards were just as strong as the first time. They more than proved it by carrying Orion three blocks away before unceremoniously dumping him in someone's front yard.

The light of a three quarters moon shone through the window of Diana's apartment. Beyond that the sole illumination was the screens, orbs, and buttons of her work console.

Without Orion around, she was finding work tedious at best, impossible at worst. The longer he had been gone, the more her thoughts turned to him. She still caught herself turning to where he had always sat to comment on something, only to be reminded by the empty chair that he was no longer around.

It was true, that without him around, there was more time for work. Taking care of him, having to train him on how to do all the things that his upbringing on this primitive planet certainly took a lot of time and could definitely be annoying. But, it had filled a hole in her life. Given her something she'd never had before, someone who needed her.

Everything was not just about her, anymore. Her every thought and move had to take into account someone else. Her time was never completely her own. But, there came a benefit she would never have anticipated. It gave her someone to share life with. The failures, the joys, all took on more meaning, more value when they happened with him. So, too late, she was realizing that though he needed her, she needed him more. Without him to see the success of her sale, it would just feel hollow.

On the side table, IO awoke from its statue form, crooked its head to the window, and jumped to the windowsill looking out, captivated by something. Diana couldn't help but get up and take a peek too. She did so just in time to get a glimpse of Orion walking up the front walk before disappearing into the building.

Her impulse was to rush down and meet him, try to work everything out. But she held herself back. No, there wasn't time to deal with him, now. There was work to be done, planets to be sold! She must stay focused.

A knock at the door and IO's familiar warning beep dissipated her resolve. She got up, stepping past her feline robot which had leapt to the center of the room and assumed an attack stance. It glared at the door with glowing eyes.

She opened the door. It was Orion. The two locked eyes. He was the first to divert his gaze.

Looking him over, she let out short gasp. His face was pallid. His eyes, underlined by black spots and heavy eyelids spoke of exhaustion. His clothes were rumpled; worn many days in a row. This was a shadow of the man she had known before. Changed inalterably by all he had seen and learned.

He looked to the ground, stumbling over some words, then gave his confession.

"I don't know…what to do."

She motioned him in and took him in her arms.

# CHAPTER XXVI
## Open House

And they came.

Visitors from throughout the universe were pouring into Diana's apartment to formally put in their bids on lot 5jie6c. From Orion's point of view, leaning on the window sill, there were maybe three or four hundred people occupying the space, yet they all managed to fit comfortably in Diana's modest two bedroom apartment.

She had not altered her place as far as he could tell and yet the visitors were able to walk around freely, intermingling with each other, and converse in pleasantries, or un-pleasantries depending on who was on which side of the conversation.

The look and dress of this odd collection of characters intrigued him, as well. It was akin to visiting a United Nations conference, except the delegations had stepped out from different times and dimensions as opposed to different countries. If there was any similarity in the way these people accoutered themselves, it was in the noticeable abundance of shiny objects: rings, necklaces, bracelets, studs, buttons, hair extensions, even teeth, and eyelashes in a few cases. There must definitely be some social importance placed on the number of shiny silver objects they adorned themselves with, he thought to himself. In fact, in this crowd, Diana seemed rather understated in her glittering ensemble, a silver scarf draped over a black and silver gown topped off in a white, feathered hat.

Diana, where was she? He looked round the room, but there were far too many people to be able to see her. What had looked like three hundred people now felt more like a thousand filling the room. It was so odd. Diana's living room could probably, at best, fit two hundred packed in tightly. But, the sea of heads before him stretched far and wide, even though the apartment's dimensions seemed to be exactly the same as ever.

Turning to look out the window, he saw an extraordinary display of luxury cars lined up on the street and around the corner. There were Jaguars, Ferraris, Aston Martins, Lamborghinis, Bentleys, a Rolls-Royce and car models he couldn't even name.

One by one, they pulled up to the front walk, the doors would open up and the occupants, in their outlandish costumes, would stream out and make their way up the front walk to the Atlas building. All that was missing was a red carpet and paparazzi, he thought amusedly to himself.

Even he was dressed up in an otherworldly suit that Diana had given him, insisting he wear it that day. It resembled a three-piece suit, except the vest was as reflective as a mirror. The buttons were black and resembled large shark teeth. The lapels, lined with long black fur, were the smoothest things he had ever felt in his life. The rest of the suit jacket was white, the pants charcoal grey, and the shoes a shiny dark ruby red. He had wanted to wear his cat eyes glasses, but Diana nixed that, reminding him of the standing rule that he was to never wear them in her apartment.

Feeling odd, playing the wallflower, he decided to stroll through the crowds to get a better look at these "bidders" who had come from all over the universe to make bids on his planet.

He looked through the door to one of the open bedrooms and was amazed to see as many there as in her living room mingling and conversing.

As he entered and gently pushed through the little cliques that had developed, he realized that even though many of the guests wore outrageous costumes and were composed of a wide range of complexions, they were all, at least in appearance, human. This was a bit puzzling because hadn't all the conventional wisdom of the day theorized that different planets and ecosystems would produce different looking creatures? These musings faded away as he picked up on snippets of conversations.

"…this place is overrated…", "…there's no one like Apollo. I know he'll get this, somehow.", "…I don't know who she thinks she is! This property is more than she ever should have been allowed to handle.", "Spiders and cats! We really are on the edge of nothing out here. Why do we bother?"

Eventually, he came across a small circle of bidders that had an opening wide enough for him to slip in.

Sureptitiously he observed the group. One was a female wearing something akin to a singing cowboy outfit, replete with silver rhinestone flourishes. Another was a tall, slender, hairless man wearing what most closely resembling a kimono adorned with metallic horizontal strips.

The last two members of the circle were, to the eye, a dark-haired mustachioed pair of twins. Both wore shiny silver turbans on their heads and Orion learned from listening to the dialogue that they were called the Rex Brothers. The odd part was that, excepting their mustaches and turbans, their brownish complexion, delicate features, and curves made them look like young Asian women.

Some of the phrases were unintelligible to Orion, but he chalked that up to things being lost in translation. Who knew what these different people's languages were or where they were from? His ears perked up, though, when the female in the singing cowboy outfit began sharing her thoughts on lot #5jie6c.

"I mean, gorillas ate my coatimundi! That phosphorous content may not be much to talk about, but it could be offset by the vegetative matter that one could shave off the surface."

The bald-headed, kimonoed gentleman interjected.

"I don't know. The surface vegetative matter may once have been something to shoot a flare about, but, the local savages have downed so much of it, you'd probably have to get rid of them and wait a number of ribs for it to grow back. Then you'd get a knock in the second hand."

The Rex Brothers nodded in unison. The first one added in a voice frustratingly gender neutral, "Yes, and then when ye've sheared it, yuh can carve out the aluminum and silver."not met, no sale was made. The property would stay in the hands of the original owner or owners, and Diana, poor Diana, would lose out on her commission. After all the work and struggle, she would leave with her career in tatters.

The rhinestone lady nodded.

"No arguing, there's a massive amount of that."

She looked to the kimonoed man.

"So, what are you really after with this lot?"

The man had not appeared to be expecting the question. He rubbed his follicle-challenged cranium before answering.

"I… would drain the core, then mine the rest of the property's elements and sell.  That's what I always do."

Orion listened to this conversation with a deadening of his spirit. The callousness with which they discussed the destruction of his home was disheartening. What made it more unreal was that they were all so matter of fact about the destruction of a populated world.

There was a question he wanted to ask but hadn't because the answer was too terrifying to contemplate. With this blasé group their calm demeanor might make the answer palatable enough that he wouldn't lose it and start hitting people.

"Talking about the natives…"

All eyes turned on him.

"What will you do with them? If you win the bid?"

Some in the circle furled their eyebrows. Others smirked, assuming it to be a joke.

The rhinestone cowgirl responded.

"Sugartime, what does one normally do with infested property? The ones on this rock don't seem to be good for much."

The Rex Brothers nodded in agreement.

"Quite right," the kimonoed man nodded, "you know, I heard they still measure time with light here! Can you believe it?!"

Cowgirl shook her head in disbelief.

"Measuring time with light? Wow! That must mean they use light for everything. Communication, observation --"

"Observation? With light? Yeah, that would be great if you wanted to see what the Rhinos Belt looked like twenty thousand ribs ago!"

Amused chuckles followed. Orion, laughed, too, though he had no idea why this was funny.

The second Rex Brother's seemed lost in thought.

"Yuh, and what would getting around be like? Imagine if ye had to travel at light speed to get from place to place."

The first Rex Brother finished off. "Ye'd be dead and long gone before ye got anywhere interesting! That's for sure."

A series of bells chimed.

The members of the circle exchanged knowing looks as the chatter around the apartment died down.

"And now it begins," the kimonoed man intoned.

The cowgirl waved it off.

"Oh, we have a little time. Has anyone seen the big players?"

"You mean Boibemad and Apollo?"

"I know Boibemad's spot has been staked out."

She pointed to the far end of the room. Orion stepped out of the circle long enough to make out two large, orange construction cones in the corner where she was pointing to.

He stepped back. The cowgirl was still talking.

"He's not here, yet. But I'm sure he'll make his entrance and it'll be grand."

"Grander than Apollo's? Now there's a showman! Remember when he arrived to that bid on Sternus inside a meteorite?"

"Yuh," the second Rex brother jumped in. "There was only five minutes left before bids end and WHAM we all look up to see a meteorite coming down on us. We run out of the way, so frightened were we. After it smashes into the surface, we look out to see what's happened. That's when Apollo most dramatically steps out of the crater, from out of the smoke and fire, as if nothing had happened. Out he comes and just casually delivers the final bid. No more than a minute before bids end!"

"Apollo may have style," the kimono man asserted," but that won't do him any good today. Boibemad really wants this lot and he's willing to throw all he's got into it. Apollo doesn't stand a chance. I don't care who's backing him!"

Cowgirl gave him a playful slap on the arm.

"Oh, don't go counting Apollo out, yet. I hear he's been getting real cozy with the broker. Taking her on long trips in his ship. Pushing real, real hard to get her on his side."

There was some tittering amongst members of the circle. Not Orion, though. He clenched his jaw, repressing an urge to tell the cowgirl to put a sock in it.

The kimonoed man smiled wickedly.

"Then I guess the smart money's on Apollo. Women don't resist him. Not even if they want to! What's her name?"

"Diana, I hear she's a real --"

Orion couldn't take it anymore. He changed the subject.

"What do you think Apollo would do with the planet if he gets it?"

The cowgirl smirked and answered right away.

"What does Apollo always do with planets, Sugartime? He'll fix it up, wait a rib or two, and then resell it for 35% more than what he bought it for. That's always his way."

"He'll sell it…?"

There was a universal nodding of heads.

Orion hadn't thought of this.

"Why doesn't he just keep it?"

"Apollo doesn't want to really have to run something. He lives for the deal, the in and out. That's what he's famous for."

The kimonoed man nodded in agreement.

"That's what his backers expect of him. The Titans, they want their profits right away. They're not the kind to wait for the slow and steady returns. No, when Apollo jumped in the fire with them, he understood that he better give them stellar payoffs, or else."

"Or else what?" Orion asked.

The bells chimed again, this time louder.

The Rex Brothers immediately gave slight bows and scurried off through the door. The cowgirl and the bald man followed along with everyone else in the room. Orion followed, though he had no idea where any of them were going.

Reaching the door connecting the bedroom and the living room, he stopped dead in his tracks. Diana's living room was now filled with so many people the furthest were out of focus. How many he couldn't say exactly. There was just a sea of heads stretched before him disappearing into other rooms. Amazingly he only felt as crowded as he might in a packed party.

A low horn played one long note. By the time it ended, the wall and the ceilings of the apartment had vanished; turning into a clear, blue sky. Below his feet, Orion felt the ground turn from Diana's wooden floor to rock and sand. The thousands assembled looked a little less impressive now that they were in a large desert of some sort. Orion couldn't say which desert Diana's apartment had transformed into, but it looked like they were still on Earth.

Another series of notes sounded. As they played, Diana's console lifted off the ground, over the crowd.

Orion couldn't see past the people around him. He clambered up a small boulder. Once on top, he found himself looking over a sea of heads. There were five thousand, maybe ten thousand.

Orion's eyes anxiously scanned the crowd. What to do? That was the question Orion asked himself. He wasn't sure his plan would work. But, he sighed, it just had to.

From his vantage point, he caught sight of what was making the crowd grow louder. In the distance, a trail of dust kicked up by a small yellow object, a dot at first, came towards them at an impossibly fast pace. People in the crowd pointed to it.

A space in the crowd parted enough to reveal the cones Orion had seen before. He could see there were four cones, placed in a square about four feet apart. In the center was a simple metal folding chair. Orion recognized them as the un-illustrious furnishings from Boibemad's tent.

Soon, the yellow dot grew. Orion didn't believe what he was seeing. An enormous yellow dump truck, the size of a two-story house, flanked by two equally massive yellow bulldozers? They were moving unbelievably fast, like a rocket car trying to break the land speed record.

He looked down at the crowd below him going wild. Diana sat above them all, oblivious to anything but her console.

He looked back. The convoy was almost upon them. In the dump truck cab Boibemad peered through the steering wheel with a half-crazed look. His bodyguards, still wearing their yellow construction helmets drove the two flanking bulldozers.

The convoy rushed toward the crowd. It was going to run right through them. Boibemad was so crazy, Orion wondered, would he run everyone over?

He looked around for something, anything that might save the crowd. He thought to shout out to them. Warn them to jump out of the way. It was too late. The convoy careened straight into the mass of people.

Orion closed his eyes. He couldn't watch. He listened for the crash, for the screams and tearing flesh.

Silence.

He opened his eyes. The crowd was untouched. The collection of construction vehicles was parked directly in front of the crowd. Somehow, the convoy had gone from a super high velocity to a dead stop. He didn't know how it happened, but was grateful it had.

Boibemad was no longer in the cab of the oversized dump truck. He was in the basket of a cherry picker with an extra-long arm that extended over the heads of the crowd. He was too short to be seen, just tall enough that his tower of poofy hair poked out over the walls of the bucket. When the bucket was set on the ground, he unlatched the door, stepped out and took a seat on the folding chair. Since the throne of cones was sized for adults, his feet dangled a few inches above the ground.

The cherry picker bucket was lifted away. The sound of applause filled the crowd.

The clapping quieted when waves of black shadows moved across the crowd. High above them, birds with enormous wingspans circled overhead blocking the sun. As one, the assembly looked up, their field of hands pointed at the circling birds slowly descending toward the crowd, circling down until they were no more than fifty meters off the ground.

Orion marveled at the beauty and majesty of these flying creatures, with wingspans the length of a bus and deep chocolate brown feathers. When the bird nearest him tipped in his direction, he saw its rider, a woman, with long, auburn hair with white, flourescent tips, flowing behind her. Her costume, what little of it there was, was composed of silver breastplates, black bottoms and white knee-high boots. She looked into Orion's eyes as she flew past.

As bird and rider circled back, he cringed, seeing that this elegant raptor was in fact a hideous vulture. Its garish, orangish-pink head with pebbled drooping skin that framed ancient black eyes surveyed the crowd below.

Then, as quickly as they had descended, riders and birds rose again, flying upwards in perfect line formation. The crowd went wild. Orion looked at Diana. She was still at her controls ignoring the amazing show.

The winged creatures lifted high above the crowds, thirty of them, their line ascended like a long lingering serpent. Its head veering left and right; the body twisted and contorted to follow.

Finally, the lead vulture and rider turned a hard right leading the whole kettle to form a giant circle. From the crowd's vantage point, the fliers made a perfect swirling ring around the full moon, which, even though it was daylight, was fully visible over the desert landscape. The effect was stunning. It was as if the moon had a wreath encircling it.

Even Orion's jaw dropped at the sight. The next sight, though, put out of mind all that had come before.

As the riders' ring rotated around the moon, the darks spots of the moon's face, the craters and depressions shifted and merged together to form a giant letter "A".

The crowd went wild. They recognized the signature of one of the most famous names in the galaxy. The birds broke off from their ring formation and swooped back down toward the crowd.

Orion stared at the moon, his precious moon, disfigured now

with the mark of the man he despised. Suddenly, the white orb that hung over the sky burst in a million pieces. Like that, the moon was gone.

Horror shook Orion to the core.

The cheers of the crowd had become a constant roar as the vultures dived toward them. From out of the flock, a lone vulture swooped over the heads of the crowd a meter over their heads. The crowd was not frightened in the least.

When the bird flew low enough, Orion could see the rider on its back. It was the same rider he'd seen before. This time, she extended her arms, her hands opened, and iridescent white dust flowed through her fingers, filling the air and coating the intergalactic masses below. The giant bird she rode repeatedly circled the crowd; magically the sparkling dust continued to flow from her parted fingers. Soon, the air was full of the glimmering white powder. Moon dust, he realized.

Murmurs of excitement emanated from throughout the crowd. Through the glistening moon dust, the silhouettes of the vultures circling overhead could be seen. Their circling pattern broke formation and they flew off and out of sight. The air was still full of the shimmering moon dust gently falling. No, Orion realized, not falling -- coalescing.

He could see the dust particles floating, drifting to a place just northeast of Diana's raised stage, about ten meters above the ground.

All eyes in the crowd watched the magical dust form like a mirage in to an amorphous shape. Gradually, the shape took the form of a man, the form of Apollo.

The ghost Apollo hovered above the crowd that went ecstatic at the sight. The undead statue of Apollo was replete with a smug smile that rode the line between solidly self-assured and totally arrogant.

the ghost Apollo lowered gently to the ground.

The crowd parted to reveal a silver and gold throne, the back emblazoned with a silver "A".

The moon glow Apollo lowered onto the throne. Once seated, an outer layer of moon dust fell from its form revealing Apollo. He gave a nod to the crowd around him. They responded with shouts of approval.

A series of reverberated horn notes played and the crowd quieted down.

Orion looked across the sea of heads and saw Diana, for the first time, get up from her chair. Seeing her reminded him why they were all there, to bid on the Earth. It also reminded him that they were, in actuality, in Diana's apartment. He desperately hoped that was true and the moon was still where it should be and in one piece. Then his plan could still work.

Diana dramatically raised her arms high above her head and spoke in an amplified voice that could be heard across the desert plain.

"The bidding for Lot 5jie6c has now begun."

# CHAPTER XXVII
## The Show

The moment had arrived. After all the working, cajoling, conniving, begging, and sleepless nights, the moment Diana had wanted so desperately, was finally here. With a few simple words she had initiated a bid for a prestige property, a sale that would put her on the map. People, from all corners of the galaxy, the best in her field, were waiting in hushed silence for her to put the bidding in motion. She watched, exhilarated, proud, as the guests shuffled to their allotted stations for the bidding.

From the corner of her eye, she spotted Orion standing atop a boulder on the outskirts of the crowd. Even from a distance, his fair hair and broad shoulders called to her. She flashed him a smile, but he was undoubtedly too far away to see it. Her smile disappeared as she remembered asking him if he wanted to be by her side during the bidding. He had declined. This hurt, but she understood. It was all too much for him. Once it was over and she had taken him away from this place, he would soon forget all about it. She would make sure of it as she took him to amazing, awe-inspiring places across the universe, where she would show him what he is, what he could be.

That would come later. Now, the auction must begin. She moved swiftly to the console which was transforming itself into three large orbs covered with screens. As they raised around her, the desert sky and landscape faded back into the floors, walls, and ceilings of her apartment. The show was over, now it was time for business.

Once all the bidders had taken their designated stations, Diana moved to proceed to the next step, but saw Orion rise from the table he was sitting on at the far end of the room, and walk through the people towards her. He stopped at the edge of the raised platform and looked up to her with an inquisitive look.

She nodded and motioned him up. Once up, he gave a weak smile.

"Would you mind a little company?"

The broad smile that stretched across her face said everything. Inside, her heart warmed and tingled. She would have him at her side, sharing with him her finest moment.

A chair extended from the back of the console. She motioned for him to take a seat on it.

Then, with a push of a button, a black energy field encircled them and the console: a security measure to block all visual and sensory connections between her and the bidders. They were now totally isolated from the rest of the room.

Her console screens came to life and bids started coming in. Twelve parsas was the first bid. Fourteen was the next. These were followed by a flood of bids. The screens tracking the bids became a blur. Lines made of undulating peaks and valleys fluctuated increasingly.

Diana's eyes were locked onto the screens. A questionable bid was put in. In a split second, she analyzed then rejected it, determining its bidder would be unable to raise the funds. Another questionable bid popped up. She looked the status over and determined that this bidder had partnered up with three others. She allowed it and their previous individual bids were cleared. The price hit three thousand parsas. Shortly, it would meet the reserve. Four more bids came in quick succession. They came in without raising any red flags. Though, her concentration remained firmly on the task at hand, the prickly twinge of exhilaration could not be ignored. Another bid came in. Then another. Another. Then...nothing.

The cessation of the incoming bids left her feeling almost like someone whose last step left them with one foot hanging over empty space. Not understanding what the problem was, her eyes darted back and forth between the screens. Maybe there was a bad connection? She checked; they were okay. But then, she saw the cause on the index screen. The readings for lot #5jie6c, were fluctuating rapidly. The core temperature was rising up and down. How was this happening? As she watched, the temperature settled back down. There was little time to contemplate. Another reading went off the scale. The mantle, the tectonic plates began shifting. All of them! Could this be from the core instabilities? Whatever it was, the plates were indeed moving. Massive earthquakes were happening all over the planet. But she couldn't feel them.

She looked back at the bidders. They had stopped. Nothing was coming in. Nothing.

Helpless, she considered shutting down the index drill transmissions. That wouldn't work. No one would bid on a blind property, especially, after having witnessed the fluctuations. The clock, the bidding period was almost up. The reserve hadn't been met. The deal would fall through.

She looked back at the property readings. Volcanoes were erupting across the crust. Massive amounts of land were being engulfed in lava. The readings showed a planet ripping itself apart.

"What is happening?!" she shouted to anyone, no one. There were no bids coming in. Time was running out.

The closing bell signaled. The reserve was not met. She had failed. Tears welled up in her eyes. So close, she had come so close.

The black field around her descended.

From his seat, Orion watched the strongest, most amazing person he had ever known break down in tears.

With a heavy heart, he pocketed the pen-shaped tool.

Somehow, the denizens of Orion's neighborhood seemed as oblivious to the mass of oddly dressed people with their luxury cars departing the Atlas Building as they had been when the same set of visitors arrived.

Even sweet, simple Uri was out front, trimming the trees and shrubs as usual. Orion looked down on his landlord from his kitchen window. All that was missing from this picture was Stan in his car frustratedly honking the horn. The sense of normalcy in seeing the old man doing what he had always done, comforted Orion, who was filled with an uneasy sense of relief; the end of his world had been, at the very least, slightly delayed.

Less than three hours had passed since the bidding for the Earth had taken place, more accurately, the failed bidding. With the reserve not met, no sale was made. The property would stay in the hands of the original owner or owners, and Diana, poor Diana, would lose out on her commission. After all the work and struggle, she would leave with her career in tatters.

Orion's heart sunk at this thought. Only a short while ago, he, too, had been swept up in those wild and crazy dreams of hers. She was going to change the night sky and he was going to be right there beside her. No project too big, no challenge insurmountable. For him, every move she made was electricity; every word she spoke a nova. She could walk on water and being with her he could, too.

A knock at the door pulled him out of his meditations. His suspicion of who it was, was confirmed when he opened the door to reveal Diana with IO at her feet.

He waved her in.

"Come in. Have a seat."

Her stiff posture and clenched-jawed expression made it clear that she was not going to do that.

He walked to the kitchen counter.

"Would you like a drink? I think I still have some champ-."

"Did you use the key remote to change the readings during the bid?"

IO jumped up to the back of the couch, its glowing green eyes aimed squarely at Orion who returned Diana's stare.

"…Yes."

"What? Why?"

"I had no choice. I couldn't see the Earth, my home sold, ripped apart."

Her eyes, still red from crying and fatigue, hardened.

He struggled for words.

"What did you expect me to do? Just let those people destroy my planet?! This is my home. These are my people. This is everything I've ever known. Everything I've ever loved...except for you."

Her hate-filled eyes glared at him. Before he knew it, the feline's eyes shot out lasers at him, pushing him violently, forcing him against the wall several feet above the ground. The air was punched from his lungs. His back pressed to the wall, he squirmed and fought to break free. He couldn't breathe. He was suffocating. The pressure on his chest was relentless. Without air, he was blacking out.

Then, just as suddenly, the lasers stopped and he fell to the floor. He lay there for a moment, clutching his chest, trying to regain his breath, feeling his ribs to see if any had been broken.

When he lifted his head, he found both Diana and IO had gone.

# CHAPTER XXVIII
## The Last of a Kind

The slow whirring sound of the Parcae Model 6 computer console filled Diana's apartment as it collated and deleted data in the final process of completely shutting down. Diana tried to block out the noise of the machine for it was too melancholy to bear, too much like the moans of a dying animal.

With the end of her business, she would have to turn in the console and surrender her license. What remained of her finances wouldn't get her very far. At best, she had enough for a one-way ticket home. Home, she sighed; she had struggled so long to get as far away as possible from there.

One of the orbs on the console was displaying a celestial map. Wistfully, she reached out to the star charts and waved her hand through them. Not so long ago, she felt that anything was possible, that she was destined to re-map the heavens. Stars were her playthings and she was master of all she surveyed. No one would care or remember where she came from, they would only marvel at

302302 Ian Adrian

what she had become.

But now she knew better. She would never be more than the little girl from the planet that no one had ever heard of. Apollo had shown he was the master of the game. The rules were his to make and break. He was to be her mentor, but in the end, he had shown her how to play the game to the end. If he couldn't have the Earth, then no one could.

A message came up on the console. Reflexively, she moved to see what it was.

It was labeled with the stamp of Apollo. A mix of emotions churned inside of her as she pulled the message up by twirling an index finger.

What she read made her stomach tighten. Apollo was offering to buy the Earth, despite its structural infirmities, for one eighth less than the reserve price.

The conceit of it all left Diana befuddled. What was he up to? Selling at less than the reserve price without going through the bidding process? She could never do that. He knew that, of course. Whatever the reason, she decided that she had to forward the offer.

She extended her left hand, fingers splayed, and twisted her wrist ever so slightly. With this action, the offer was relayed to the owner. She would wait for a response.

It didn't take long. The reply message, though, was not what she expected.

Just as Diana was about to leave the apartment, another incoming message came in. It was not from Apollo, but from Hephaestus, the purchaser of lot #4o83q. There was an emergency and Diana was needed at the Tran Asteroid Belt immediately.

She pondered the message. As her job was done, she did not have to go. But, despite everything, she was still the broker who had overseen the deal.

The transportation sent for her rolled up to the front of the building and she made her way down.

Before stepping into the silver-toned sports car she looked back to the Atlas Building, half hoping she might catch a glimpse of Orion. She hadn't seen him since their confrontation a week ago. But the window was blank.

She knew something would eventually have to be done about him, but her emotional state wouldn't allow her to think about it now. Everything in her life had crumbled apart.

The ride was a little bumpy. She realized she had become a little too accustomed to Apollo's ultra-luxurious mode of transport these past few months. Anything else was a letdown.

She surmised the transport must be pushing itself to the limit to get her there as fast as possible and it wasn't long before, through the windshield of the sports car, she could see the volcanic rock surface of the asteroid appear. She had arrived at lot #4o83q, otherwise known as the Tran Asteroid Belt.

Due to the low priority she placed on it, she had never actually visited the asteroid belt, only virtually visiting it through the simulation of the index drill readings. The drill had been inserted not here, but in the belt's most central asteroid.

Looking around, she found the view quite different than the one depicted in the index simulation. The size of this particular asteroid varied from the drill insert site. Judging by the horizon line, it must be the size of a small moon.

The history of the asteroid belt came back to her. A large asteroid had hit a planet, breaking it up. This began a cataclysmic chain of events as the orbital paths of other planets in the solar system were thrown off and several of them collided. The end result was the creation of this asteroid belt.

Seeing no one to greet her, she went ahead and put on the outfit provided to protect her from the environment. Stepping onto the rock surface she spotted in the distance a small, one story white structure, about two hundred meters wide. Why had the transport vehicle let her off so far from her destination?

Her question was answered when she saw the mighty orbiting Skylar ships hovering a few kilometers over the asteroid's surface. The vessels, which looked like enormous metal balls with their bottom halves cut off, were used for the immolation of celestial bodies.

The massive, oblong Skylar ships hovered ominously a few kilometers over the surface. The hazy effect between the ships and the ground below indicated that the dynafield was on.

The Skylar ships used the dynafield to deconstruct the planet's core, triggering the target's core to collapse in on itself. A second Skylar ship would be required to contain the implosion. Diana knew that the presence of two of these giant machines meant that the rock she was standing on would be completely destroyed.

Only the first Skylar ship's dynafield was active. This meant it was in the process of extracting a valuable element. To do this, the dynafield penetrated the crust of a celestial body, usually to the outer edge of the mantle. The energy was calibrated to specifically break down to the subatomic level the desired element in the field's range.

Once broken down, the targeted element was extracted from the crust into the Skylar ship. As the element slipped through the matter that made up the crust, an energy bubble was left in place of the extracted mineral to prevent collapse.

After an extended walk, Diana became fatigued. Her supplied suit provided protection, but was heavy and awkward. Reaching the modest white building, she still had not seen a living soul; the energy door identified her and slid open.

The interior was comprised of two cavernous rooms both relatively empty. Some small machinery lined the wall in one room and two miniature, block-shaped hover vehicles occupied the other. Overhead, the glorious night sky sparkled through the transparent ceilings.

At the far end of the second room was Hephaestus, his face and towering body covered in a long robe. He was energetically talking with two white suited geo-deconstructors. He saw Diana enter and motioned her to come over.

He waved off the engineers and removed his veil, revealing his scar torn face.

"Diana. Hello. Isn't this beautiful?!"

She forced a smile, tried not to cringe at the sight of his face.

"I guess."

"No, not my face," he laughed heartily. "I remove my veil because you have already seen how I am and to show respect as you have traveled all this way to aid me. What I meant is how beautiful it all is?"

He waved to the giant Skylar ships that could be seen through the ceiling.

"In less than a day, all the precious elements from this rock have been extracted. We are ready to move to the final step; immolation."

Diana nodded.

"Sounds good. Your message. It indicated there was an emergency."

Hephaestus pointed again to the sky.

"It's the neighboring planets. My engineers tell me that the immolation might destabilize the asteroid field too much, altering the balance of the solar system it surrounds. With the volatile history of this system…"

"You need to know your coverage."

"Exactly."

Hephaestus gave a coy smile.

Diana pulled a small, pen shaped computer out of her pocket.

"Here are the agreements drawn up with the owners of the other planets. Any damage must be compensated for at an amount of no more than ten thousand parsas per celestial body."

"Sweet star shine! That's all I needed to hear."

The cheery disposition of the man before her was in such contrast with the monster like personality she had dealt with before, that it had Diana's mind spinning.

"Why did you need me here in person?"

Hephaestus gave a coy smile which stretched the sides of his face, elongating several of the larger scars, one of which seemed to be seeping.

"If it had turned that there was no liability protection, I didn't want our neighbors to know. They listen in on our transmissions here." He added, "And it made for a nice excuse to meet up with you, again."

He raised a mischievous eyebrow and looked her up and down.

Diana quickly changed the subject.

"Let me go over this with your engineers," she said stepping away as quickly as she could without being obvious. "Make sure they're okay with this."

She found the two geo-deconstruction engineers huddled together in the next room, a shorter than average male and a stout red-haired female. They were your typical deconstructionists, wanting to make sure every "i" was dotted and "t" crossed before they began. Considering the finality of their job, their attitude was understandable.

At the end of their business, the male engineer extended his arm to Diana.

"Thank you."

She took it by the wrist.

"No, thank you."

She was about to leave the pair, when a question popped into Diana's head.

"Do you think you will be able to deconstruct this planetoid safely?"

The female engineer bristled at this. Straightening, she pushed her red hair back defiantly.

"Of course!"

The male signalled his colleague to relax.

"Yes, with the Skylar ships there should be no problem. Now, in the old days, it was all so less precise."

"How did they do immolations back then?"

The female engineer shouted the response.

"With chemicals, of course!"

Diana put her hand to her chin, suddenly remembering.

"Oh, yes! You introduce chemicals that react with elements of the structure to be de-constructed."

The two engineers nodded.

The insides of Diana's mind became electric as a flurry of thoughts and ideas hit her all leading to one, unmistakable realization.

"Would it be possible," She addressed both of them. "To use the chemical process to implode an asteroid without it being detectable afterwards?"

The female responded almost before she had finished.

"Of course!"

"How would you do that?"

"Oh, well, first you would find what the asteroid's made of and-"

The male engineer grabbed his co-worker's arm to stop her. He started pulling her away.

"I'm sorry, we don't have time, right now. Things to do."

The female looked miffed at being interrupted but relented, allowing herself to be pulled away.

A low booming laughter caught Diana's attention. It was Hephaestus in the other room. His spirits were so high, she thought, because, in the end, he had gotten everything he wanted. The property for a steal.

It was time to depart the white structure, she decided and walk back to the parked silver sports car. As she did, the enormous white Skylar ships overhead parted, each one moving to take their place around the asteroid.

Never having seen this process before, she could not help observing the dynafields increase in intensity until even the ground below her feet began to shake.

Less than a hundred meters from where she was standing, a small fissure opened as the ground was coming apart. What looked like gas rising out of fissure spewed out. But then it shifted in a purposeful direction towards the nearest dynafield and then turned and began moving straight towards Diana.

As it neared, she realized the mass was a swarm of insects approaching her at extreme velocity. There wasn't time to get into the car. Instinctively she raised her hands as the swarm flew towards her.

At the moment of impact she closed her eyes. The wind from the tens of thousands of insects flying past pressed against the protective suit she wore.

Opening her eyes she turned to the see the swarm flying off and disappearing into another newly formed fissure.

From out of the roof of the white structure, one of the mini-hover vehicles rose up and flew towards her. The tiny ship landed about forty meters away from where she stood.

A door lifted open and the two geo-deconstruction engineers emerged and walked to a pre-identified point, inserting an electronic pointer into the ground, an indicator for the ships above, a marker of the insert point for the dynafield process.

The Skylar ship moved toward them. As it neared, it began to emit a bright white light. It wasn't long before the landscape turned bright as day. Through squinted eyes, Diana could see the female geo-deconstructionist running towards her.

"You have to go!" the woman shouted over the roar of the ship above them.

"What?" Diana put her hand to her ear.

"The immolation. We're about to strip the atmosphere off! You can't be out here."

Diana nodded and made her way back to the transport that had brought her here.

She turned to take one last look. The engineers, too, were returning to their small craft to escape before the surface atmosphere was burned off.

Before she could enter her transport Diana spotted an insect on her arm. It wasn't huge, just large enough to startle her.

Instinctively she started to swat it but, looking at it, stopped realizing this had been one of the creatures in the swarm. As it crawled down her arm, she watched it, transfixed by the little legs and antennae. So, there was life on this asteroid. This rock, the size of a moon really, would be large enough to support life and had originally been part of a planet. This little bug and its kind had survived their planet being torn apart. Astounding!

She gazed at the tiny creature, its dark violet skin speckled with white spots. It had wings, a throwback to when it lived in an environment with trees and foliage.

Still on her arm, it crawled erratically, cautiously towards her hand then paused. Diana was mesmerized by this little creature; amazed, because it had dawned on her that this was a real, living organism. Its species had survived the impossible. Now this little organism would be eliminated with the rest of its kind.

# CHAPTER XXIX
## Closing the Deal

The sun came up that morning as it had every day for the last four billion years. Orion's eyes were already open, savoring the morning light as any day might be the last.

Out of bed, he fixed his breakfast, more out of habit than for any sense of hunger or need. Thirty minutes later, Stan arrived. Twenty-two minutes later he was sitting at his desk, staring at a computer screen spreadsheet; rows and columns of numbers, now as meaningless as the tasks and duties being acted out by everyone in the office, in every office, everywhere.

Hours passed steadily until it was five o'clock. On the drive home, Stan tried to strike up a conversation with him a few times, but each attempt fell flat.

Getting out of the car, Orion mechanically thanked his friend before walking up the front path to the Atlas Building. The sun was beginning to set. Seeing it, he took a seat on the front porch and watched it until the orange mass dipped below the horizon and the sky turned dark.

In his kitchen, he prepared dinner, again, more out of habit, than necessity.

Through the front window, he saw Apollo's Bentley pull up. Orion clutched his stomach and shook his head, smiling sardonically. Lest he be allowed to forget the peril the Earth was in, something like this was here to remind him.

A knock came at the door. He answered it. It was Diana.

Seeing her was like a knife in the heart. Somehow, miraculously, he had been able to push her out of his mind. Not permanently, but for short stretches of time. With her standing before him, the stress of everything was too much.

Realizing IO was at her feet, he instinctively backed up.

Diana's eyebrows lowered, seeing the dismal state he was in: blonde hair greasy from being unwashed, clothes disheveled. She wanted to tell him so many things but ended up telling him what she had come to say:

"I'm going to sell the Earth. The owner has graciously allowed me another chance."

She watched his eyes turn downward.

"It's out of my hands. I'm sorry. If it wasn't me, then it would be someone else doing it. The owner's going to sell no matter what. I'm just doing my job."

He turned his back to her.

The farther he moved from her, the faster her heart raced, the more she wanted to touch him, hold him, hear him say something. "I know this doesn't seem right to you because living on this planet is all you know. But, this is how the universe works. People buy and sell property. Then they develop it. This is how economies work.

How civilizations rise and fall. This is life."

Orion's face burned as hot as his feelings.

"This is how it works, huh?" he repeated. "You'll just take this planet, sell it, and tear it apart. What about the people who live here?! What are we supposed to do? You wipe us out? Lock us up somewhere? I don't want to die."

"But, you won't die. You're not…"

She took a step towards him. He pulled further away until she ceased attempting to come nearer.

A glint came to her eye and her head cocked slightly. Slowly, she pulled out a pen shaped object and held it before her.

"Your glasses." She pointed to the cat's eyes glasses he was wearing.

He didn't understand, just stood motionless.

She extended the silver and black pen shaped object.

"What do you see?"

His jaw was still clenched in anger.

"Look, I don't want to play games."

"What do you see?" she spoke calmly, firmly.

"Your key remote."

"Anything else?"

He said nothing. She answered for him.

"No, you don't. Now, take the glasses off."

He resisted the order. She repeated it.

"Take the glasses off; then tell me what you see."

Reluctantly, he complied. To his astonishment, he saw an energy orb projected from the end of the key remote. It fluctuated from pale red to green, a half foot in diameter. He replaced the glasses and the orb disappeared.

Diana nodded.

"For as long as you can remember; you've never fit in. When you were in a crowd, the voices came together too much. More often than not, you just kept from talking because you didn't really know what was being said, just caught bits and pieces. It was always hard to see things like television and computer screens. Digital watches were doable, but cell phones, with their screens full of mish-mosh, were all but worthless. You never were like the others."

He wanted to refute her, but couldn't. Everything she was said was true. Every word she said hit him like punch in the gut.

"You never knew why, never fully realized how you perceived things differently from others. Never realized that while they could only see six colors of the spectrum, you could see eight. What they saw, you could see and then some. What's more, your eyes interpreted the colors differently, more efficiently. Your ears could pick up both higher and lower frequencies than theirs. Your senses never fit on this planet. It's as if they were developed on a different planet. Well, they were."

She let the last line sink in. The strength in Orion's legs had given out. It was hard to process all she was saying. He leaned back against the side of the sofa.

"I don't...understand."

A hint of frustration came through her voice.

"That's why I gave you the glasses. To force you to see. The glasses don't improve your vision, they handicap it, filtering out everything that a native wouldn't see. I gave them to you to let you see like they do. I thought that once you realized how limited their world is, you'd finally accept who you really are."

"Who I really am?"

"Yes, Orion. You who share a name with a constellation, a nebulae, a gravity hole and a galaxy. Deep inside, you have always known you weren't of this planet. You could never fully connect with the people here, so you struggled through life, doing just enough to keep going, but really having nowhere to go. You had no drive because there was nothing to obtain. One day you saw something you'd never seen before. One of your own kind."

"You."

She nodded, smiling tenderly.

He inhaled deeply. He had been so caught up in the moment he had forgotten to breathe. Suddenly, a life full of hidden anxieties, differences and problems he could share with no one, rose up, unable to be suppressed. Finally, he could speak freely, sharing it with someone who understood.

He looked straight into her eyes. "Seeing you was like someone had turned the lights on. I was seeing myself for the first time. My entire childhood, I had waited for my parents to tell me I was adopted. It seemed so obvious, but the moment never came. You are right; I just went through the motions, doing what I was told, because I didn't really know what I was supposed to do. That all changed when I saw you that night."

"I spotted you, too, standing by the car with that odd native friend of yours who drives you to work in his ridiculous four-wheeled contraption. How could I miss you? One of my own; I had no idea who you were or what you were doing here. And Apollo, of course, seeing the two of us must have been like-."

"I didn't notice him at all. Not with you in my sights."

Her eyes darted down as she blushed.

"Then you came to my apartment to fix some doodad or the other.

I guessed you were up to something, possibly a spy for one of the bidders, so I went with you for that dinner."

Orion smiled, remembering the dinner.

"What changed your mind?"

"It turned out you couldn't be some bidder's spy. You were too genuine and so ill-prepared to gain my attention. And you made me laugh, really, really laugh. It had been so long. I think I had almost forgotten how."

"I loved making you laugh. Seeing you smile makes me the happiest man in the universe."

"But, then, after the night you fell out of my apartment--."

"When I sat on your console and IO tried to kill me?"

"Yes," she laughed a little. "I realized you didn't know where I was from. Didn't know what you were. With the sale of the Earth, the surface, at the very least, would be stripped off. You would have to leave. But you knew nothing about life outside Earth. So, I decided to prepare you."

"That's what all the lessons were about?!"

She nodded.

"You had to be acclimated as quickly as possible. I couldn't just come out and tell you everything. Who could handle that? Finding out your life is a lie. What that would be like, I could barely imagine. It pained me that I would have to be the one to tell you."

She reached out the delicate tips of her fingers brushing his cheek.

"But, it was wonderful. Showing you everything, watching your eyes light up each time you witnessed something new and spectacular. Through your eyes, I was seeing everything for the first time. I was giving you a new life."

"At the price of my old one."

She saw the anger returning to his eyes.

"It's out of my hands. The owner is going to sell. If it's not me, then it'll be someone else."

Taking a step back to the door, she put her hand on the knob.

Orion caught her glancing at the window. He turned round to see Apollo's chariot waiting.

He stood up.

"Him?! What is he doing out there?! Is he the new buyer?"

Diana didn't respond. She opened the door to leave.

Orion moved to grab her, but IO sprang in-between them, its eyes turned fiery green.

"IO, wait!" she commanded.

"Diana, don't!"

"Good-bye."

She closed the door behind her, IO following her out at the last second.

At the close of the door, Orion's mind sprang to life. The console, he thought. If he could get to the console, there might be a chance.

He grabbed the doorknob and yanked. It was locked. He turned the lock handle, but the door still wouldn't budge. Diana, he realized. She must have sealed the door shut.

He rushed over to the window in time to see Apollo's Bentley pulling away. He pulled on the window. It didn't budge either. He looked and it wasn't locked. Had she sealed everything in the room?

Grabbing the coatrack by the door, he ran over and rammed it against the windowpane. Instead of smashing the glass, the result was the splintering of the coatrack.

He grabbed a hammer from under the sink, banged it against the glass. No effect. Another thought came. He stepped up to a spot on the drywall that he knew was hollow and slammed the hammer into it as hard as he could. The hammer's head snapped off, bouncing off the wall almost hitting his face.

Throwing down the hammer handle, he examined the spot he had struck and found not the slightest sign of damage. Everything was protected. She had sealed him in completely.

Apollo was unusually gregarious as he handed his favorite smoky concoction to Diana. His vehicle had an almost unlimited supply of beverages, a point in which he took great pride.

"A toast to a beautiful deal and an infinite future, my lovely."

They clinked their glasses together, Apollo noticeably the more enthusiastic of the two.

"I'm so glad the owner has agreed to my buying the property."

"Agreed to hear your offer for the property, you mean?" Diana corrected. "You didn't even meet the reserve. Why should the owner sell below the reserve?"

"The owner doesn't have a choice. No one else will touch lot #5jie6c, now."

She opened her mouth to speak but he quickly added, "Worry not, Diana. I'm just having fun with you. So, who is the seller, anyway? You can tell me now, right?"

"Someone wishing to remain anonymous. Why do you ask? Want to go around me, again?"

A smirk crossed his face.

"Not now, at least. My offer is the reserve price. But, that's my final offer."

Diana pursed her lips. She couldn't keep her feelings in, anymore.

"So, now you offer exactly the reserve price? I see. I guess this was how your plan was designed to work."

He put his hand on his chest feigning shock.

"Plan? Why, whatever do you mean?"

"Your elaborate scheme to acquire lot #5jie6c."

His eyebrows rose and mouth fell open as if shocked by what he was hearing, and waited for what she would say next.

"First you, the great Apollo, came to be my mentor and helped me sell the first property. Convinced, no doubt, that in your presence long enough, I would fall madly in love with you and give up 5jie6c voluntarily."

"It was worth a try, yes."

"When that didn't work you offered to buy lot #4o83q if I threw in #5jie6c at the reserve price, a fraction of its real worth."

"To help you."

"To help me? By then destroying q6, the only asteroid with any real value. No doubt you introduced ckatelim into the ilithium deposits. The massively excited ilithium particles tore the planetoid apart. That's what was happening when we arrived. That is why ilithium was spraying out of the surface. You being there with me was a nice touch. It let me believe that we were both in peril as we made the dash for the your transport. But, you were prepared for such an event. Why else would you have lumi-spectacles on you? You knew when and how q6 would rip itself apart? You choreographed and timed our visit perfectly."

Apollo opened his mouth to answer but Diana kept speaking.

"You planned it so well, but then I found Hephaestus, a super rich industrialist who could salvage the deal."

"And when he decieved you, I intervened to save you."

"You intervened because you believed I would be so indebted to you that I would fix the 5jie6c bid in your favor. But, I didn't because I put the client first."

Her eyes grew fiery.

"And that leaves your final manipulation."

"Which was?"

"The diabolical way you convinced Orion, an innocent, unaware of the ways of the world, into sabotaging the deal."

"Why would I go to so much trouble. I could just outbid the others."

"Yes, except for Boibemad."

Apollo's hands tightened into fists at the name. He took a deep breath.

"Yes, that was quite a bind you put me in. Bringing in my most hated opponent, the only one who could outbid me for that piece of rock. I thought I had everything set. I could acquire this asset and use it-."

"To settle the financial mess you're in with the Titans?"

"You know about that?"

"I researched all the prospective bidders, Apollo, including and especially my 'mentor'. I was able to ascertain that your amazing Lathius 9 deal fell through. But, not before you had overextended yourself and found yourself deeply indebted to the Titans."

"It's nothing I can't handle."

"No, you handled it, alright. You convinced Orion to sabotage the bidding."

"He didn't need much convincing."

"Thus plunging the Earth's value and ridding yourself of rival bidders. With the competition cleared away, you could swoop in with any offer because you knew the owner couldn't sell it for scrap. Once you'd acquired the Earth, you could resell it and clear yourself with the Titans. Then you, the great and mighty Apollo, would once again demonstrate why you are the master of the game. You got exactly what you wanted. We were the game pieces and you played us perfectly."

"You sound upset."

"I am mad... at myself for not seeing it coming. Now, you'll get the property at a steal and I will have failed my client."

She turned away from him. She just couldn't bear to see his smug face. But, she heard nothing. An extended silence ensued. Still, she could not bear to look back at him.

"You are right," he finally said, voice softening. "The Lathius 9 deal fell through a while ago."

"Even before you took me there to show it off?"

"Yes... I had been misinformed on certain details and my partners, at the slightest hint of trouble ran off, leaving me to turn the wheel. I was in it up to my neck, gasping for air. Well, when one deal collapsed, it pulled the foundation out from under the others. I had to act fast, you must understand that, salvage what I could. I was going to lose it all. I had never been in a spot like that."

She turned round to see a much different Apollo. His face contorted, shoulders hunched forward, not so tall and proud as usual. The look of a person not quite contrite, but at the very least, being forced to look at himself as he actually was.

His voice cracked just slightly with each word.

"But, I had taken a calculated risk. If Lathius 9 had worked, I would have, would have been…"

"A Titan." She finished for him.

He nodded.

"Yes."

The slowly emerging specks of light from outside the tinted windows were the only indication that they had reached their destination.

Slowing, imperceptibly, the Bentley stopped, its doors opened and the two stepped out right in front of the silver and ebony skyscraper that was Apollo's lair.

He looked at his own building, his eyes shot straight to the top, to the skyscraper's dazzling crown covered by brilliant gold suns on each side. He could hear them up there. The Titans.

Diana could hear the same fleeting wisps and traces of conversation, laughter, and music that she had heard the last time they stood outside Apollo's dark, marble citadel.

She looked across the car roof at him and was struck with the feeling that she was seeing the grand and mighty Apollo for the first time. Despite his business dealings with them, he was still entranced by those people at the top. He would give anything to be with them. But, she could tell that the sounds of their chatter and singing were as incomprehensible to him as to her. Though, he strained to make out what they were saying up there, he couldn't. Apparently, no matter how many stars, planets and nebulae he bought and sold, no matter how insanely successful he became, in the end he was still a small, little boy standing on the outside, looking in.

As she observed him, she reached into her handbag for her remote key on which the paperwork for lot #5jie6c was stored, but came across a slip of paper that she had put in there a long time ago. Glancing at it, she immediately recognized what it was. The picture of a mountain landscape on the front, the name of the organization written just below, it was the flyer Orion had left at her place.

Her first thought was to put it back in her pocket, but curious, she started reading it.

Apollo finally broke his gaze away from the building and turned to her.

"You know, there is one part of my plan you didn't mention. I spoiled the bid to solve the problem you instigated by bringing in Boibemad. But, then I came back and offered the reserve price even though I know I can get the property for much less. Why?"

She thought a second.

"For me?"

He nodded. "I wasn't going to let you lose your deal of a lifetime."

She crooked an eyebrow. "That was really part of your plan?"

"That was the whole plan.  We both needed to win."

"Because?"

He smiled as he made his way around to her side of the car, "A victory's no fun if you don't have anyone to share it with."

His hands gripped her arms, his eyes looked into hers.

"This can be our beginning. Together, we can possess all we see. We'll rewrite the stars and when we look out in the night sky, know there's nothing out there we can't possess. If we so decide, we can snuff out one star and place a new one somewhere else."

"All that?"

He pointed up to the skyscraper's crown high above. "With the power of the Titans all that is possible and more."

"But, you're not a Titan."

"Those fools up there. They're really not that smart, just only children, really, who've been given too much power. We can twist and bend them to do whatever we like. Eventually we'll be one of them. We'll have infinity. We'll have forever."

As he spoke he had kept his hands firmly locked on her arms, his face pushing ever closer to hers. His power still held an intoxicating effect on her. She needed to get distance.

She pulled back a little.

"First things first.  Lot #5jie6c. That's what we came to talk about, right?"

He remembered himself and released her.

With head bowed he extended his hand to lead her through those black revolving doors that slowly and continuously spun.

She did not take his hand.

"And lot #5jie6c?  What will you do with it?"

"Whatever is required. Its newly gained reputation as an extremely volatile planet excludes it from being made a resort. I can't sell it whole because I wouldn't get anything for it, now. That leaves extraction and immolation. The materials and energies will be more than enough to restore my financial situation."

"There's no way to keep it intact?"

"No, of course not. Why does it matter?"

She didn't respond.

He looked to the building. The ever-spinning revolving doors beckoned them to enter. He stepped next to her and put his hand on the small of her back. He gave a slight push.

"Shall we go in?"

Sensing her resistance, he pointed up to the top of the building.

The two story towers at the top, filled with swirling lights and music that could be heard even from so far down below.

"They await you. I've told them all about you. You will meet them, the ones who control all. The powerbrokers, the dream makers, all that is bought and sold in the universe, they have a hand in it. Come, join them."

He took her hand and started to pull her towards the spinning doors.

"Join us. Where you belong."

She hesitated once more, standing firm. The music rose slightly from above. She lifted her eyes from his gaze to the towers at the top of the building.

Feeling her resistance fade, he pulled her through the revolving doors and into his abode.

# CHAPTER XXX
## The Man Who Sold the World

As Diana knocked on Orion's door she had no idea if it would be answered. Ten seconds of silence passed, she knocked again. The sound of footsteps came to the door then it opened.

When he answered, she almost gasped at how beaten down he looked: his brow permanently furrowed, sallow complexion, and eyes with heavy bags underneath them. It was so distressing that she just had to tell him the news.

"Lot #5jie6c, I mean, the Earth, has been sold."

His head sunk even lower than it had before as if she had struck him with a bat.

She reached out and took his arm.

"The buyer was the Sierra Club, a land preservation group. You know of them, right?"

At first he didn't hear what she was saying, just felt her hand touching his arm, giving a gentle squeeze. But then the meaning seeped in.

"I don't get it." His eyes searched her face. "You sold it...to the Sierra Club?"

He looked confused. She smiled.

"Yes, though I don't think they quite realize what they own. The owner and I talked it over. We agreed they would be excellent purchasers."

Orion was still running this new information through his mind. "You've sold the Earth to the Sierra Club... The Sierra Club? The environmental organization?"

She nodded. "They are the owners now. I got the idea from that scrap of paper you brought home that day. They were seeking funds to make land preservation trusts. So, why not let them make the whole planet a land trust? I contacted them, had them sign on and we extracted all the ammonium acetate from the lands they currently owned as their payment. They don't really know what they got from the deal, but it doesn't matter. The Earth is theirs now. As I was saying, the owner is fine with this. He was only selling the planet because he's lonely and ready to move on."

She studied his face but couldn't make out what he was thinking. She nodded.

"It was Apollo's doing."

Orion looked even more incredulous. She continued:

"He believed that rules weren't meant for him. So, when he broke them, I was free to start a new game with my own rules."

She studied Orion's dazed expression.

"Was this, okay?" she asked.

Giving his head a rapid shake to try and take it all in, he smiled.

"Yes, that's more than okay."

He opened the door wider to let her in.

"Wanna drink?"

She nodded, entering a bit trepidatious, and took the drink.

He motioned to the couch.

"It's new. Everything's new."

She eyed it leeringly.

"That's okay, I'll stand."

He lifted up his glass. "To lot #5jie6c."

She pushed her glass against his but was distressed, seeing tears form in his eyes. He lowered his glass, his face reddening, body convulsing. He turned his back to her, but she could hear his quiet sobs.

A puzzled expression came over her face. Laying her hand on his shoulder, she stepped around to the front of him, saw the tears in his eyes. He turned his face away again, but she grabbed hold of him and wrapped her arms around him.

"What's the matter?" she asked.

Still sobbing, he struggled to speak. Finally, he managed.

"Thank…you."

She pulled back enough to study his face. She could see it, now. His tears were not sad. They were of immense joy and relief. This planet really had meant so much to him. Seeing him like this, she could feel tears coming to her eyes, as well.

The two of them embraced for the next few minutes, alternately crying and wiping tears away from the others eyes.

When the tears ran out, they kissed and let go of each other.

In an almost trembling state, Diana looked for a place to sit and seeing nothing but the couch, conceded by sitting on the arm. "You know, now that this planet will stay the same, you can stay here."

Orion was wiping his face with a paper towel.

"I can? I hadn't thought about it."

"There's no owner who would like to eject you. You're free to live here for the rest of your life."

He contemplated this. She rose from the couch.

"Or, if you'd like. You could come with me."

She saw his eyes widen.

"There's a whole universe that you've never seen out there. I know you'll love it... if you're willing to give it a chance."

She stepped up and kissed him.

"Will you come with me?"

He pondered this as she gave him another kiss.

"I..."

She kissed him again.

He took her in his arms, pulled her close.

"Well, maybe."

"Maybe?!" she cried.

He kissed her this time, long and hard. Picked her up and twirled her around.

"Bees and butterflies!"


Diana, her small bag in hand, listened amusedly, to the loud banging of luggage down the lobby steps. Orion had insisted on taking his personal effects with them. She still didn't understand his attachment and sentimentality towards such small physical things. There wouldn't be much use for them out there. At least he wasn't bringing his furniture!

She had wisely not lent him one of her bags that would have easily fit the contents of his whole apartment in it. No, let him use his own suitcases. That way he was limited to bringing only what he could physically carry. When he saw the world beyond, he'd understand.

As she held the front door open for him, she was chagrined to watch him successively drag out three large suitcases.

"No, no. That's okay. I can…get it." he quipped.

She shook her head.

Along with the small purse that comprised her luggage, he noticed a glass case in her hand. Inside it was a little alien-looking winged bug, dark violet with white, perfectly square eyes, crawling around on a small volcanic rock.

"What's that?" he asked.

"Just something I picked up. The last of its kind."

She held it up so he could see the bug she had brought back from lot #4o83q. Sensing too many eyes on it, the bug flapped its wings and scurried to the underside of the rock.

"We have to drop this little creature off at an animal park." She continued, "They'll be able to get it to reproduce. In a couple of RIBs, there will be hundreds of them again."

"I don't understand."

She eyed the glass case.

"I don't think I quite do either."

The honking of a car drew their attention. It was Stan pulling up in his Honda.

Orion waited as his friend got out and ran over to them before chiding him.

"Oh my gosh, Stan! You're just getting here!? You almost missed us!"

Stan caught his breath.

"Oh, man, I'm so sorry. Lorraine needed help moving her dresser in to my place and…" He caught the smirk on Orion's face, gave his friend a punch in the arm.

"Oh, yeah, look who I'm apologizing to about being late."

Stan saw the giant suitcases at Orion's side.

"Need help with that?"

Orion pointed to the front porch. "There's another back there."

Stan moved to get it. Orion stacked the massive cases on top of each other and clumsily dragged them to the street, joining Diana who was waiting there.

A taxi pulled up. Diana pointed to it.

"Our ride is here."

"Is this a real cab?" he asked.

The passenger door and the cab's rear trunk opened by themselves as if to answer his question.

He stacked the massive cases on top of each other in the luggage compartment.

From behind them Uri, his gray hair disheveled, ran up to them.

"Diana, Orion. I'm so glad I caught you. I just wanted to say goodbye."

Orion was touched.

"Oh, Uri, that's so nice of you."

The two exchanged a quick hug.

Eyeing Orion and Diana, Uri's smile turned wistful.

"You know, you two remind me of when I was young and in love. But, that was a long time ago."

Stan came up, struggling with the overly large suitcase.

"Here you go. This weighs a ton. What you got in there?"

"More than he needs." Diana quipped.

Orion lifted the bag without much effort and threw it into the trunk. He faced his old friend and gave him a hug.

"Thanks, Stan. I'll never forget…how you were always there for me. Whether I deserved it or not, I could count on you to have my back. I just wish…I could have been a better friend."

"No, problem, buddy…" Stan was flushed a little from the sentiment.

"Jeez, you don't have to get so emotional. You're only going on a trip. We'll see each other in a little bit."

Orion forced a weak smile as his eyes looked down.

Stan's phone could be heard ringing from his Honda.

"I," Stan's head spun around to the car. "I think I should get that… Lorraine."

Orion gave an understanding nod. His friend gave a "what are you gonna do" shrug and hurriedly rushed to his car.

Uri eyed the cab. "So, where are you two heading?"

Orion stepped in-between Uri and the cab, hoping to distract him from the fact that it had no driver.

"Oh, uh, we're not sure, yet."

Diana corrected him, "We're traveling to Batelaxion."

Uri smiled knowingly. "Ah, yes. Make sure, though, that you stop by the third moon. It's lovely!"

"Oh, thank you," her eyes widened, "I would have forgotten about Theos. My little Earthling here," she patted Orion on the arm, "won't have ever seen anything like that."

"Oh, there'll be a whole universe of things he's never seen. Maybe, I'll run into you two out there when I figure out my next step."

Orion was utterly confused as Diana shepherded him into the taxi. He resisted for a second, seeing IO in the front passenger seat, eyeing him ominously with I'm–watching-you eyes, but then he got in. Diana followed and the cab, driverless, pulled off.

Still dazed, Orion turned round to look through the back window at Stan and his ex-landlord, both waving broadly with twin opened-mouthed grins.

"What did-? How did Uri…?"

Diana smiled coyly.

"Oh, Uri. Well, he loves the earth, but he knew it was time for him to move on. That's why he sold it."

"What!? You mean, Uri…?"

"Uripedes. Yes, he and his wife owned the Earth for most of their lives. When she passed away, this planet became too painful a reminder of his loss. That's why he had to sell it."

Orion's jaw dropped in disbelief.

She nodded, "I think that's why he stayed here with you in the Atlas building; to be close to one of his own kind."

Orion looked pensive. "What is my kind? I don't really know."

She put her hand on his, gave it a squeeze.

"He tried to subtly educate you about the universe, but I'm afraid his methods were very limited."

It dawned on Orion that that was why Uri was always showing him astronomical pictures and lecturing about the universe.

"He was trying to educate me?"

"He was lonely. A friend, someone to talk with about things, that's all he probably really wanted."

"I was a lousy friend; always trying to dodge him."

"Don't blame yourself. You didn't know."

"But, I knew he was lonely. I could have easily hung out with him, drunk his tea and looked at his slides."

Still overwhelmed by it all, Orion turned back to get a last glimpse of the man he never really knew - Uripedes - the man who sold the world.

The adventure continues...

*THE PRETTIEST STAR*
Available Fall 2015.

Published by Wingways Productions.

# Further Acknowledgements

*In writing this book, I learned that writing a novel is, despite common perceptions, a truly collaborative process.*

Thanks to Marc Stern, a selfless, good and honest man who I am so proud to call Dad. I will be lucky if I became half the man you are. Your help in so many ways made this book possible.

To my brother, Orion Adrian, I appreciate you allowing me to use your name for the book. If you hadn't I don't think I would have had a story.

Thank you, Virgilio Aponte for your continual support with this artistic endeavor and being great sounding board. You're the best!

Jesse Burne, my appreciation for reading through an early, not very well written, draft and letting me know it.

Special thanks to Stephanie Chen for your super helpful edits and pointed questions which prompted...sigh...major rewrites.

Aaron Cohen, thank you, thank you, thank you, for using your commute time to read and edit the manuscript. Your comments really helped me improve the story.

Much appreciation to Rob Genadio who sacrificed quality time with his wife and two lovely kids to take the time to read and edit the manuscript.

Thanks to Mike Everette who, through his wonderful Screenline group, enabled so many of us to learn the art of storytelling.

To Elinor King, who so bravely and graciously read and edited a very early draft and gave suggestions on how to handle the character dynamics.

Merci beaucoup, grand-mère Barbara Stern pour ton soutien. Ce projet n'aurait pas été possible sans toi.

Stefan Swanson, thanks for reading an early version and being a good friend.

Last, but not least, thanks to Laura Woodford for reading an early draft and confirming that the ending works.

Ian Adrian

Born in Kansas City, Ian has lived in many parts of the United States - good and bad - finally settling down in New York City.

*The Man Who Sold the World* is his debut novel, but he is writing more books because he hopes to get enough money to buy a new hat.

*The Prettiest Star* comes out on-line and in stores Fall 2015

CPSIA information can be obtained at www.ICGtesting.com
Printed in the USA
BVOW01s0542290914

368525BV00001B/3/P